Burger Bar Dad

BURGER BAR DAD
Ian Butler

MP PUBLISHING

BURGER BAR DAD
First print edition published in 2013 by MP Publishing Limited
6 Petaluma Blvd. North, Suite B6, Petaluma, CA 94952
12 Strathallan Crescent, Douglas, Isle of Man IM2 4NR
www.mppublishingusa.com

Copyright © Ian Butler 2012
All rights reserved.

This book is sold subject to the condition that it shall not, by way of trade or otherwise, be lent, resold, hired out, or otherwise circulated without the publisher's prior consent in any form of binding or cover other than that in which it is published and without a similar condition including this condition being imposed on the subsequent purchaser.

The scanning, uploading and distribution of this book via the internet or via any other means without the permission of the publisher is illegal and punishable by law. Please purchase only authorized electronic editions and do not participate in or encourage electronic piracy of copyrighted materials.

Your support of the author's rights is appreciated.

Jacket Design by Alison Graihagh Crellin.

A CIP catalogue record for this title is available from the British Library.

ISBN-13: 978-1-84982-263-3
ISBN-10: 1-84982-263-8
10 9 8 7 6 5 4 3 2 1

Printed and bound in the United Kingdom

Also available in eBook.

To Heather, Ben, and, of course, Sammy.

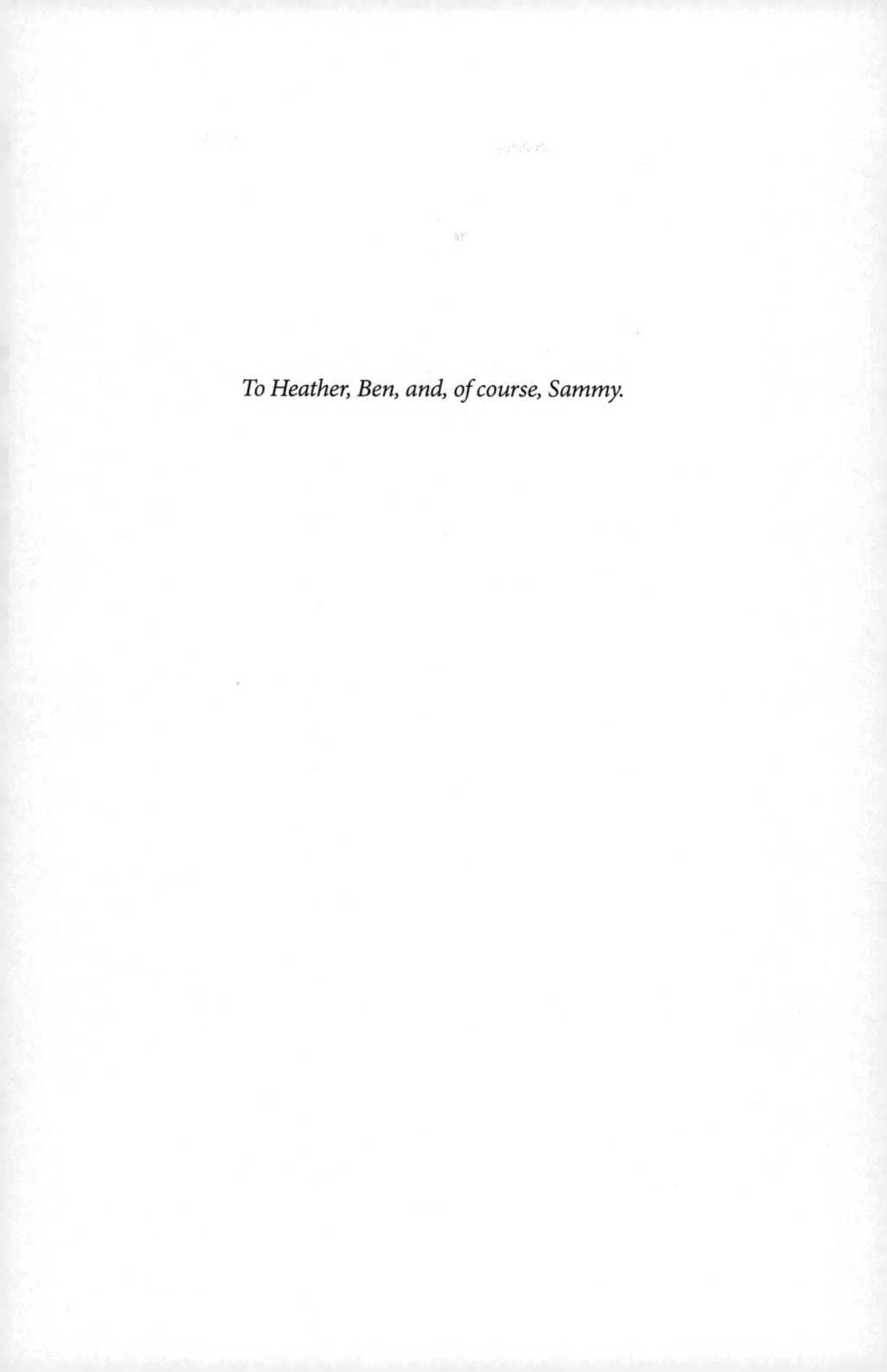

Chapter One
Burger Bar Dads

Whatever we do and wherever we go on Saturday, Jack and I usually end up in a fast food place. I know: I can already hear all the tutting, but he loves them and needs to eat, and frankly I'm not going to waste the precious time we have at the weekend cooking. Anyway, as I say to my sniffy friends, I'm not committing a crime and there's plenty of time to give him better food habits. Right now, though, I want my time with him; our precious Saturdays together. Middle-class value judgments about fast food are all very well, but they're time-consuming. Anyway, if I made him a nut rissole, would that make me a better dad? All this self-justification is obviously a defence mechanism, as transparent as Lady Gaga's blouse, and it gives you an indication of what a knob I am sometimes.

Today's no different from any other, and after watching a great movie full of robots, explosions and mayhem, we're going to eke out our last hour together at some fast food joint. Even superheroes have to have some downtime, and Jack and I shoot off in my car, recalling the epic explosions we've just seen and competing to see who can make the best farting noises.

Today we're in McDonald's: the Golden Arches, the archetype for burger bars everywhere. Jack, I think, loves this place above all others, but it's a marginal choice. We pull into the car park and, as usual, it is full of wrappers, burger boxes and paper cups, and I always get a little grumpy, as no matter how many bins are provided, some people just can't be arsed to put their rubbish in the bloody things. Forgetting that for a moment, and as usual on these occasions, I ask him, "You want to eat in, or drive through?" I always try to phrase this so as not to indicate my preference.

"Eat in today, Dad; it's too cold." He answers quickly and I make the necessary noises to hide my disappointment. My dream is that one day he will say, "Let's eat in the car today; I want to hear the football scores." Well, that dream will have to wait, and as they say, there's always another season.

After parking the car, we get out, hungry and ready for our food. The car park is small, and in a moment we're in through the big glass doors. It's when you're inside a place like this at the weekend that you see them: dads like me, enjoying the last few minutes of their own family life. The Burger Bar Dads, trying to find a space to have some time with their estranged kids.

For me, it's where I get to hang out with Jack, my son, and have a Mega-Guilty Pleasure Meal with large fries. It comes with a free gift of my ex's disapproval at us finishing our contact here.

You see every type of dad here, and today's no different. Over there is Guilty Dad, the one with a face liked a slapped arse, looking like he's just inherited the national deficit: he's nearly always on the verge of crying as, after this meal, he has to drop his kids off and spend another evening wondering if he's done the right thing leaving his wife. Across the way is Indifferent Dad: he is the heartbreaker with the vibrant orange tan, who doesn't give a crap, and Saturday afternoon with his kids is a drag. He's looking at his chunky watch to see how much time he has left before he hands them back and can get to the gym. Naturally, I hate guys like this, as you can imagine, and looking away I quickly spot Caring Dad. He's fussing and overcompensating and can easily become Guilty Dad, if he doesn't watch himself.

So: the burger bar or the pizza, chicken or ice cream place. It's where kids meet and get to know their dad's new partner and her kids. It's also where dads get to find out and be jealous of their ex-partner's new love interest. It's where they find out about school and what's happening at home. If they're like Caring or Guilty Dad, they're trying to make the kids understand that in divorcing or leaving their mother, they weren't divorcing or leaving them.

We get in the queue and begin my little game. Jack has a favourite meal for every fast food place we go in and the game's based on that. It goes like this: "So, Jack, what do you want today?" I'm not sure the reason I do this, but I guess it's just a habit.

"Happy Meal with chicken nuggets, please!" It's the same order every time we come here.

To start the game off, I always reply, "You don't want a Big Mac?" Obviously this varies, depending on where we are eating, and yes, I know it sounds stupid. It's just one of those things that dads do to stop getting bored in very long queues. I always hate the queues in these places: I mean, they're just chaotic, and it's murder when someone jumps in front of you, and somehow they always do.

Jack replies, as usual, "No, Dad."

Here we go: the game can get going in earnest.

"A Quarter Pounder, then?"

"No, Dad." A little more exasperated; he can't recall why this used to be funny, and its constant repetition certainly doesn't help him remember.

"A McChicken Burger, then?"

Obviously this has endless potential for annoyance. I don't know what I would do if he caught on and said, "Yes Dad, I'll have that instead!"

However he just says, "No, Dad." He's starting to look around to see if anyone is watching, and trying desperately to see if his dad is embarrassing himself.

"I know: what about a Filet-O-Fish?"

"No, Dad." He's definitely more rattled now, so probably time I stopped this: but hey, it's a long queue!

And so it goes on, until we get to the counter and the assistant wishes us a good afternoon and asks us for our order in a bit of a practised voice. At this point, we order the same thing we do every time we go to McDonald's.

"A Happy Meal with chicken nuggets and a quarter pounder with cheese meal, please."

After that, Jack smiles and holds my hand, waiting for his food. He loves ordering our Cokes and always makes sure they come without ice. Somehow, he has learnt that it's chilled anyway and that if you order it without ice you get more. This always secretly irritates me, as it is exactly the sort of thing his mother would do. It's the banker in her and "banker" in my vocabulary is another word for anally retentive, hard-faced, stony-hearted, money-obsessed bloodsucker. My profound apologies to all bankers out there who are not like that, but the only one I know is my ex-wife, so she's my template. Needless to say she speaks very highly of me!

My boy always likes to sit by the window, and today is no different. For the last thirty seconds he has been scouting for an empty table for us to sit at. For some reason, he's very good at this and even if the place is full to bursting, he will get us a seat.

"Come on, Dad!" he says, as I'm handed my plastic tray. He runs off to the table leaving me in his wake, carrying our food and drinks like a waiter very much under pressure. After reaching the table, it takes a little while for us to settle down and sort out the bags, boxes and bundles that make up our meal. Before we start we always look at the toy that comes with his kid's meal. It's invariably some figure from an upcoming movie that McDonald's is helping to promote, and recently he has begun to look fairly disappointed at the reality behind the brightly coloured pictures on the box. At this point he usually remembers his meal and then we both tuck in.

And this is where we talk: about school and life, and what's happening in his world and what's happening in mine. We talk about the latest films and what's on TV. Then we chat about books he's read and stuff he wants for his birthday, all of the bits and pieces that make up the busy life of a lively ten-year-old.

About a year ago, he began to talk about the Ex's new partner. For a while, it was John this and John that, and I felt usurped as a male role model. Unless you have experienced that, it's impossible to describe. Those feelings stopped when Jack got hurt playing some rough-and-tumble in the school, and his first thought was to ask for me. That was a great feeling and made me feel like a real dad for the first time since the divorce. That night, I made it my business to make Jack feel great, with a slap-up meal as a thank you for his unconscious affirmation of me as a father.

Today he's quiet and, as there's usually a lot of chat between us, I ask him, "Hey, Jack, anything up?"

There's a distinct pause and he looks down at his Coke.

"No," he pauses, "not really." Never slow to see an invitation to butt in when I see one, I jump in.

"That normally means that something is up." I look him straight in the eye as he peers up from his drink.

Jack puts another chip in his mouth and digests this with the knowledge that I know he is upset. He's ten and a pretty switched-on kid. OK, I have to admit I'm biased, but what dad isn't? So he looks at me with one of those expressions—a sort of exasperated tolerance—then sighs and says abruptly, "It's my school report; Mum shouted at me." He stops and takes a drink. "She told me I would grow up to be a loser if I didn't work hard at school."

Alarmingly, I feel myself getting angry and I know, I just know, I have to keep that under control. "What's wrong with the report, Jack? Your mum hasn't talked to me about it." Calmly, I say this as if it were a concrete reality, his mother actually contacting me about his schooling, as opposed to the non-communication that we actually have.

"She said that she was going to talk to you before the Parents' Evening on Tuesday." He looks anxious: worried that I know nothing about this; worried about this casually cruel thing that his mother has thrown at him. If I were to describe the thing that really upsets me about my ex-wife, it'd be this: she has a pre-disposition for hurting people with hasty, ill-chosen words, which she's usually much too stubborn to take back.

"OK, I'll talk to your mum, but you need to hear this." I pause to make sure that he is listening. I want him to hear what I have to say and that it comes from my heart.

"What, Dad?" He's trying to hide his disquiet about the revelation of his mother's hard-heartedness.

Smiling, I look in him straight in the eye, and pause for the effect that I want. "You will never, ever, *ever* be a loser."

He smiles. Sometimes I like to think that Jack has a bond with me, above and beyond that of father and son. It's like I'm his ally against the anally retentive toss that his mother frequently comes up with.

"We'll say no more about it; let's finish up and get an ice cream, OK?" In the circumstances, a bit of a gee-up isn't a bad plan. Jack breaks out into a huge smile, and says, "Yeah!"

I change the subject and, whilst walking over to the insincere counter assistant to grab some McFlurries, begin penning in my head the email I'll send his mother tonight.

Chapter Two
Battle Lines

When I think about the Ex and me, there is always a danger I will lapse into a remembrance of *that* argument. It's always *the* argument: the one that began sounding the death knell of our marriage. Depending on my mood, it's either poignant and sad or ironically funny. It can certainly make me smile, remembering my Ex turning into a manic, Basil Fawlty–like character right in front of my eyes.

It was before Jack was born. I'd driven home, got out of my much-dented Citroën, and lit a cigarette. She used to ask my friends how I could double the value of my car. With an ill-concealed scowl she would bark out the punchline "fill it with petrol!" and not wait for anyone to find it funny before dissolving into a cackle. Anyway, that day I took a long drag on my cigarette and watched as she pulled savagely into the drive, looking very unhappy. Well, unhappier than usual.

You have to understand that I tried to lighten the mood as she got out; it seemed that my main function in the marriage, at that point, was to try to make her laugh and help her de-stress. This had become much more difficult to do, and the reality was that I had almost given up trying. So as a joke, but mainly to myself, I said, "Oi! Don't scratch my car."

Her withering look should have told me to shut up. Ex was not one to mince her words and, on reflection, it was a mistake to ask my next question: "What have I done wrong?" Ex always had a temper. It seemed to come from some deep place inside her; imagine, if you will, Vesuvius erupting.

"It's you and your loser car!" She decided not to pause for breath. "You're holding me back, and the result of that is *that bloody witch Deborah-bloody-Hamilton-Finch* has got my promotion!"

I opened my mouth to offer a platitude. You know, "Bad luck; there's always next time!"—that sort of toss. However, before I got there, she ripped into me again.

"Don't speak!" she rasped. It was a step up from the usual "shut the fuck up!"

I took this as a good sign, but that thought didn't last long.

"You spend all day volunteering to do this and that, helping some yobbo or that flea-bitten theatre, when you're not working on that rag of a local paper. You get paid buttons, mooch around like a loafer, and drive your shit-heap of a car."

These were fairly familiar arguments to me, as I had pretty much lost sight of the gentle, beautiful girl I fell in love with, as she climbed up the corporate ladder. However, this day was a little different, as I had not anticipated the level of her anger, which seemed to be raging and focused purely on me. Usually I had a laid-back way of letting this stuff go past me and, at that stage, tried to use humour to deflect the excesses of her temper. You know the sort of thing: "Hey, Mr Ed, why the long face?"

Her face was reddening, and a wicked thought struck me: was this from her not breathing, or she was genuinely upset? Then another humorous thought struck me: what if it was both? I began to get worried, as I am crap at CPR.

Then, oblivious to the risks to her health, she continued ranting and raving: "Deborah-bloody-Hamilton-Finch's husbands plays golf and has lunch with my boss—what do you do to help my career?"

Still not really understanding why all this anger was focused on me, I toyed with the idea of offering to join the Masons, but thought better of it. You see, I can't help making humour my first weapon in conflict.

"You know I got thrown out of the Conservative Club for my Trotskyite leanings," was my more considered answer, and even this gentle use of humour didn't go down too well.

"Ha, ha, bloody ha! You are so amusing. My career is in the dustbin and all you can do is laugh. Thanks a fucking lot!"

I opened my mouth again, to give my thoughts on the inherent unfairness of capitalism. She must have sensed this and sadly these thoughts were stillborn.

"Oh, just shut up!" With that, she stormed into the house, leaving me finishing my cigarette alone in the driveway, and while I was doing that it began to dawn on me that my wife had changed so much. It occurred with some violence that her values and dreams, whilst never quite the same as mine, were now wildly different.

These were the battle lines over which we stormed for the next couple of years. We could have gone on like that for a lot longer, but during a similar row, she announced that she was pregnant. That was rapidly followed by her stating that she wasn't going to give up her career and that I would have to look after the kid.

That pregnancy conversation was the start of a brief hiatus in our rowing, whilst we settled down to prepare for Jack. We fell into our allotted roles after his birth: me the doting househusband father, her returning to high-flying in the bank. I have to say from the start that I loved, and still love, being a dad and the idea that I could fulfill a non-stereotypical caring role was very appealing.

That's largely based on the fact that I was, and still am, unbearably unfocused about my life. To some extent I envied the Ex: she knew where she wanted to go and nothing would be allowed to stop her. I, on the other hand, have passed forty and still don't know what I want to do. Probably the best "job" I ever had was writing for my Student Union magazine. I had a great funky, slick, clever writing style and I loved creating. It made me feel clever. Essentially everything has been downhill since then.

I'd arrived at university full of hope, left it half full of dope, and woke up this morning twenty-odd years later still looking for a purpose beyond my Saturday trips out with Jack and the odd byline in the local rag. The whole househusband thing was great for a couple of years, as I greatly enjoyed fatherhood and could still write some pieces for the paper. Ex was climbing the greasy pole at work and though that was partly annoying, it was manageable. However, what soon surfaced was a nagging tension regarding my lack of support for her career and my dearth of ambition. Despite the fact that my role gave her the scope to develop her career, I don't think that she could ever escape the disappointment of me not being a successful writer.

I think that realisation came to me as I waited for her to arrive home from the bank every day. Her return would be marked by a bombardment of acid-tipped anecdotes of who had done what to whom, and I was expected to know the intricacies of her office politics. Then she would begin to search around for jobs I had not completed correctly, or not done at all.

Now, without opening the whole man vs woman debate, Ex is fastidious and was never slow to criticise. That was hard and always a source of tension between us. Was I dilatory in my housework? I don't think so, but I just think, at that time, everything I did annoyed her. By the end of our time together, we hardly fought at all. Her carping at me got worse the higher up she got in her career, and my responses became more muted, until I decided that I couldn't do this anymore.

Every night I would experience the same tension as the clock raced towards 6 p.m. It was a realisation that I was starting to hate myself and beginning to doubt everything I did. Then one day, I snapped and decided that something would have to change. The catalyst was a huge rant that she started about Jack having spilt a drink. It was just about six o'clock, and she walked in a microsecond after it had happened and assumed that I had done nothing about it. She went ranting on about my "slackness" and how this was precisely what was wrong with my life, blah, blah, blah. I let that ride for a bit, until it began to bounce back at me, to a point where I could no longer stand being quiet.

I decided to approach her later that evening for a make-or-break meeting and she jumped, and I do mean Bob Beamon-like, at the chance of a break-up. That says an awful lot about my negotiating skills! Except for the pain of losing Jack, it was a relief really. She got a nanny and I got my half of the house and, when the divorce came through, the only question my solicitor asked me was why we got married in the first place.

That was a bloody good question, as we were at each other with some antipathy during the divorce, but reflection is a useful tool. I suppose that I'm fairly attractive, or certainly was when I met her at university. I was cool then and at the heart of student life. At that time, she was unbearably beautiful. We used to talk for hours about art, fashion and just stuff. We read *The Face* together and she laughed at my jokes and we shagged for England. We exploded together, then spent ages drifting apart and, when we eventually hit the rocks, there were three of us and two lifeboats. Sadly I was in the lifeboat without Jack in it, and I got left with marginal parental responsibility and Saturday and Wednesday night to be as good a dad as I could be. As much as possible, I made the best of it, but the reality was that it was a terrible wrench and I hated her using him to get a quick divorce. So I guess I settled for second best, in the hope that the time Jack and I had together would be quality time and that he would value it as much as I did.

The trouble with remembering that argument, the one that started it all, is that afterwards we ended up having fantastic sex. She always said I was really sexy when I was trying to be funny, and I said she always looked great when she got passionate. There is always the constant nightmare in my head that Jack was conceived after one of these fights, during a furious bout of make-up sex. For some reason that bothers me, though I can't fathom why.

So, this sort of remembrance goes on and on, and I still haven't begun the email rant to her in my head; the one about the school report. That's the trouble with sex: it ruins everything. Even when I'm manifestly justified in my anger at the Ex, who used to nag the arse out of me, reducing me to a quivering wreck of nerves and misogyny, up pops up an erotic memory of her in little white panties, and I'm sunk.

When it comes to her, I really need to learn that I have to think with something other than my knob. Looking at Jack, I realise I need to stop thinking about anything other than focusing on the rest of my time with him. The bloody email to the Ex can wait.

Chapter Three
Tears Before Bedtime

We have just about forty-five minutes left before I have to return him home. We're finishing our ice creams, and he catches me looking at my watch. I do this not because I am bored, but know that we will get a deathly look if we are more than thirty seconds late. Ex is always looking for a stick to beat me with, and I could say "Bugger it!" but I don't like arguing in front of Jack as that has happened far too often, so I keep my head down and get on with it.

"What's the time, Dad?" He has obviously seen me looking at my watch and understands, I think, that this is about us not being late home.

"5.15. It's nearly time to go." This is the time I really hate; the last hour of Saturday with Jack. His response produces one of those awkward moments that can break your heart. You know, the kind the questions that can only be answered by causing him, and therefore me, masses of pain.

"Can I come home with you tonight?" He says it in a pleading tone that pulls terribly at my heartstrings. It's agony, this; I mean, put yourself in my shoes. All I want to do is take him in my arms, put him in the car, and drive him home. Instead I play the reasonable parent. What does that make me: a coward?

I suppose so, but I can't see me running off and sparking a manhunt as Jack and I scoot around the West Midlands, like Thelma and Louise without the Grand Canyon ending. Mind you, there aren't too many deserts in the M6 corridor.

"Sorry, Jack, we have to take you back to Mum. Why don't we ask her if you can stay over after the Parents' Evening?"

He smiles at the possibility. "OK, great!"

Somehow I get away with that, and put some additional sugar on the pill. "You can bring a DVD, and we'll eat some popcorn."

"Fantastic! I'll bring my favourite film." It's nearly too much for me. It breaks my heart, all of it breaks my heart, to see him so pleased with so little. I want to grab him and cuddle and kiss him, and I would if he wouldn't find that incredibly embarrassing.

For the next few minutes he talks about films, and we draw up a list of stuff he wants to see. He loves lists and that sort of thing. Luckily he changes his mind a lot, and by Tuesday he will probably have a different film at the top of his pile of favourites. His current number one is a Disney, a saccharine-riddled piece of nonsense, which most kids love, of course, but which I suspect in my heart is a vehicle to make the filmmakers and toymakers loads of money. I'm already really looking forward to the day he wants to see *The Godfather* or the director's cut of *Blade Runner*. He's ten, so I guess I've a bit of time to wait for that, and then all my favourite films will look very clunky and dated. Of course, some of them are already. We do have some great times, though, and, when he was about six, Jack had a flirtation with *Thomas the Tank Engine*. Despite their cack-handed attempts at political correctness, the animators made a good job of it. We used to sit for hours with Ringo Starr narrating *The Flying Kipper* and other stories with Henry, Edward, Percy, and, of course, Thomas. Then, if that wasn't brilliant enough, he discovered *Thunderbirds*. His joy at the adventures of the Tracy family and Brains has connected us for years. It just seems that generations of boys have identified with those puppets, and they keep on delighting them and their dads. I have a sneaking liking for a lot of other Gerry Anderson stuff, but *Thunderbirds* is my favourite.

In the past I used to try to have a little influence over the stuff he watched and the books he read. Sadly, I retired from that battle, badly mauled by a stream of abuse and negativity from the Ex. She has an agenda based on the educational value of everything. If she feels something is frivolous or not "developmentally appropriate", then it has no value. Ex seems to feels that he has to be prepared for life outside, even though, after all, he's only ten. There was a time when I tried to talk to her about the value of children just playing and having fun. Ex was having none of it, until she read it in a magazine or something, and even then she never really grasped the concept. It's like asking her to be nice to a subordinate at work: she knows it's good for morale but she struggles letting her guard down. It's impossible for me to think of her playing games and just enjoying herself, unless it's *Monopoly* or *Risk*.

At this point I want to say nice things about the Ex, but the memories of her saying "I don't want my son growing up to be a loser like you" come back to me and still really hurt. That sort of vision crowds out the good stuff I can say about her. However, if I am really forced, I can point to the fact that Jack has a pretty good home life, albeit that Ex is a bit anally-retentive and everything is a bit regimented. Breakfast at this time, lunch at that time, homework now, and you must read before bedtime. Now I love the thought of him reading before going to sleep, but her way makes it a chore and not a joy for him.

By the way, I'm serious: she really does say that kind of stuff to me. It's clear that I truly am a loser in her eyes, but I'm sort of happy, unlike her. By no means do I view success in the same Thatcherite way she does. For some reason, her materialism is coupled with the Iron Lady's finger-pointing and hectoring. So my attempts to encourage theatre and help kids on the margins are dismissed as pointless, my job on the paper as demonstrating a lack of ambition.

Now I admit my hackery on behalf of the paper is pretty pointless, but all that I require from it is a way to feed the mortgage monster. Anyway, someone has to report on the Midland Knicker Snatcher's progress through the courts. Then again, I often get a byline, and the recognition is a cool part of my job; getting a column now and again is great too. It also means that I get paid for writing (my first love, career-wise anyway)—and what business is it of hers what I do with my life? At this point I need to move away from this self-justification and ask Jack a bit more about Parents' Evening.

"Is your mum going with John on Tuesday?" I'm actually not sure why I'm asking this, but deep down I feel conscious that I don't want to be replaced as a father figure by Ex's newish man. Especially as I know he is a bit of a financial whiz kid, up his own arse and therefore perfect for the Ex. In short, someone who knows the exact date his company BMW will be replaced and the state of the Japanese bond market, but has no idea who Xenophilius Lovegood is or the date that *The Hobbit* is being released. Of course that's unfair, but at this stage of my life I don't give a bugger. As far as I'm concerned, Ex can sleep with whoever she wants to and all my concern is focused on what's good for Jack. Actually I formed the impression that, despite my class-based critique, John is OK with Jack and they seem to get on, after a bit of a rocky start. I'm not sure what went on, but I got the feeling that Jack thought that by liking John he was in some way betraying me.

He shrugs. "Don't know. Do you want me to ask?"

Thinking of Ex's reaction to that question, I rush to take that responsibility away from him. "No, I will do it tonight when I drop you off." Not a conversation I'm looking forward to, I grant you, but better than Jack asking it. Out of the corner of my eye, I can see his mind turning over stuff, and I start to worry that it might be about his report again. To stop this happening, I go for a change of subject to take his mind off school reports and his mother's reaction.

"You finished here?" I point to his tray full of paper, bags and whatnot.

"Yep!" He looks pleased, as he knows what's coming. At the end of every Saturday we go for a drive before parting at his house. For some reason he regards this as a highlight of the day.

"You want to go for a drive?" I know the answer to this, but I love asking the question just to get the response.

"Yesssssssssssssss!"

He adores my 1971 Citroën DS Super as much as I do, delighting in the hydro-pneumatic suspension that raises the car when you switch on the ignition. He's also obsessed with the headlights that move whenever you turn the steering wheel. My DS is black and, for the uninitiated, that's by far the best colour. It looks like a huge, dark shark, and I love it. Weirdly, I catch myself looking at it from time to time, and it sometimes takes my breath away. My love is repaid by the ride and the easy way it performs and drives. Even forty years after it was built, and over fifty years after it was designed, it looks really cool in a Gallic, roll top sweater, Jean-Paul Belmondo sort of way.

As we walk across the car park, he starts our little routine, as he does every time we get in the car. He waits outside whilst

I put the key in the ignition and he counts down, "Five, four, three, two, one!" Then he claps with joy as the car raises itself up on the suspension. He says it reminds him of *Thunderbirds*, then he jumps in and shouts, "Thunderbirds are GO!!!"

Today's no different, and as always, I find myself dreading the day that he is too old or too cool to get pleasure out of just being in my car. At that point he'll probably have gone into that hormonal "Kevin the Teenager" surly oik phase: that stage of life in which the only communication between parent and child is abrasive, unless it's a request for a transfer of cash. However, I am nowhere near that time yet, and I'm determined to enjoy every minute of his pre-teens; then I'll deal with his teenage years as they come, rather than worrying about them now.

Jack loves looking at maps and he always plots a route home for us with the maximum amount of turns, so he can see the headlights move. Tonight he plans a typically twisty route, and we set off, enjoying our last few minutes together, each of us desperately hanging on to our final bit of today's joy. We approach corner after corner, with Jack giggling as the lights move in tandem with the steering wheel. As ever, I wonder whether Citroën understood that when they designed this innovation, it would give so much joy to small and not-so-small boys for generations to come.

As we get nearer the Ex's house, my stomach begins to tighten. This happens most times, but it's especially tight tonight, as Jack's report is weighing heavily on my mind. The whole thing is still there for me, and the fact that she has been living with John for a year now hasn't mellowed her ability to turn me into an emotional wreck or ruin any confidence I might have gleaned over the previous week.

The Ex's house, which used to be our house, formally

known as home, looms into view. It's a 1930s detached, with a bay window and stained-glass over the front door. For this part of Birmingham it's a substantial piece of real estate. We park outside and Jack scoots over the bench to give me a big hug; I hold him tight, rubbing his hair. "Love you, Dad!" he says, and I reply in kind, hating this part of the day, knowing I have to keep it together and not let him see how fucked-up I become when we have to say goodbye.

As I gently kiss his forehead, we both get out of the driver's door. Instinctively, I know that he hates this part of the day too, and, when Ex opens the front door, he quickly runs inside shouting, "Bye, Dad! See you on Tuesday!"

"Tuesday?" Ex asks in a confrontational way, which instantly gets my back up, and I fight hard to reel my feelings in; a task made difficult looking at the features of my former wife set in a rock-hard grimace.

"Yeah, I said I would ask you if he could come on over after Parents' Evening." Struggling, I try to keep it friendly. This isn't in any way in deference to her, but almost like an exercise for me in good manners. Obviously there's the point of not allowing Jack to see us arguing, but it's also demonstrating to her that she hasn't the power to upset me.

"I suppose so," she replies grudgingly. By asking Jack, I have removed her veto, and she always appears to always take this badly. However, as the philosopher said: "It's easier to say sorry afterwards than seek permission beforehand." Wise words indeed!

"I wanted to chat to you about that." I'm still trying very hard to keep it friendly. Her face appears not to acknowledge my efforts, and my stomach's tightening, waiting for her next sentence. I don't have long to wait.

"I hope you're not trying to wriggle out of it?" She's clearly not trying to keep it friendly, as I'm obviously not worth the effort. Taking a breath I count to ten, as the last thing I want to do is let her see that she's got to me, but it's incredibly hard. It's stupid, I know, but I'd really like her to think it isn't worth her while trying to wind me up.

"I'm coming, of course. Can I see his report? For some reason, they haven't sent me one." She's looking at me and trying to stop herself calling me on it; blaming me for the school's failure.

She settles for a clipped "OK!" and turns on her heel and walks down the hall into the lounge, leaving me on the doorstep. At this point I feel about as welcome as a cowpat on a bowling green. Emerging from the lounge, she hands me a buff envelope. Her face is full of disdain and I really do feel like an interloper, on what used to be our front doorstep.

"Will I meet you at the school?" I'm hoping that she doesn't want a meeting beforehand. I can see that would be a non-stop tirade on my slacker tendencies, and my inability to inspire Jack as a role model

She snaps, "OK, seven o'clock?" and I try really hard not to show my relief. As you have no doubt guessed, I've no desire to spend any more time in the Ex's presence than I absolutely have to.

"Yes, that'll be great," I say, as pleasantly as I can muster, and with that she closes the door not with a slam but a very loud thud. It's the usual end to my Saturday excursion to the former marital home.

"How to win friends and influence people!" I mutter *sotto voce* and climb into my car. The journey from here to my flat would normally be about fifteen minutes at this time of day. Whenever I drop Jack off, it takes a little longer, as I need a short stop to dry my eyes. Today's no different.

Chapter Four
Parents' Evening from Hell

There's a weird truth at work with pretty much all divorced couples. No matter how many metaphorical lumps they have kicked out of one another beforehand, civilities must be maintained in front of doctors and teachers.

Ex appears to be the exception that proves this rule, as we emerge from our cars at the school car park. Getting out of her BMW, she looks, as usual, with disdain at my Citroën. Like I said, she has always hated it.

There's a discernible "tut" that I decide to ignore as we give each other a barely audible "hi!" and walk through the front door. Jack's school decor is bright and colourful and, like every other school, filled with the artwork of its current crop of students. Each wall is dedicated to a story or subject that one or other class is being taught. As we move towards the hall, we see *The Oceans*, *The Night Sky*, and *Living Together*, and I smile at how this subject seems peculiarly inappropriate in relation to the Ex and me.

The signs eventually direct us into the main hall, and we go past the various teachers holding court until we see Jack's, in earnest conversation with another pupil's parents. We sit down in the chairs, which are carefully placed so you can hear some, but not all, of the conversation.

The teacher is earnestly addressing the couple, although the father looks bored and trying hard to appear interested. He needs to be told that he's crap at it and that, by the state of his partner, he'll be in trouble later. She looks unlikely to hold back the urge to tear into her child as a result of the lecture that's coming from the teacher. Her facial expression is alternatively mortified, furious and embarrassed. I wouldn't be her kid tonight for a million quid. Eventually the parents rise, say "thank you" to the teacher, and march off to sort out little Johnny or Jemima, who won't see the business end of a PlayStation for a couple of weeks.

Very soon we're beckoned over and we sit in front of Jack's teacher, Ms. Williams. Her name is indicated by a little card in front of her but her current marital status is blanked out by her title, although her lack of a wedding ring speaks volumes; I'm at a loss as to why I'm mentioning this.

"Hello, so you are…let me see…oh yes, Jack's parents." It's said in a pretty neutral tone, but deep down, I detect a faint hint of edge. That doesn't sound too good and I can mentally see the Ex starting to get rattled because, I suspect, she's picked it up too. We both mumble an affirmative and the teacher ploughs on.

"Well it is clear that Jack is a very clever and talented boy." I sense a "but" coming and it circles the room, waiting to crash onto the table. By this time I'm already feeling like I've done something wrong. "However, Jack appears to have some issues at the moment which are preventing him from realising his potential." The "but" lands on the table with a bone-shaking, jarring crunch. Just as I'm coming to terms with this, the next blow rains down. "We at the school are wondering if something is amiss at home?"

I suspect that the teacher already knows the answer to this question, but the Ex doesn't even pause before spitting out:

"No! Jack is perfectly happy at home."

Ms. Williams doesn't seem fazed by this warning rattle and ploughs on, regardless of the danger she is in. I feel like hiding under the table as Ex starts to stiffen. "It's clear that Jack's performance has slipped during the year and, whilst he is still among the best in his class, we are keen to learn whether there are any reasons behind his dip in performance."

I can practically feel the hostility coming from the seat next to me as this sentence is delivered. Mischievously, a thought runs through my head. At this point it would be a great time for me to say, "Your new partner moved in this year, didn't he?" It would be a devastating quip, the dénouement an obvious solution to the problem. The answer to the mystery of Jack's dip in performance: John did it! What's more, I suspect that this analysis is right on the money.

Sadly, as usual, I bottle it. I'm convinced sometimes that I'm completely full of shit. So I play it safe and, in doing so, provide some cover for Ex, and she goes instantly on the offensive. Really bristling, she spits out, "Perhaps he's experiencing difficulties at school; have you looked at that?" Surely the teacher wouldn't ignore two death rattles? I know the Ex and I've seen this before. For some reason, it's almost as if she enjoys spoiling for a fight.

"I've spent a lot of time talking to Jack and it is clear to me that he is very happy at our school." Ms. Williams's response does not have the required effect of mollifying the Ex. However, you have to hand it to her: she is either suicidal or crazily brave.

The Ex takes a deep breath, and I have to work very hard to resist the temptation to stand up and shout, "Tin hats, everybody!"

"Jack is very happy at home, and I'm not going to sit here and have you imply that our domestic arrangements are impacting his education!" She's practically bellowing it, and I can see that a couple of parents are looking in our direction.

At this I think that I ought to intervene, if only to stop the smug looks from the others in the hall, who even now are thinking at least things with their kids aren't as bad as that couple with Ms. Williams. The only problem is that I don't have one sensible thing to say, so bemused have I become with this clash of the Titans.

The teacher decides to change track: maybe she wants to find new ways of upsetting the Ex. "Perhaps we could look at some of his work from last year and this year to illustrate what I am worried about."

The Ex decides to hold back the launch of a broadside, mumbling sullenly, and I'm hoping against hope that she might see reason if she's given proof. I think this display will forever put me in love with this dark-haired, wide-eyed teacher.

"These are last year's spelling and reading ages and, as you can see, they have fluctuated downwards all year. Similarly, his maths and science scores have only held constant." Ms. Williams hands over the books with what can only be described as a rather smug expression on her face. My eyes look down at the books and a silence descends between us.

Sadly, instead of listening, looking at the books and taking this stuff on board, the Ex uses this pause to marshal her indignation. "I'm still not convinced that he's not being affected by something at school."

Ms. Williams looks sadly at her, and this, I think, is a little bit of a mistake.

Ex decides to move in, sensing weakness. "I will be speaking to the Head." She takes a breath to let this sink in. "And in addition to that, I will be asking for a review of your teaching methods, which I suspect are at the root of Jack's performance."

The Ex stands up, gathers up her bag, and stomps out. As she leaves the hall, the focus of the whole place turns to me. As you can appreciate, I'm in a bit of a dilemma. Do I leave to go after her? Try to get her to return and risk the teacher misunderstanding the gesture as acceptance of Ex's position? Or do I try to sort some stuff out here to help Jack?

As a complete coward, I decide on a holding pattern. I need to have a word with the teacher and then at least try to talk to the Ex, whom I suspect will be raging in the car park. "Ms. Williams, I need to speak to my ex-wife; can you bear with me?" The slight emphasis on the "ex" clearly has the result I was looking for.

"Of course," she says kindly, sensing my predicament. At this point she comes out with the killer line of the night: "Do you think I've upset her?" I resist the temptation (and it's very hard, I might add) to laugh out loud and say, "No more than I do."

Trying hard not to smile, I glide away, not too quickly, to try to find the Ex. As expected, she's in her BMW fuming and looking through the window; it glides down silently, very much at odds with its occupant.

"I'll have that bitch's job; you see if I don't!" I'd like to say that her anger is all for Jack's benefit, but I suspect that it's much more to do with the teacher getting one over on her.

"Calm down or you'll have a coronary!" was my very ill-considered response. Sometimes I hear these lines coming out of my mouth and wonder what on earth I'm doing. I'm like the drinker who gets to the point of drunkenness, where he knows what he's doing but can't stop himself.

I'm regretting my humour straight away, as she proceeds to give me both barrels of her verbal shotgun. "That's typical: I get insulted and you tell me to calm down." I let her rant on. "That's oh-so-you, letting people walk all over you." This is another one of her favourite sticks to beat me with. Apparently my lack of achievement is closely linked to my inability to stand up for myself. I consider this a bit harsh, but let it ride. My silence doesn't mollify her. In addition, I'm a little miffed that she expects me to jump to her defence.

Before I have time to process all this, she goes on another rant. "The problem with Jack is that he has you and your slackness as a model. The more time he spends with you, the worse he becomes; now his work is suffering."

Getting annoyed, I decide to grow a pair. Not a common position for me, I grant you. "Listen, Jack was doing great at school and the only thing that has changed this year is your relationship with John." As an answer, it isn't half bad and it isn't that bad a guess as to the real substance of Jack's minor dip in performance. However, I'm not expecting Ex to see this issue in the same light as me, and so it turns out.

Imagine, if you will, the attack on Pearl Harbor. She practically explodes with fury: "I can't believe that you are suggesting that John has got anything to do with this terrible school's treatment of my son." I know that as soon as she uses the words "my son", I'm in trouble. It's a kind of statement about me, and her view of me as a hopeless parent. Then I open my mouth to speak and the staccato bark of "Shut up!" rings out across the car park. This is the way that she gets on. Nothing must get in the way of her point of view; it's definitely "my way or the highway".

"In any case, John has offered to send Jack to a private school and after this shambles, I won't have him here for one more week." This is a clear breach of any sort of parenting agreement we have, so I decide to remain in possession of my newly grown pair, definitely out of character.

Barking back, I make my views known. "I won't have him

move school without any discussion with me, and frankly I know he won't like that." A fair summary of my legal rights and a pretty good summing-up of what I genuinely believe Jack's reaction will be. I'm actually getting angry now, and my face is very near to getting into hers.

She brushes aside my fair summary with a devastating and witty bit of badinage: "Bollocks! He'll do what he's told."

She starts the car and leaves me looking into a non-existent car window. Suddenly I jerk upright, looking like a complete idiot and realising that ten feet away is Jack's teacher, Ms. Williams.

Chapter Five
Aghast in the Car Park

Ms. Williams is in her coat and it's clear that she's heading home. My mind is still fighting with the Ex and I'm a bit loath to admit this, but for some reason my knees are wobbling. "Hi!" I blurt out. It seems the only thing to say in the circumstances.

"Hi!" she says, and there's a pause that seems to last for several hours, particularly as I have nothing of any substance to contribute. Then she laughs, and this act of kindness breaks the ice, allowing me to relax a bit. "You're having a difficult night."

Trying not to resemble a lost puppy, I look at her and answer, "Yes, but it isn't the first and it won't be the last." Then, trying to play it down: "I hope you didn't hear too much of that?"

She smiles. "Sadly, a bit too much." I'd like to play it cool but catching me looking through a non-existent car window has closed off that particular option.

"OK," I laugh, "but first let me say, it isn't always like this." Lying isn't my default position but I don't want her running away with the idea that the Ex is a one-dimensional monster, or I'm a spineless jellyfish with a thumbprint on my forehead.

"I certainly hope not!" With that, she laughs again. Two laughs in a row: bonus! "Is your wife…"

"Ex-wife!" I cut in quickly, to remove any doubt that we are in any way connected, except through Jack.

"Sorry, *ex*-wife, is she always that touchy?" This seems to be a question only someone who doesn't know my Ex would ask.

However, I try to look thoughtful, as if I really need time to consider this question, before I answer.

"Yeah, kind of," I smile, and look into her eyes. "Listen, I'm sorry about all that: between ourselves, you touched a nerve. She has a new man and that might be upsetting Jack." She nods. I really don't know what has prompted me to say this and I'm starting to wonder if it was to demonstrate my complete separation from the Ex.

Therefore I feel a sudden, guilty need to restore some balance. After all, John isn't a monstrous stepfather stereotype, as far as I know, and I'm confident that Jack would tell me if he was. My real problem is my sincere belief that anyone who's compatible with the Ex must have some sort of character flaw. However, I decide to keep that a secret and tell her instead, "Don't get me wrong: he seems like a nice bloke. Anyway, Jack would tell me if he wasn't."

"I sense a 'but' here," is her reply.

Deciding to choose my next words very carefully, I opt to speak in platitudes. "Well, you know these things are difficult, and Jack's a little sensitive."

"Sure, I understand; did you want to talk some more about Jack?" Of course I do. Additionally, I want to make sure she understands that I don't think like my Ex.

"Well, yeah, but this doesn't seem the time or place." I've always been good at stating the bleeding obvious.

She laughs, and I join her. "I suppose not. Can you make it in after school tomorrow?" This sounds intriguing, and I am beginning to notice that Ms. Williams is quite attractive. Even now, I know I need to stop myself because I have to focus on Jack and this kind of stuff doesn't help anyone.

However, I jump at the chance of seeing her again. "Of course, but not till four; I'm in court tomorrow." She looks aghast, and I realise my mistake. I sometimes use "I'm in court tomorrow" to shock people as a joke, but this is pure thoughtlessness on my part and is indicative of the mood that I'm in. "Sorry, I'm the legal reporter for the local paper; I have to attend the sessions tomorrow." I hope that this will be an explanation that she believes. Thinking of me as a villain isn't what I'm aiming for.

"Oh, I'm so sorry. Did I look all horrified?" she says in a giggly, girlish voice that is very attractive.

"Not too much!" I lie. "What did you think I was up for?" Smiling, I'm aware that I'm flirting now but can't really stop myself. People have always said that I'm very charming. It's after they get to know me that the rot sets in!

Laughing, she says, "No idea, but being a rascal probably comes into it!" Wow! The woman's teasing me and responding to my flirting; definitely a bonus for the evening, which frankly started very badly.

She looks completely at ease and I don't want to push it, so I look at my car. "I have to go; I'm picking Jack up."

"Oh, of course! See you tomorrow."

"Sure! See you then."

I march over to my Citroën and unlock the door. Then I turn to wave, and she looks at me and says, "Nice car." Needless to say, I'm a bit lost at that remark and it occurs to me, as I get in the driver's seat, that the idea of me even asking this girl out has absolutely no future. Quite apart from the inappropriateness of going out with Jack's teacher, I'm not in any emotional place to consider a relationship at the moment, especially if I have to gird my loins and fight with Ex about Jack's education.

The car splutters into life and I drive off, but can't resist waving to her as she gets into her anonymous hatchback. She waves back and, despite everything, I'm very keen to see her tomorrow at the very least. My mind then embarks on a Ms. Williams–inspired daydream, and the drive to Jack's is finished in no time. Although the familiar tightness of the stomach is still there, my son's teacher has rescued this from being a terrible night.

Standing on the doorstep, I ring the doorbell and hear Jack running down the corridor to open the door. "Hi, Dad!" A hug follows and he says, "I'll just get the DVD and my bag."

"Of course; what is it?" I ask, fervently hoping that he has changed his mind about the Disney movie.

He shouts "Harry Potter!" as he runs down the hall to where his stuff is piled neatly, awaiting my arrival. He grabs his bag and yells goodbye to his mum and John, and I hear them replying.

"I've got popcorn at home. Have you got a book?" Obviously I have loads of books for him at my place, but I don't want any fuss at bedtime.

"Yeah!" He seems really jolly and I just feel happy that he is this excited about spending time with me. To be honest, it always makes me feel great, and I give him another hug as he arrives on the doorstep.

"Let's go, then, but I do need to say 'hello' to your mum before we go."

"Mum!" He shouts for me. "Dad wants you." He then takes his stuff to wait by the car. I hope that he only has a sixth sense about what's happened tonight.

Ex arrives at the door, wearing a furious look on her face,

and I sense that I need to be careful. Rattled, she's not a pleasant sight—or sound, for that matter. As much as I was appalled by her petulance and aggressive behaviour, it's clear that she can't see the difference between that and genuine assertiveness.

"You OK?" I ask, in the friendliest way possible.

"What do you want?" Her hostility is evident, and I'm irritated that I have always had to march around her moods. Standing up to her is not going to help Jack, and I decide to be conciliatory.

"We need to talk about this evening. Can we arrange a chat, as this clearly isn't the time or place?" Ex looks like she just wants to bite my head off, but clearly the danger of the neighbours overhearing holds her back. Obviously, it's very clear that I'm not her favourite person at the moment.

"You can email me; make sure Jack is in school on time."

Letting that slide, I say goodbye. Quickly, I turn as the door shuts with a bang next to me. It's all forgotten as Jack is waiting by the car for our usual routine. Thunderbirds are GO!

Chapter Six
Harry Potter and the Email of Doom

Driving home with Jack is a complete joy, compared with the trials of the Parents' Evening and the frosty reception on Ex's doorstep. Jack's excited, chatting about the movie and about Harry Potter and the gang. After he started reading the books, he struggled with the movies when they deviated from the story by even a word. It took me ages to explain how long films would be if they were exact copies of the books, and he finally got his head around it. Even so, he talks about the differences between the films and their source material, and this lasts till we arrive at my flat.

Compared to the regime he has to endure at the Ex's house, my flat must be like a fun palace for him. He gets to watch the stuff he likes and use my Xbox, which I guess makes me a pretty cool dad. There are some boundaries around homework and bedtime, but they are dealt with in a caring, non-dogmatic way, which I imagine is at odds with what happens at his mother's.

We go into the lounge, and I say to him, "If you want your movie on, we have to do it now. Otherwise you'll be in bed too late."

"OK, Dad. Will you watch it with me?" He always asks this and it makes me happy just to see the joy when I answer in the affirmative.

"Oh yes," I say with relish, as I love sharing stuff with him. "I'm really looking forward to it." It's a pleasure to say that, and Jack smiles back as if sensing my sincerity.

"Brilliant!" he squeaks, already at the DVD player sorting out our evening's entertainment. It's great that he feels at home enough to do that, and cool enough about treating the place as his own. He loves the fact that he never has to ask my permission to eat a biscuit or get a drink. By the same token, he knows not to push it, and is really good about his eating and drinking. In fact, he's a bit of a health freak, and I make sure that there are lots of healthy things for him to eat. This seems a bit weird, considering his love of fast food places, but I never question that. That, I think is for later, and right now I don't want to restrict any activity that gives him pleasure.

"I'll get the popcorn and be back in a jiffy." It takes me only a few minutes to get this sorted, thanks to my stock of microwave popcorn (who says the human race isn't moving forward?). In no time, we're sitting on the sofa together, ready for the evening's entertainment, which turns out to be two hours of the best of Hogwarts' finest versus Voldemort, with my son holding my hand during the scary bits. Obviously, this is unbelievably touching for any dad, and I'm no different. As the movie progresses, I try to refrain from mentally comparing his mother to the Dark Lord. However, the temptation to point out the similarities between her and Dolores Umbridge is beyond endurance, so I mumble "I must not tell lies" *sotto voce* right at the end of the movie.

Jack doesn't hear that because he's very tired, and getting him to bed involves carrying him to his bedroom. It takes a little while to get him into his pyjamas and pop him into bed. After I've achieved all that and tucked him in, I kiss him goodnight. He sleepily murmurs, "Love you, Dad!" and yet again I realise that contentment is sometimes a very simple concept.

Having had a great night with Jack, I'm forced into thinking about what happened earlier in the evening, and I'm obviously feeling less happy. Wanting to sort some stuff out in my head, I walk back into the lounge, trying desperately to separate my nascent feelings for Ms. Williams and the job I have to do. There's a desperate desire for me to prevent the impending doom of Jack being packed off to private school. That's a complete nightmare, of course, and putting a spoke in that wheel is my first priority. However, to do this I feel the need to mollify the Ex and try to keep her on side. This, as you can imagine, would be difficult at the best of times, and it really seems impossible in her current mood. However, I have at least got to try to get a grip on this, because if I do nothing Jack will be away from me in the blink of an eye. The trouble is that at the moment, I'm angry at her high-handedness and her assumption that I will just roll over and accept this. Cursing at myself in my head, I vow to stop this type of thinking, as I've never found that this helps me make decisions. However, I know it's based on a long history of conciliation in the face of Ex's fierceness.

Eventually I sit down at the computer to type an email. Instinctively I know that at all costs I must not upset her more than she is already, as this is only likely to harden her resolve. At this stage, I think I have a chance of delaying this idea, but if it catches hold and she starts planning, I'll be sunk.

The reality, of course, is that I've worked myself into a state, and my first email attempt, which starts "Why don't you wind your neck in, you stuck-up tart?" proves a little too direct. Also the "I'll fight you and your upper-class wanker boyfriend with every breath in my body" version is rejected for similar reasons.

By now it's 10.30 and I'm tired, and the vision of the Ex and John snogging pops into my head; for some reason it upsets me. It isn't often that I feel this way. In fact, I very rarely think of her in any other way except as my angry ex-wife and Jack's mother, and that's usually enough to be going on with. Somehow tonight, though, and I can't think why, the thought of her and the boyfriend together bothers me.

It's not that I miss her, or am pining for her, or jealous of John, but I think maybe it's because I'm lonely. These feelings have been creeping over me a lot lately and they are beginning to piss me off. In a world based on couples, it's quite hard to be single. That can be true at twenty-five, but at forty-two, it's sometimes bloody terrifying.

Right now I know a lot of thirty-plus single women, and I am fairly *au fait* with their loathing for commitment-phobic men. What's less known, though, is that the thirty-plus single men are usually hiding their loneliness in football, beer, curry, and vomit, all topped off with pizza. Now I have to ask myself: is this me? Maybe, I suppose, and I have to admit that the whole bachelor lifestyle thing is much less appealing than it was before I was married. Obviously, I want an awful lot more than that. However, I'm supposed to be carefree, and it's hard to express this stuff to someone who isn't in that boat. Every day lately I'm aware that I want someone to care about and someone to care for me, and I really like the whole romance thing, which since the divorce that has been a bit of an issue for me.

The school thing is a trial too, and I know I have to hold myself together for Jack's sake. Lately I look at him on his way in life and wish I could be more than an all-day-Saturday, one-evening-a-week, Burger Bar Dad. Even though I try hard to get more access, Ex puts up any number of obstacles to prevent that. This is the thing, though, and it's the one thing that really hurts: Ex is an assertive woman and I'm a conciliator. For the Ex and car salesmen, that translates into "easy touch".

You see the picture? It's depressing to think that I might have to fight her to prevent this private school idea from taking off, and what really bites me is the almost certain knowledge that if it does get off the ground, I'll lose him. It all goes round and round and the more I think about it the more I need to focus on the email. After about twenty redrafts, I come up with this:

> Hi,
> Whilst I appreciate that the teacher at the Parents' Evening wasn't very tactful, I do feel that your anger won't help Jack at school.
> His performance still puts him near the top of his class, and I am afraid that he may not see that if you criticise him for a relatively minor downturn in his performance.
> I am also alarmed about the idea of taking him out of his current school and putting him in a private school. You need to be clear that I want, and expect, to be consulted, and I am sure that Jack would have very strong feelings about leaving his friends and familiar surroundings. Of course I am open for discussion about the way forward and, like you, want the best for him. However, I want him first and foremost to be happy and contented, and would not like that to be compromised for an illusion of academic success.
> Lastly, I hope that we can meet soon to discuss all the ideas we have for Jack's progress.
> Paul

Pressing "send", I shoot it off into cyberspace: a gentle, measured appeal for Jack and my wishes to be considered when his future is being decided. Let's keep our fingers crossed that it makes an impact.

Chapter Seven
My Socialist Principles

Imagine, if you will, the Battle of Waterloo. Ex calls me at work the next day, wasting no time in deriding my literary efforts in the email as pathetic. She screams down the phone that if I want the best for Jack then I won't stand in her way. Apparently, John went to private school and he had a great time. Whilst she is ranting on, I can feel my left-wing principles wrestling with other types of feelings, including jealousy, anger and frankly a bit of working-class reverse snobbery. I try to hold all of this back, but the task is too much for me.

"Ooooh! John went to public school. Ooooh! Well, that makes everything so much better!" Childish and stupid, but I'm angry and it just floods out.

Raging, she bites out a retort. "What the hell is that supposed to mean?" This doesn't improve my mood and I'm barely holding it together at all. This type of question isn't one to be answered with anything other than care. At such a juncture, a well-rounded reply would be in order: something like, "What was good for John twenty years ago may not be the best for our son now." That would have done it.

Instead my razor-sharp brain comes up with, "John's a private school prick." Which, given the efforts I made to be conciliatory last night, is clearly the voice of an arsehole. As it's coming out of my mouth, it sounds frail, childish and stupid. That certainly isn't likely to make Ex any more measured, and so it turns out. The last I hear is a few screeched four-lettered Exocets, before the phone is rammed down at the other end.

Shaking my head, I chastise myself for losing it and really start beating myself up. It doesn't take long, though, before I realise how fruitless that is, and go outside and have a cigarette. Smoking is a very calming thing for me at times, especially when I'm not worrying about what it's doing to my health. The calmness obviously comes from dealing with my nicotine craving, but there's something else.

Going outside to smoke gives me an excuse to put my day on pause, to think about stuff and walk away, however temporarily, from situations that are bugging me. A pitiful excuse, I know, and I will give up soon, I hope. At the moment, though, everything feels like it's getting the better of me, and this is on my mind as I walk down the stairs at the office and meet the other social outcasts huddling in the doorway. Right now I don't feel like talking, and I just nod and don't interrupt their fascinating deliberations on the latest reject from *The X Factor*.

Smoking down here is an opportunity for me to turn things over in my mind and attempt to understand some essential realities, and I do this sort of stuff quite often the truth be told. It's very much part of what makes me reasonable, or a pushover, depending on your point of view, but I like to work out things in context and get some perspective.

Today my thoughts work like this:

1.) I sort of dislike my job.

2.) My Ex is a high achiever and judges people by what car they drive and how much money they earn.

3.) I like being a writer; I really am quite good, despite not being particularly successful.

4.) I don't want Jack to be the president of the Mega-Rich Bastard Bank Co.

5.) Ex wants Jack to be the president of the Mega-Rich Bastard Bank Co.

6.) Her anger at me stems from her disappointment with my lack of success as a hack and a writer.

7.) She feels cheated, as I was a really cool guy at university who looked likely to be very successful.

8.) John is much more successful than me.

9.) Ex wants Jack to be more like John than me.

10.) Ex who used to make my pants explode now makes my head explode.

All this stuff is going round in my head, along with the real killer: Ex was very unhappy as a child, and very poor. Her drive comes from a highly forceful mother who basically kept everything together. Her motivations are understandable and, when she was younger, were incredibly exciting to me. The trouble is that I'm too flexible. She took that for me being happy in the past and, these days, as a licence to do what she wants with Jack.

A lot of my unhappiness at work stems from my experiences of being a writer. I wrote and wrote and eventually got sick of rejection and, on reflection, started "lowering my sights". Dreams of writing a novel became relegated to the practical task of earning a crust on the local rag. My thoughts of writing for the RSC turned into the odd one-act play for the local amateur company. Truth is, the hopes and dreams of college were replaced by my voluntary work in the local fleabag theatre and helping kids in trouble at my mate Gerry's local youth project. It isn't well paid but it makes me content, and that drove Ex mad, and she is probably still bemoaning my lack of ambition.

While I was struggling professionally, Ex's career bloomed with her relentless enthusiasm, zeal and drive to succeed. The result of this was that she moved away from me financially, emotionally and politically. I had been, and to a large extent still am, left-leaning, but she was apolitical. As her career moved upwards, she became a paid-up member of the "I'm all right, Jack" style of Toryism personified by Teresa Gorman in the eighties and by Nadine Dorries now. Quite, quite nasty!

This trip down memory lane is interrupted by the realisation that I am due in court in ten minutes. Luckily, the journey is not onerous and, if I get a move on, I can make it in time. Stubbing out my cigarette, I hoof it indoors to get my notepad ready for today's brush with the justice system.

When I get there, the court is full and the waiting room is, as usual, populated by baseball-cap-wearing, tracksuited youngsters. These are the kids who, all too often, fall through the cracks in the welfare, education and social paternalism that make up modern Britain. It doesn't help that they're sometimes jumping on those cracks and it also may be significant that they're the offspring of parents who spent their teenage years with their arses on the same benches, waiting for "justice" to be done.

I've spent rather too much of my working life in the courts and I've always had the view that the court system is one long joke at the public's expense. The stereotypical image of Perry Mason and Rumpole working hard in the interests of their clients takes a massive dent every time you witness the real execution of justice. What happens is a mere procession of names, followed by a charge being read out, then a date being fixed for a hearing in this or another court. For every five examples of this, the public, the paymasters of this ridiculous circus, get to have one case dealt with.

That's usually the result of a motoring offence: a mumbled guilty plea, followed by the requisite sentence. About one in twenty cases involves some fracas or other with drunken youths or a minor crime of dishonesty. The sum total is that about one case in fifty is for something vaguely interesting to the readers of a local newspaper. So, as far as it concerns me, I get to write loads of "Mr X of So-and-So Drive got six points and a £300 fine for speeding". Not exactly reporting the cut-and-thrust of cross-examination in a jury trial and later the dramatic pause as the twelve "good men and true" are ushered in to render the verdict. So my working life is, on the whole, pretty boring, but it does at least pay the bills.

My first taste of court reporting promised a lot more, and I remember going to court with an old hack who left me to report on a car theft while he nipped over "to another case". At the time, I didn't know that was reporter's code for a case of beer. The defendants were a couple of brothers accused of ringing cars. That meant they bought insurance write-offs and then stole similar cars, so they could swap their identities and sell them on at a massive profit. Apparently you can't do this any more as the insurance companies closed that loophole with the DVLA.

Sadly it was rife then and the yard operated by these lads was full of dodgy motors, as the prosecution barrister laid out before the jury. However, what was truly memorable was the same barrister questioning one of the defendants.

He started with a gentle approach: "Mr. Smith." The defendant looked at bit confused at being addressed in such a formal manner.

"Yeah!" came a grunted response.

The barrister was looking through his papers absent-mindedly before asking his next question. "Can I ask you about your arrest on the fourteenth of May?"

"Yeah." The defendant was clearly not one of the world's great conversationalists.

More papers were shuffled and, after a short while, another question popped out. "When you were arrested, did you have anything in your possession?"

I saw the jury looking at their watches; clearly they didn't know where this was going.

"Urr, what?"

"Any personal possessions, papers, keys?" I saw the judge looking at his watch, as he clearly didn't know where it was going either.

"Urr, dunno." It's hard not to laugh at the memory of the defendant's inarticulacy. I shouldn't do it, but sometimes I can't help myself.

"Perhaps I can help you. Did you, by any chance, have a number of vehicle licence documents, more commonly known as log books?"

The jury start to focus as they can see what might be coming. The judge, however, is still looking at his watch.

"Dunno, might have had a couple!" came the answer from Birmingham's answer to Oscar Wilde.

"Well, Mr. Smith, what would you define as a couple? Two, perhaps? Three?"

More paper was rifled though in that absentminded professor way. The barrister seemed almost distracted by the answer from the poor bloke in the dock.

"Yeah, I suppose so."

The barrister took his time, rifled a bit more and then, after a little pause, came in for the kill—a masterpiece of his art.

"In fact, Mr. Smith, when you were arrested you had in your possession 287 vehicle log books."

The jury fell about, and even the judge was smiling. And so it went on—terrific stuff, as you can imagine—and I made hay with it on the third page of the Rag:

Brothers Arrested with 287 log books.
by Paul Castle

All good knockabout copy, and it probably raised a couple of laughs in and around the town.

Those days are few and far between, and therefore most of my days are filled with feeding the mortgage monster with the fees from "Mr. Y was banned for twelve months after being found one-and-a-half times over the legal limit." Not very glamorous, but needs must.

Chapter Eight
Skateboarding Punk Rocker

Perhaps the only good thing about being a court reporter is that, unless you have a deadline or it's a big national story (lots of cash but no byline), you get to bunk off at 4 p.m. Today's no different, and I rush down to Jack's school to see Ms. Williams. At this point I have a complete headful of thoughts and emotions running through me. The principal one is trying to get through the meeting without mentioning the fact that Ms. Williams looks like Michelle Shocked circa 1988. Now, I have to admit that I had a crush on Dallas's finest daughter, and that marked me out from most kids. They were still looking at girls with exploding hair and garish make-up, but I wanted substance rather than style and Michelle Shocked really delivered.

Anyway, Ms. Williams has really dark, short hair and big eyes and a brilliant endearing smile, just like Michelle's. Like I said, it's hard keeping that out of a parent-teacher meeting. It makes me nervous as I walk into the school and ask for the way to Jack's classroom.

The school is like any other, I suppose, with every wall used for children's art, inspirational messages and the usually ignored exhortations not to run in the corridors. Jack's classroom is at the end of one of these and I have no difficulty in finding it. I pause at the open door, taking a deep breath and promising myself that I will at least try to focus. Then I knock discreetly and she looks up from her desk, smiles, gets up and walks over to me, offering her hand.

"Mr. Castle, thank you for coming." She says it with a big smile, which I return, trying hard not to look like a grinning halfwit. Hopelessly, I try to think of something intelligent to say, or mumble at the very least.

Eventually, "Hi! I hope I'm not disturbing you!" comes out of my mouth. Not Noël Coward, I grant you, but better than nothing.

"Not at all! I was waiting for you."

D'oh! Of course she was…and now I genuinely feel like a dullard.

"Hope I'm on time!" is my next effort and, as it's accompanied by me walking into one of the classroom chairs, my attempt to focus looks doomed, but she skirts over that and gets right down to business. This is, after all, her workplace.

"Shall we sit?" It's like a request, but it isn't really. We both go to her desk, and I can see Jack's books and some of his other work. Her desk is neat, but not too neat. It has a feeling of teetering into either chaos or anal-retentive tidiness. You can imagine that I deeply approve of this, and with that happy thought, I sit down.

"Now, Mr. Castle…" She starts the meeting in a very brisk fashion; in fact, my arse has barely touched the chair.

"Please, call me Paul. You calling me Mr. Castle makes me feel old." I try to get a grip on the conversation, and also haven't forgotten last night's feelings of attraction: "Mr. Castle" isn't fitting into that at all. This clearly isn't what she's expecting, and for a moment she seems rather knocked off her stride.

"Oh, er, well yes. Paul." She seems rather discomfited by this informality.

Apprehensively I continue, and vow to say something close to, or approaching, intelligent. "Last night wasn't fair on you, and my ex-wife was a little brusque. I'm concerned for Jack, but know that this is a temporary blip in his work."

"It is good you can see that, Paul. Sadly, it seems you and your ex-wife are somewhat at odds, because she spoke to the Head Teacher today and has formally complained about my teaching methods." That, I'm thinking, would explain her formality and businesslike attitude. My Ex at her worst, crashing into anything she can.

I'm angry now, and vent some frustration towards the Ex. "I'm not very happy about it at all and I want to keep Jack here, if possible. I'm confident it is in his best interests." At least this bit is sincere and it's clear that there is agreement as she's nodding. There's a pause and I get a look that suggests I'm about to be told something I may not like.

"I feel that you need to agree on a plan for Jack. Forgive me, but at the moment that sounds quite hard for both of you." Ouch, that hurts, but at least she doesn't mince her words.

I'm trying desperately to resist the urge to say "bugger her!" and just about manage it. "Well she is very assertive!" Her smile returns, as the memory of last night is obviously coming back to her. Pausing for a moment, I attempt to find ways of describing my dilemma other than "she's a bitch and I've got no balls".

Instead of that I come up with, "I'm sorry but all this has been sprung on me and until I can sit down and work this out with her, we will be divided on this issue. I'm very much against taking him out of this school till the end of the academic year." At least that actually sounds like I know what I'm talking about and I'm not completely spineless.

She looks at me, and I sense she's a bit intolerant of my wimpy side. That may, of course, be a bit of an assumption on my part. Ms. Williams makes a face that indicates she is not going to let me off the hook regarding the Ex. "Jack needs some stability, and I would suggest that this matter is sorted out sooner rather than later."

I'm nettled by this, but not enough to forget that she looks like Michelle Shocked. In fact, what would Michelle do in my predicament? That's an interesting thought, which goes unanswered as my daydreaming has led me to miss Ms. Williams's last statement.

"I'm sorry; I missed that." For God's sake, I really must learn to focus. I get a bit of a look, which confirms my last thought about paying more attention.

"I was asking if you would like me to talk to her." Her question is quite clipped: not annoyed, but not far away. I feel the need to work hard to get back in this conversation and decide to use humour to see if that gets me anywhere.

"Good God, no! You are much more useful to the community than a reporter. If one of us has to die, it should be me." She laughs. My gamble has paid off and I'm back. "Seriously though, I know she has strong feelings, but she loves Jack and only wants what's best for him. I think she's wrong here, and I'll try to talk to her so we can come to an agreement that suits him."

"Jack's a lovely boy and I am sure he will appreciate that." She leaves it there.

The thought pops into my head that I want to ask her out. It seems wrong and is probably very wrong. Maybe if I can sort out this issue with the Ex. However, I don't want Ms. Williams to think that I am using Jack as a dating opportunity. "Thanks for seeing me and I will talk to my ex-wife and get back to you, Ms. Williams."

"Please do, Mr. Castle."

"Paul. Please call me Paul." I feel awkward insisting on this informality and I'm sure that it's having little or no impact.

"OK!" is her answer, and it's clear there's a desire on her part to seem enthusiastic about it. At least, that's what I'm convincing myself.

"Goodbye then, Ms. Williams. I'll keep in touch." I hold out my hand and we shake. Her warm hand lingers in mine, or am I just imagining it?

Just then another teacher walks in and says, in a completely insincere way, "Sorry, Michelle, are you busy?"

She's bloody called Michelle—would you believe it? Of all the names, it had to be that one!

Michelle *Not* Shocked looks at me and then replies to her colleague: "No, we're finished here." That feels like I'm being dismissed and I'm never one to outstay my welcome, so, using as much pleasantness as I can in my smile, I then turn to go.

"Goodbye. Please keep in touch." She says this in an offhand fashion, but it gets me thinking. Shouldn't she have said "about Jack" at the end of that sentence? Yes: she should have said "please keep in touch about Jack", not "please keep in touch". Am I seeing things that are not there? That's something to think about as I walk towards the door.

Just as I get there, I look back to see Ms. Williams, Michelle to her friends, look up at me and give me a small smile.

Chapter Nine
Reflections

I love my flat. It's a kind of bachelor haven, only it's clean. I insist on having a housekeeper and she's great, which makes my life very easy. My payoff from the Ex was bordering on generous and my mortgage is therefore quite small, so I live a pretty comfortable life.

The trouble is, and it's something that needs to be acknowledged, that since the divorce I've been very crap at sharing things. That isn't to say I'm mean—quite the opposite, really. It's just that having lived under the totalitarian regime of the Ex, I needed to escape that kind of emotional fascism. That has essentially put a brake on any but the most fleeting of emotional involvements. When the Ex and I first separated, I rented a flat and leapt into bed with a really great girl called Susan who worked for the paper. I'd started working part-time again when Jack went to nursery, and by the time I got divorced, he'd started primary school. Susan was lovely, attractive, empathic and all that, and knew I was really unhappy so helped me a great deal through the pain of my divorce. It just seemed natural to move to the next level. Then when I got this place, I found I wanted my space; I just wanted time to be with Jack and think about it all. She discovered that I was unwilling to share my life with anyone but Jack at that time, and she ended up getting heartbroken.

Being wise after the event, I just wasn't ready, and she was moving too fast—not that I'm seeking to use that fact or absolve myself from guilt. There was also the concern about what the impact would have been on Jack. Yes, I know that I'm probably using that to make excuses, but that was genuinely a factor at the time. In the end it got a little bit nasty and Susan accused me of using her. Sadly, I have the feeling that might be true, but, believe me, it was unconsciously done. We somehow managed to stay friends, but it is not the same: just nodding acquaintances, really. Genuinely, I hope she finds someone really nice, who will treat her very well.

Arriving home from the school visit, I pick up my bills then leave them on the coffee table. These days I pay all my stuff online, but it always makes me laugh that they send you the bills anyway. New technology: waste of time, really! The kettle is turned on and I check my emails: one glares at me from the usual spam offering cheap Viagra and penis enlargement. It's from Ex and I open it with some trepidation.

> *Paul,*
>
> *John and I are looking at schools for Jack for next year as I think that it will be impossible to find a more appropriate school at such short notice. I don't want to exclude you from this, but it is clear that you have an objection. However, I am determined to have him educated privately and I want you to understand I'm doing this for his benefit.*
>
> *In addition to looking at schools for Jack, I have made the Head aware of my feelings about his teacher. I expect you to support my decision in this.*

Well, what can you say to that? I sit there stunned and cannot take in the pace of her decision-making process. From Parents' Evening to private school. Poor Jack: do not pass go; do not collect £200. There is no room for manoeuvre; no room for dialogue. Bewildered, I go to the kitchen, and think about getting a beer, but I want to keep a clear head. There is at least a clear thought that I don't want to get pissed, get angry and fizz off the best email I'll ever regret. I settle down for a coffee and put on some lounge jazz. That normally helps to calm me down.

After this, I begin to assess the implications of Jack attending a private school. Apart from the class thing, which is not my strongest card to play, I admit, it's the uncertainty of it all. Where will it be; how often will I see him; will he be happy there? On top of that, I want to be his dad and the idea of John and Ex picking his school really gets up my nose.

The reality of all this is that I can't do anything because I don't know anything. There is the additional problem that I don't want to be involved in any discussions because that feels like I'm endorsing their decision. Sadly, the class thing rears its head again and whilst I don't want to be a militant Bolshevik warrior—if such a thing exists anymore—surely private school isn't what Jack needs. Feeling angry, I think about him turning into some silly upper-class twit. You know the type: all stiff upper lip, walking around like he has a poker stuck up his arse. I know it's a ticket to the old boy network, but I want Jack to be something special, not a yah boo stockbroker from Cheam.

In order to prevent this I have to cause some waves and fight the Ex. Not an appealing prospect, because, well…I'm a bit of a wimp. Not as assertive, not as uncompromising, not as self-assured, and definitely not convinced that my arguments are 100% irrefutable. In short, I'm a bit of a wanker.

Ex, on the other hand, will be prepared. By the time I have

marshalled my forces, she will have shed-loads of school brochures backed with statistics on school performance, league tables and all manner of other shit that she thinks will assist Jack in his future life. The trouble is I know that, from her point of view, my wishes will seem like I want Jack to end up like a stoned slacker. In addition to that, I doubt she could resist the temptation to add, "I don't want him to be a loser like you." Oh bollocks, what a mess!

The jazz CD finishes and my coffee is cold, and if I keep on like this I'll drive myself dotty. Trying to think constructively, I attempt to imagine what Jack would like and how he would react to Ex and John's plan to make him an upper-class, emotionally retarded twit. They're actually going to have to persuade him about this, and that will be a tough ask: Jack likes his routine and he likes his school. The trouble with that is that he is ten and leaving this year for high school. Sure, he will miss his friends, but Jack never had problems making friends. The fact that he's leaving his school anyway might make the private school argument seem OK.

This is a big mess and if I'm not careful I'll end doing what I usually do, which is sit on my arse and hope for the best. Then the decision will be made and I'll be sidelined. With this in mind, I decide to get myself together and really do something that will show my resolve and ability to assert myself. I decide to make another cup of coffee.

Yep. This is my big plan: have a coffee and think some more. I may actually radically alter this and have tea instead. Faced with an emotional crisis, I reach for the kettle. Priceless. All the time I'm beating myself up, I'm still thinking about making progress on this issue, and then eventually I put together a great plan: I'll procrastinate. It's an excellent plan, full of merit, and I rush to the phone to put it in action.

Chapter Ten
Football, the Opium of the Masses

Yes, like constipation, procrastination is the thief of time, and my oldest friend, apart from my mate Nick and my Parker fountain pen given to me by an old girlfriend. Therefore, I pick up the phone and call the Ex, and with my stomach tightening I hear it ringing. There's a click and Ex answers.

"Hello," she says in a friendly way. She obviously hasn't looked at her caller ID.

"Hi, it's me." I can feel the frostiness coming down the cable. I'm not too bothered about this, as, let's face it, I've been here before.

"Did you get my email?" She had decided to skip the pleasantries; again something that I'm intimately familiar with.

To keep the peace, I choose not to make an issue of it and answer, "Yes, and I think we need to talk before we discuss this with Jack." Which isn't a bad opening gambit, if I say so myself.

Ex pauses and then, miracle of miracles, I get a response not dripping with rancour. "Yes, that seems a good idea." She seems surprised that I want to talk about it, even forgetting the hostile tone. "When would like to do this?"

"As soon as we can, we need to sort this so Jack doesn't end up being unsettled." Which, after all, is my first concern.

She seems to realise this and she says, in a much more conciliatory way, "OK, I'll email you some dates."

Feeling lucky, I decide to push it. "I would like us to be in full agreement about this before we tell Jack anything. Can we agree on that?" There's the sound of her hand being forced round the receiver, and it strikes me that she's discussing this with her boyfriend. As I don't know what type of relationship they have, I decide to keep quiet and let her sort that out. Eventually she comes back to talk to me.

"I can agree to that as long as you're not going to be your usual difficult, time-wasting self." This seems to be progress and I rejoice at this concession, despite the dig, which in the interest of harmony I decide to ignore.

"I promise I will listen and come with an open mind," I lie.

"OK, look forward to seeing you soon."

"No you won't!" is my first thought, which I sensibly leave unsaid. However, I'm still happy, as we've managed to end a conversation without rancour, certainly on her part.

Almost in a sense of rapture, I put the phone down with an air of satisfaction. There you go: procrastination! It's bought me some thinking time, put her off her guard and made me look reasonable.

Job done! Back to the coffee and jazz.

Sticking in another CD, I start reading a script that I wrote some time ago, and which a director I half know has half promised to read. The writing has some life, real zest and humour. The words rip along and I'm pleased with the pace and plotting. It needs a polish and I want to make a few changes here and there, but it reminds me I can write really well when I put my mind to it.

Sometimes, when I look back at the stuff I wrote some time ago, it produces two emotions: pride and anger. The pride comes from reading and enjoying the way I can put this stuff together. The anger is that I lack the balls to get it out, to do anything with it. The essence of this is that I'm afraid. Sure, I can write, but knocking out a court report is different from a novel or a play. That requires a thick skin, which I'm not sure I have any more. Bizarrely, I don't mind the rejections that much. In fact, they prevent what I fear the most. Imagine getting a publisher, getting a book deal or a play produced, and then it gets panned by the critics or even worse ends up in the remainder shops, unread.

That would be the ultimate failure for me, and In comparison to that being called a loser by the Ex is a walk in the park. One of my plays got put on a few years ago and from the moment that rehearsals began I was in a terrible state. Fear of failure: just awful, mind-crushingly awful.

Before I go too far down that road and end up pouring petrol on myself, the phone rings and I check my caller ID: it's my mate Gerry. He manages a youth club for kids excluded from school. This is where we first met when I began volunteering about fifteen years ago, and we hit it off straightaway.

"Hi, Gerry." My voice is upbeat, partly from my successful implementation of the procrastination plan, and partly because it's a mate on the phone whose company is always enjoyable.

"Paul, how are you?" he asks with a laugh in his voice.

"OK, kind of. You?"

"I'm great." Whatever mood he is in, Gerry makes the best of it. Tonight, although I'm fairly upbeat after my last phone call, I'm not into that level of relentless bonhomie, as my issues aren't sorted yet. However, it's hard to scowl when he's in the room or on the phone.

"Cool!" I answer. "What's happening?" Whatever it is, I have a suspicion that it's likely to cheer me up—that is, if I allow it to.

He sniggers. "I'm off the leash tonight! Fancy a pint? The football's on in the pub." He says the magic words and I decide that I can give myself permission to enjoy an evening out.

First, though, I make the decision that Gerry isn't going to get off unscathed.

"Gerry, you've never been *on* the leash!" He laughs, and it's the laugh of a man with something to laugh about. Gerry married Jenny three years ago, and they work well together. She's an artist and he's a youth worker. They don't impose on each other and give each other space to pursue different interests and friends. They're so cool together and every single one of his married mates is wildly jealous of him.

"So are you coming or what?" he asks, still laughing. It's clear he's expecting me to say yes.

"Of course! White Horse?" I'm not about to disappoint him, as it could be a good tonic for me. After all, life's too short, and going to the pub isn't going to impact on my ability to derail the plans for Jack.

"See you at seven!" He laughs again, and it's clearly infectious as by the time I get to say my goodbye and all that guff, I'm laughing too. The power of friendship should never be underestimated.

"That's great. See you then!" I put the phone down. This is actually just what I need: a few beers and some overpaid prima donnas to shout at. Bliss!

However, a night out with Gerry needs some preparation, and I pour away my coffee and instantly start. You need a good stomach lining, so I cook an omelette with potato rösti. I love food and I particularly love cooking for others, so this isn't a chore, as I have a well-stocked fridge and larder.

When I've finished cooking, I sit and eat my meal with a glass of water, which I'm hoping will act to dilute the alcohol somewhat. Gerry is a real drinker; I have long since refused to keep pace with him, much to his amusement. Every night out with him is punctuated with the words "party lightweight!" and I am completely OK with that. I mean, he works in the evenings and I work in the mornings.

However, I've made it a rule that whatever I drink in the evening and however rough I feel in the morning, I get to work on time and in reasonable shape. Although I have lots of issues with work, I'm not a slob about it, insisting on putting my hours in, so there are absolutely no duvet days for me.

Quickly, I get a shower and change, deciding on jeans and a rugby shirt—which is, after all, perfect drinking attire. Then I phone Jack and say goodnight and head for the pub. Later, as I'm getting nearer in the cab, I realise this is the perfect antidote to the Ex: beer, Gerry and football.

Beer.

Ah well, I love it just because for a few minutes, it makes everything seem OK. Gerry and I are good drunks: it makes us stupid and funny and really good company. Obviously, being a journo, I know all the downsides, and I'll never let alcohol rule my life the way it does some of my colleagues'.

Gerry. He's my closest friend at the moment, although I have other long-standing mates. He's also a great emotional confidant and for fifteen years, he's seen all my troubles so he really could be called Ex's archenemy. It will be a good release to spill all my fears about Jack to him tonight. He loves my son, and knowing Gerry he will come up with about twenty plans to deal with the problem, all of them involving a Heath Robinson contraption delivering a ten-tonne weight on top of Ex's head. Despite this, there isn't a nasty bone in his body.

Football. Well, as far as I'm concerned, it is the opera of the working-class, despite the attempts by satellite TV and the middle-class to ruin it. I've always loved it, and Ex hated it, of course, which gave me not a moment's pain. It is the one place I can rant, rave, scream and shout without anyone raising an eyebrow. For me it's the ultimate pressure valve.

Whenever I think about football, it brings back brilliant memories like being with my mate Nick watching an England game. Our much-vaunted striker missed a complete sitter. Nick jumped up and shouted, "I've been telling you he's a useless cunt for two years!" No one batted an eyelid—despite the fact that we were in the boardroom of his company and the place was packed with his clients. It's football: the place where men and now women can shed polite overcoats and for two hours rediscover the cave-dweller within. Of course, I realise this is a bit of cod-psychology, but there we go. Football's brilliant and I love it, and I don't need or want to apologise for that.

Yes. Beer, Gerry and football: a top night in store, with the added possible bonus of a curry.

Chapter Eleven
Dream Result: Me 4, Ex 0

The pub is crowded and Gerry has bagged a table near the screen; a Beck's is waiting for me. We embrace and, as we're here to watch football, that's OK. Actually, I'm very tactile and have no problem embracing either sex in public. However, the modern world isn't welcomed by everybody and The White Horse is still bit old fashioned. We chat about the usual: work and all that. Then he asks me to do a couple of shifts—as usual, he sorts out his rota when we meet and I work as and when he wants. This is usually to plug staffing gaps and cover holidays. The truth is he wants me there full time but I prefer just a few shifts rather than a career change.

Then he asks the question: "How's Jack?"

I decide not to launch in, but to hint about my issues, then he can decide for himself what he wants to hear. "Hmm, how long have you got?" I try to make sure he knows what he's letting himself in for.

He laughs and says, "Don't tell me his mother has locked him in his room for breathing too heavily?" We both laugh, and he cracks on. "No, don't tell me: her sales projections are 1% behind the forecasts and she's taking her workers on a team bonding course to refocus them, and she's insisting Jack comes along to get a taste of corporate life?"

There's a glint in his eye, and he can't stop himself. "No, wait. He spilt his drink in her BMW and she's stopped his pocket money in order for him to learn the consequences of carelessness and respect for others' belongings?"

My eyes are watering as I roar with laughter and hold up my hand, as I want him to be serious. "Come on, tell me what the Wicked Witch of NatWest has done now!"

That's his favourite name for her, and whilst it doesn't make me laugh out loud much anymore, it's still bloody funny.

"Why do you assume it's to do with her?" I ask this like it's a sensible question and I'm expecting a sensible, worked-out reply.

"All your problems revolve around her, that's why." Which, given Gerry's usual replies to that question, has at least the merit of brevity. It also has a lack of four-letter words, his usual *lingua franca* when discussing the Ex.

I quickly skirt over his answer, and that's for two reasons. First, he blames all my problems on her all the time, and this is familiar ground we're treading. Secondly, I've a solid suspicion that he's right. Whenever he advances this argument, I laugh, nod furiously and change the subject. The truth is that I'm scared to analyse this as I'm terrified about what I might find out at the end of it. Changing the subject slightly, I decide to let him in on what's troubling me.

"Jack got his school report this week and it was not as good as last year." For the next half hour I talk about that, the open evening and the threat of her putting Jack in private school. All of this is punctuated with Gerry venting his fondest swear words, usually reserved for Arsenal's centre forward. To end the tale, I tell him about the Michelle Shocked lookalike and my feeling that I could go out with her.

"Wow! So your ideal result is more homework for Jack and home tuition for you?" This is Gerry's reading of my situation.

"Be serious!" is my reply.

"I am being serious: you need home tuition more than any other man I know."

Not wanting to acknowledge his new euphemism for sex, or my chronic need for it, I try to steer the situation back to Jack. "What do you think about him going to private school?"

He looks at me with a frown and switches into a vaguely sensible mode for a moment. "How serious is she about all this?" he says, confirming that he's on-message.

"Very bloody serious by the sound of it." I hope that my sadness is communicated in that sentence, and he realises what this means for me.

"Well, my advice, between ourselves, is to hire a hitman and kill her." I know that Gerry is trying to cheer me up by using humour, and that means he knows I'm really upset.

I decide to play along, confident that he will get to the point eventually. "Gerry, how long have we known each other?"

"Fifteen years, off and on."

"How many of those years have you been telling me to kill her?"

"Fifteen years, off and on." He laughs. "Which just goes to show you what bloody good advice it is."

"Well, look, I'm serious here."

"What makes you think that I'm not? No jury would convict." We both laugh but he becomes grave quite quickly. "Whatever you do, get some legal advice. I know her, and more importantly I know you."

"You mean I'm a wimp, don't you?" I say this almost without thinking; self-deprecation is my default position.

"No, I don't, you idiot." He pauses and takes a swig of beer. "You are a wise, lovely, brilliant, human being and I would trust you to the end of the earth."

"I sense another sentence coming here." My turn to swig, and when I finish I look him in the eye. "Come on, then: out with it." I hate this lecturing even from Gerry, and I want to get it over with. The reason I hate it is that I'm much better at lecturing myself than any of my mates.

He decides to crack on and give it to me straight. "It's like this. You always look to include people and you're always ready to sacrifice your interests for the good of those around you."

"Most people would think that's a good thing!" is my not unreasonable response.

Gerry leaps on that instantly. "Yeah, and your ex-wife fucking loves it! She's won the battle just by taking a position."

"Yes, but…"

"No, Paul. You can't be a nice guy on this. If you don't want to see Jack in a private school, you have to fight; and don't take this the wrong way, but you're rubbish at fighting."

Which is a pretty good summary of the situation, all told. Attempting to take this in, I want to come on all grouchy and defend my pugilistic skill but I know that he's correctly got the essence of this. The landlord puts the football on, and Gerry reaches over to put his arm on my shoulder.

"You're like a brother to me. Whatever you decide, I'll back you. But please, please, promise me that whatever you do, you'll run it past a lawyer. Promise me! If you lose Jack, it'll be a disaster. This is one fight you cannot afford not to win."

He's right and I know he's right. The volume comes up on the TV and the football starts, and I raise my bottle to him. He reciprocates, and our bottles meet and we both shout, "Cheers!"

The game kicks off and the analysis of my life is put on hold until half time.

The match is dire but the banter with Gerry isn't. Guiltily, I have to admit that is part of the attraction. The worse the game is, the wittier he becomes. At one point, a terrible tackle lays out one of Gerry's most hated players. He raises a tremendous laugh in the pub by shouting, "Have another kick: he's still fucking breathing!" Top stuff, I think you'll agree.

The ref blows for half-time and Gerry runs to the bar to get a round in. My phone beeps, and, looking at it, I find a message from a friend offering a dinner party invitation on Friday. Bonnie and her partner are a cracking laugh and great company, so acceptance won't cause me any pain. That is, unless she is trying to fix me up again. It's not that they invite inappropriate women; I just don't do spontaneous. There is a need for me to get to know someone slowly and not under any pressure. So a fix-up usually sees me clamming up and looking surly, which isn't really me. It's just that I don't like meeting new people in that sort of social situation. Does that sound weird? Probably, but it's just one of my foibles. The evening usually includes me spilling soup down my shirt or knocking the wine over. It's just that I get so wound up and probably don't make a good first impression. However, a meal with friends is always a pleasure and I text back a reply saying yes, then look for Gerry to see whether he and Jenny have been invited.

He comes back with the drinks and says, "Has Bonnie asked you to dinner?"

I answer in the affirmative and ask him, "How do you know?"

"She's just texted me. Is she trying to fix you up again?" He knows it's a favourite pastime for Bonnie, and he does try to help.

"I bloody hope not!"

He nods, as he is familiar with my inability to do spontaneous. "I'll try and get the guest list from her."

My sense of relief is palpable, but all I can manage is, "Thanks, mate." We both take a drink, and I'm not that keen to reopen our conversation about Jack. Instinctively Gerry seems to understand this.

"This game is shit." This, I guess, is his attempt at moving away from the Jack conversation.

As a diversion, it's just right and I answer with relish. "Yeah, completely."

"Let's hope the second half is better than the first."

Thanks, Gerry: what a mate! He really gets the whole male communication thing. So off we go, chatting about nothing till the match restarts and we can shout at the telly again.

When the game gets into injury time, Gerry asks me if I'm up for a curry. The omelette was a long time ago and I love that idea. The final whistle blows and he starts to get ready to go for the food, and I know I'm going to get my ear bent about fighting the Ex.

Chapter Twelve
Life in a Recession

It's Friday, and the court is struggling its way through the usual round of traffic offences, minor public infractions, and the normal petty larceny.

Trying my best to focus, I scribble it all down and ensure the public knows about the wrongdoings of their neighbours. One day, I know I will be reporting on a big murder, but in my fifteen years the most I've ever got was an armed robbery in the post office and a near-fatal domestic dispute involving a knife.

The situation with Ex is no better, and she's emailed me a couple of dates for a meeting. I've replied with a yes for Monday evening. We'll be meeting in a pub, as I insisted on somewhere neutral. Jack will be looked after by the nanny, so John can be there. Strictly speaking he's nothing to do with this and I could in all fairness have told her that. However, I decided to let that ride. My logic is that if he is to be a part of Jack's life (if he isn't already), I need to allow him to participate in his future.

Meanwhile, I have the weekend to marshal all my arguments and put forward a convincing case.

The notion that I have got a chance to change their minds is pitiful, but I do have the ultimate game-stopper in my bag, if it all goes badly. That's the threat of legal action. OK, it's a nuclear option and I don't want to use it, but I have to think of Jack's best interests and I'm convinced that this private school nonsense is nowhere near any good for him.

The court drones on, and as I'm no good at doing more than one thing at a time, I decide Monday will take care of itself as I have to worry about tonight first. This dinner party at Bonnie's has become worrisome. Gerry dropped me a text yesterday saying that Bonnie was noncommittal about fixing me up but that she's knocking out dinner for eight people.

This means that apart from Bonnie and Jim, her partner, there is me, Gerry and Jenny and probably Archie and Shona, a couple of teachers that have entered our circle relatively recently. That leaves one space unaccounted for. A sure fix-up opportunity for Bonnie. Bollocks.

Even though I'm cross, I'm a little intrigued by the possible occupant of that seat at the dinner party. There's even a chance that one day it might be Ms. Right, but what with the whole Jack thing going on, I'm not really in the frame of mind for a new relationship, especially one based on a blind date.

The court plods on, and I'm scribbling my usual drivel to translate later when a sudden thought pops into my head. What about Michelle the teacher? That would be someone I could really get my head around: funny, funky and attractive in a Michelle Shocked skateboarding punk rocker kind of way. Now that would be a great blind date, and one that I could get enthusiastic about.

Absentmindedly I start daydreaming. Michelle Shocked-a-like looked roughly mid-thirties and that isn't much of an age difference, so I begin to picture us meeting tonight. The surprised helloes, the questions about how we've managed to arrive in the same social circle, and all of that guff. Sadly my musings are so intense that I have to ask another reporter the name of the defendant up next for six points on his licence and a £200 fine for having no insurance. Shamefaced, I resolve to get a grip. My new resolution prevents me from thinking about the blind date trial ahead and I hunker down to the proceedings at hand.

Lunchtime arrives, and the magistrates rise and the court suddenly troops out. The dinner party returns to my thoughts and I light up before walking back to the office. After a five-minute dawdle, I see some of my colleagues outside. They all look pretty sullen, and I ask the inevitable.

Jim the photographer gives it to me straight: "We've all got a memo from the management, and they're looking to lay some staff off. They want volunteers first. Volunteers! I mean, who wants to be unemployed in this nonsense of a recession?"

Amazed, I look at him and blurt out, "Oh my God, that's terrible! How many are they looking for?"

"Fifteen," he answers. "About a third of the staff." That's a load of workers in what is a small regional paper.

"That's shit." Genuinely, I can't think of anything else to say. A sad reflection on my communication skills, but after all I'm really stunned.

Jim just shrugs in a resigned fashion. "Yeah, completely shit." My first thought is how the Union are going to stop this. However, given that Jim is a convenor, he would tell me straight off if anything was going on, so I'm assuming the Union is as gobsmacked as me.

Standing there in silence, I notice the other smokers also aren't talking and I think about the possibility of redundancy. Though I don't particularly like my job, I'm not thrilled with the prospect of unemployment. I look at Jim again. "When will we know if we're for the chop?"

He looks miserably at me. "If you want to volunteer for redundancy, you've got till the end of the month. Then we'll be told a week after that if we're getting the elbow."

"Thanks, mate." This begins to put my worries about tonight into perspective and forces me to consider work. It's a recession, but I thought the paper was doing OK.

Walking to my desk, I see the editor in his office, and I cross the newsroom to see him. As I walk up to him, he knows what's coming and goes onto the defensive straightaway.

"Look, it's nothing to do with me. All I can say is that I tried to fight for all of you." Not the most impressive opening, but I guess he thinks he might get away with it.

"Very good speech, Doug, but save it for the gullible. What's the real story here?" I'm not impressed and I want some answers. Actually, despite my alleged lack of assertiveness, when it comes to asking hard questions, as a proper reporter should do, I'm not too shabby.

"The owners are rationalising; they want to consolidate income and beef up the bottom line." Every day he sounds more like a corporate accountant, and from a newspaper editor it's the last thing you want to hear.

As you can guess, I'm definitely not happy, and I spit back: "So they are using the recession to squeeze more money out of the paper!"

That seems to be the position in pretty much every business that isn't failing at the moment. My dad had a very sharp view of life in a recession, and he was always saying that the biggest firms make the same amount of profit in the hard times because, at the first whiff of a downturn, they start gouging workers and upping prices. The turnover will drop, but the bottom line stays the same.

Doug, oblivious to my musings, drones on. "Look, Paul, I don't have any power in this. It's a hard world." This is his perennial position: "it's tough out there". He uses that to excuse any attempt by the paper to screw people.

My experience of being assertive with the Ex has borne fruit and I refuse to let his point go by unanswered. "All I can say is that if standards drop, circulation will follow, and then we're all fucked." I'm definitely angry now and Doug's attempts to weasel out of any responsibility aren't helping.

"I know, I know." He fixes me a little conspiratorial stare and says, "Look, I've got an agreement that I cannot cut the newsroom too badly, so you're pretty safe."

There's an anger growing in my stomach and I'm a bit disgusted with the thought of others being pushed out of the door before me. That's what the Ex would call my hopelessly wimpy side. My face has a look of disdain and I say, "Well, you never know—I might take you up on the voluntary redundancy." With that, I walk out to my desk and leave him looking crestfallen or shocked; either way, it looked pretty good to me.

Chapter Thirteen
The Middle-Class at Play
(and I have to include myself in that even though I consider myself working-class)

Dinner at Bonnie's is always a good night, even if she makes the occasional cack-handed attempt at partnering me up. She always keeps a good table, and she and Jim are vivacious and really fun to be with. He's cool and often comes out with Gerry and me calling it "playtime" or "the men's group", like a support network for oppressed victims. Which, considering we arse about, shout at the football and eat curry, is pretty ironic.

Gerry and Jenny are coming, and that'll be great, as I love them like a brother and sister. As a couple they shouldn't work but they do, and they're very different from Jim and Bonnie. Gerry, apart from being a blokie sort of guy who can occasionally be much too frivolous, is a bloody hard worker. He runs the youth club with a passion that really surprises many people who only know him socially. The kids love him, but more importantly they respect him. That's all the more admirable because some of those guys have come from terrible backgrounds. Realistically, I like to think I have a rapport with the kids, but next to Gerry I'm an amateur.

His partner Jenny is very different: as quiet as he is loud and ethereal to his earthy. The one thing that keeps them together is their love of helping kids. Jenny uses her art to help disabled children, and occasionally works with some of Gerry's youth group doing one-to-one projects. Her artistic work, outside of the community art, is sublime and has an indefinably light touch. Tonight's meal, it turns out, is a little gathering to celebrate the opening of another exhibition of her paintings, which I'm attending tomorrow after I've dropped off Jack.

Also there will be Archie and Shona, a Scottish couple who teach locally. Shona works with Bonnie, and to be honest they came down to the Midlands last year for work and they're a bit homesick. Archie is a gentle giant, who is really worried about upsetting people, but a man of strong opinions. That sounds contradictory, but it isn't. He's a proud Scot and we all banter with him, with me occasionally arguing with him about his Scottish Nationalism. He'll never get anywhere near personal abuse, unless he's had a few and then he'll spend the whole of the next week apologising. Gerry, as you can imagine, has a great deal of fun at his expense. Shona, on the other hand, is a gentle, quiet, caring hippie chick. It's lovely to talk to her as she has a kindly manner and it's clear she has great empathetic qualities.

Which leaves "X", the unknown quantity, a.k.a. my blind date. In the past Bonnie has invited a diverse range of unattached women to fix me up with. Whilst most of them were "nice" and none of them would be unsuitable as a partner, I'm not at this point looking for any love interest, even if I could get over my clumsy shyness. This is usually at odds with the unattached women who are invited to Bonnie's dinner parties.

Suffice to say that I've gone out with a couple that could see past my diffidence, and they were nice enough, but to be honest I'm a bit unsure about women these days. OK, the Michelle Shocked-a-like Ms. Williams would be in my top ten list of desirable women at the moment, but what with the Ex and her being Jack's teacher it's just a pipe dream.

Which is perhaps why I really fancy her? The unobtainability makes her a great fantasy object, but shelters me from the reality of the whole relationship thing. That's especially attractive as she will at some point find out I'm a bit of a wanker, and blow me out.

So as I'm in the cab driving to Bonnie's, I while away my time on the reasons why I shouldn't go out with Michelle Williams and her skateboarding punk rocker hairstyle. In my head, I go through the pros, go through the cons and realise that this is after all a displacement activity; a conscious diversion from the reality that awaits me at Bonnie's house. The closer I get, the more I think that this is a bad idea and that any romantic involvement with Michelle or anyone else outside of my head is just not worth considering. After all, I will need all my emotional energy to sort out Jack, and the Ex's weird idea to send him to the modern equivalent of Greyfriars to be bullied by the next David Cameron.

Arriving on the doorstep, I'm in my funny-peculiar mood, and the fact that I might be fixed up just adds to my emotional fragility. Shaking my head, I knock on the door, and Bonnie is all smiles, taking my bottle of wine from me without looking at the label, which slightly annoys me every time she does it. I spend a great deal of time picking wine for friends and like them to at least acknowledge that. If Jim had have opened the door, he would have given it a once-over at the very least. As you have no doubt noticed, I am not in the greatest mood, but I'm way short of full-on grumpy bugger; I'm just nervous, especially as I have not seen the mystery woman yet.

We go to the kitchen and she offers me the usual choice of red, white or beer and I select a red as her white is an Aussie Pinot Grigio that I don't fancy. The kitchen smells excellent, as both Jim and Bonnie are bloody good cooks, and whatever happens with Miss X, I know I am in for a good load of nosebag.

I slope towards the dining room, and the mystery woman is a brunette with big brown eyes: as I instantly note, very attractive. Not as thin as a supermodel, which is great considering I once had a brief, ill-thought-out relationship with a beautiful woman with a supermodel figure. Honestly, she was really, really vain, and as for lovemaking, it was like sleeping with a bicycle.

Miss X is sitting next to Archie and is very intently chatting to both him and Shona. My shout of "Hi, everyone!" gets the usual acknowledgements, then Archie gets the introductions out of the way.

"Listen, Paul, this is Gillian; she's doing some supply teaching around here. Gillian, this is Paul, who writes for the local paper, and he's the author of a load of other stuff as well." That actually makes me sound quite cool.

She holds out her hand and I shake it firmly. Her skin is very soft and the grasp is warm and firm but not bone-crushing; then I stupidly ask, "What subjects do you teach?" Oh God, is that the best I can come up with? Practically every person she's ever met must have asked her that question. But she shows no sign of rolling her eyes, so at least I know she's polite!

Gillian answers brightly, "English Literature and English. I've moved up here to be closer to my daughter. She's at Birmingham University."

"Cool!" I respond. Oh God, what a Muppet I must sound! Archie helpfully adds that I write the court reports and I wince, as that is hardly the picture of crusading journalism that I'd like to portray. "Well, it pays the mortgage," I add, attempting to be nonchalant. Gerry is sitting at the table holding a Beck's, which I secretly want to drink, and he fixes Gillian with a grin.

"Don't listen to that old guff. Paul's a great writer. He wrote a couple of plays and loads of other stuff. Brilliant it is, honestly." Blushing, I silently curse him, as I hate being bigged up. I'm out of control of this conversation and it's only a few sentences old.

"Really?" Gillian asks. "Have you had them put on anywhere?" She actually sounds genuinely interested.

"I've had one done locally." The play was one of my best, and Jenny helped me put it together for a local experimental company. They loved doing it, and it truly was one of my proudest moments as a writer.

Her face lights up. "That's fantastic! I love the theatre. I know this is presumptuous, but can I read it?"

Oh God, I'm blushing again, and I'm desperately hoping that I don't look quite as discomfited as I feel. There's a strange noise coming out of my mouth as I explain that it wasn't that good and blah, blah, blah. In short, my self-deprecation is kicking in, and instead of making a good impression, I've started to look like an idiot.

Gerry laughs, and Jenny playfully slaps him on the top of his head.

Gillian asks, "What 's so funny?"

Gerry leans over, puts a hand to the side of his mouth theatrically, and says in a whisper you could hear in the next street, "I'll show you the reviews; it was brilliant." Everyone around the table laughs at this gesture, except me of course.

What's going on in my head is impossible to describe, and

I've no idea why I feel compelled to say, "No, it wasn't. It was definitely not brilliant—average at best."

Gillian turns to Archie and Shona. "Did you see it?"

Shona says lightly, "No, we were still in Scotland when it was on here."

"Lucky you." This is my attempt at dry humour, and it occurs to me that I must stop this.

Gerry jumps in: "Shut up! Bonnie!" She arrives at the dining room door. "What was Paul's play like?"

"Brilliant; made me cry." She is all smiles and puts her hand on my shoulder, and then goes back to the kitchen.

I make a face at Gerry and then look at Gillian. "She didn't tell you it was a comedy, though, did she?" Everyone laughs and, unbelievably, I actually start to relax. Miracle of miracles, by the dessert course I confess *sotto voce* to Gerry that I am having a really great time.

It helps that Gillian is lovely, witty, interested in everyone, not afraid to express an opinion, a bit left-wing, and really at home in this company. In short, the sort of girl who would be perfect for me. Now the panic starts to mount as I realise that I have left thoughts of Ms. Williams at the first course. I start to go wobbly and begin to think about whether I dare to ask Gillian out. Do I? Well, no, to be honest. I want to get a grip on things and I know that when I fall in love, and I could see myself easily falling in love with Gillian, I go a bit mad. You know the thing: heart beating, cold sweats, talking nonsense and dribbling.

So, at the moment I need to be focused on Jack and I don't know if I can make an emotional commitment of the magnitude required. Does that sound like a load of bollocks? Of course it does. This is typical of me, dreaming about having a relationship with a woman I've just met and imagining asking her out, and then thinking of all the reasons I shouldn't.

The cheese board comes out with the coffees, and Gillian asks me about my play again. She's interested in what it's about and the central characters, and I talk, with some passion, about the plot, where I got the idea from, and how I wrote it. In short, I'm a writer enthusiastic about his work, not a hack hiding behind my cynicism. It's been a very long time since I've been with a person who has been able to pull off that trick.

The evening comes to an end and Gillian is whisked away by Shona, but not before she gently pecks me on the cheek when saying goodbye, a gesture that leaves me in a trance for a few seconds. In fact, I only just hear Jenny, who doesn't drink alcohol, offering to drive me home. As Gerry steers me out of the door, Bonnie kisses me goodnight with a knowing look in her eye.

"What?" I say, knowing pretty much how she will respond.

Bonnie does not disappoint. "Gillian's nice, isn't she?" It's not like she hasn't been dying to say this ever since I walked into the lounge to introduce myself.

However, I decide to have a bit of fun, in the spirit of things. "Stop that! Now!" I say in mock horror. She laughs and I laugh too, and pretty soon we're all laughing. "And yes, she is very, very nice."

Winking at her, I allow Gerry and Jenny to take me home. I smile to myself as we hit the traffic in the city centre. It's an ironic, wry grin, as Bonnie has introduced me to a woman whom I would actually love to go out with and with whom I can imagine spending lots of time. Sadly, she's done it at what is likely to be the most incredibly inappropriate, soul-destroying time of my life.

Chapter Fourteen
Time Flies By
(When You're the Driver of a Train)

The next morning finds me dozing in my bed, until I'm woken by a call on my mobile. It's Gerry, and he wants to know what I think about Gillian and how she compares to Michelle Shocked-a-like. I have a bit of a hangover and have just under an hour to take a shower, get dressed and pick up Jack for our regular Saturday jaunt. This time issue prevents a full-scale discussion with Gerry and I tell him I'm in a hurry and I'll call him back, but yes, Gillian is lovely. He reminds me about Jenny's exhibition at the gallery in Birmingham tonight and I agree to pick him up after dropping Jack off.

I arrive at the Ex's on time. Jack's really happy to see me and laughs as he points out the shaving foam I've missed below my ear, and I wipe it off with a tissue, laughing too. He waves goodbye to his mum and then the usual "Thunderbirds are GO!" routine sees her scuttling indoors. It wouldn't be going too far to guess that she frowns on anything that gives approval to my car.

Jack and I have no plans for today, so drive for a while and make suggestions about what we are going to do. "What about a movie?" I ask him.

"Nah." He has obviously given this some thought or otherwise he would have asked for a list of what's on.

"Tobogganing at the SnowDome?" This is in the nearby town of Tamworth; it has real snow indoors and is a great attraction, if you like Alpine sports. Apparently it was one of the first in the U.K., and I can't imagine how on earth it arrived in Tamworth of all places, but there we are.

Jack makes a face and says, "Nah." He isn't really that into sport or physical stuff, so this answer doesn't comes as a surprise to me

"What do you want to do?"

I ask this stuff every week, and at least once a month he says, "I want to go to Toys"R"Us." This isn't that much of a problem as he has a great way about him and doesn't have childish fits about every toy that he can't have.

"Really?" I ask in mock-surprise, and he responds with a high-spirited shout.

"Yeah, really!"

"OK, but we need to do something else first, yeah?" That's my answer every time he asks this. "Can I make a choice today?"

He nods with some hesitation and answers, "Only if it isn't rubbish."

We both laugh, and I head towards Leicestershire for a day out on the Battlefield Line and a ride on a steam train. This is, in my view, a perfect day trip for boys of all ages. There's a list of activities I keep and think that he would like, and I always make sure they're open a couple of days before. He asks me where we're going and I keep him in the dark, hoping he will be thrilled about the surprise. We drive through the leafy lanes near Market Bosworth and onto Shackerstone. Spring is beginning to lay a veil of green on the landscape, and Jack and I chat about this and that and the coming of summer.

We twitter away and laugh about stuff that connects dads with sons, and I distract him while we pass a brown sign directing us to the railway. So when we pull up to the station, he's surprised, and when he sees the steam engine he whoops with delight at the prospect of a train ride. Jack loves the past and the steam engine is like a magnet, so he very quickly drags me into the station to see it. He gets impatient, as we have to wait to buy tickets, and he's practically hopping with excitement until that task is completed and we can finally get up close to this mechanical marvel from the fifties. After a close inspection, he is beside himself, and wants to know when we can get on and what time it's leaving. I've bought a couple of return tickets, and we look at the timetable and find out that the train is leaving in half an hour.

He's so excited, and we walk back down to the end of the platform to look at the locomotive again. It's a tank engine, in a black livery with the old fashioned British Railways emblem sporting a red lion rampant, immediately taking you back to a time of life taken at a slower pace, with cakes, afternoon tea and bicycle clips. The smell of oil and burning coal and the steam from the boiler fills the platform as I take pictures of Jack on my mobile, then the engine's whistle blows and Jack grabs my hand and looks down the train.

"Come on, Dad, let's get a seat!" It's not a request; it's almost a demand from a thoroughly excited boy who is desperate to experience a ride in a steam train. We walk down the platform, looking for a place that's empty and has a seat near the window. He looks excitedly into the various carriages and selects one for us to ride in. It's old-fashioned, with a corridor, and he soon finds the empty compartment for our journey.

After sitting down, he starts to get excited at the smoke and steam wafting down the platform, and I ask him, "Is this a good day out or what?"

He looks at me, eyes burning with happiness. "Yes, Dad, it's fantastic!"

Just at that moment, the guard begins to close the doors, and when that's done he takes a deep breath and blows the whistle. Jack is very excited and is constantly getting up from his seat to look out of the window. There's a slight jar, and the engine makes the unmistakable chuffing sound beloved of every male under the age of 150. With a hearty cheer from Jack and me, the train moves out of the station.

As we leave the platform, people are waving at us, and Jack and I wave back enthusiastically. The train begins to pick up speed and we pass some sheds and the old rolling stock: some obviously useable, some in a sad state of disrepair.

That is soon left behind as the train reaches full speed, and we settle back to see the countryside fly past the window. Consciously I look at Jack, and he is staring ahead, trying to get a glimpse of the engine as we navigate a bend. He is just the archetype of an excited, curious little boy who is innocently taking in his surroundings and finding joy in situations that his elders would find cheesy. Sadly, I know he hasn't long to go before he becomes a teenager and discovers ironic detachment, and the world will have one more spotty youth mumbling "whatever".

That thought hits me hard, and I'm very emotional and so flooded with good memories of Jack and me that I can feel myself welling up. Silently cursing, I shake myself out of that mood and get a grip. Obviously I don't want to be crying in front of Jack, especially because I'm being wistful and frankly a little bit soft. That thought stiffens me, but not enough to forget that I love my boy and want to get the most out of watching, however temporarily, his continuing joy on a day out with his dad.

Chapter Fifteen
Art for Art's Sake

After our outing, a quick breeze around Toys"R"Us and another Happy Meal, I drop Jack off and head for Gerry's.

He and Jenny live just round the corner from the Patrick Kavanagh pub in Moseley. They own a fantastic Victorian place, typical of the houses round there. Naturally for the home of an artist, they have kept loads of the features and bought or renovated beautiful furniture, and it looks just perfect. The hallway is tiled and leads into a lounge/diner with a period Victorian fireplace. It's a great house, but I have the suspicion that Gerry isn't that comfortable in it. It's a bit too perfect, too respectable, too *House & Garden*. Secretly, I think he wants some rug rats running round the place, and bumping the elegant period skirting boards with remote control cars and footballs. I don't know why he didn't have kids with his first wife, but I think that the reason he puts so much time into the youth group is that it is a displacement activity, a way for him to fill the void. As I said, it's only a feeling, as he doesn't talk that much about it; in fact, he doesn't talk about it at all.

Jenny is a great artist, in my humble opinion, but she hates the London art scene, and although she does exhibit there occasionally, she says she makes more than enough in the

Midlands and her happiness is more important. That makes her a comrade to me at least.

Actually, she fitted in brilliantly with our social circle, and all she requires from Gerry is his support of her artistic endeavours and acceptance of the fact that she'll never be a housewife. So Gerry does some of the chores and he shares my cleaner for the rest. Her studio in the attic is the one place he isn't allowed to clean, and he seldom goes up there unless invited. Jenny is very intense when she's working and will, if disturbed, lose her temper.

Her exhibition tonight is in the former Bird's Custard factory in the centre of Birmingham. It's surrounded by what used to be foundries and industrial buildings, which were the hammer on Birmingham's anvil of industrial greatness. Now they are rundown and decrepit, except for the Custard Factory—a phoenix from the ashes, if you like. In essence, it's a vibrant collection of galleries, shops and music venues, and a seriously cool place to hang out.

I pick Gerry up in the Citroën, and after a short drive we park up in the side streets near St. Basil's, a rather lovely Italianate church that now acts as the headquarters of a housing charity called, imaginatively, St. Basil's Housing. Whatever the limitation of its name, it does brilliant work, and I've often covered their annual sleep-out, which raises them much-needed cash.

Gerry's full of nervous energy. He always is on the opening night of Jenny's exhibitions. He really loves her and on the surface Jenny is so cool about her work; given the intensity she puts into its production, she's unbelievably aloof when it's being exhibited. That's why Gerry is so useful, as he talks to everyone while Jenny floats around, almost oblivious to what's going on.

In no time we get into the gallery, and Jenny's there, looking like she's in a daze. Gerry hugs her and she smiles, then she turns to me and we embrace as she whispers, "Thanks for coming."

Smiling back, I say to her, "You know I love your stuff. Just wish I could afford it." She smiles at my joke as I have at least four of her paintings, plus some sculpture and a couple of line drawings. In truth, I have to beg her to let me buy it, as she hates taking advantage of our friendship. This is a courtesy she extends to everyone who is close to her. Jenny, on the surface, is the complete opposite of Gerry. He is a tall, big man, while Jenny is slight and delicate. He is blond and she is dark, and he seems like a bear to her mouse. However, they are both very passionate, and they give each other everything that they need. She gives him space and he gives her an emotional platform so she can create. It's symbiotic, it's perfect, and it's how love should really be.

The gallery fills up with the usual pretentious arty-farties, whom I pretty much dislike on the whole, but I see Shona and Archie and shuffle over to them. They smile when they see me, as in this company they look a little lost. The pleasantries completed, we stroll round the gallery, taking in the atmosphere and the free nibbles, and discuss the exhibition. Jenny mainly works in oils, but in this exhibition she has worked a lot in charcoal and it has produced some bold, stark images. They're not overwhelming but very dynamic, and the gallery owner, with whom I have a nodding acquaintance, seems very full of herself.

On our way round I chat to her: "How is it going?"

I'm hoping for Jenny's sake that it's OK, and that even in a recession there's some money about.

"Very well. Jenny always does good business here." The answer is fired back with a smile as she knows I'm a friend;

she asks to be excused and the three of us continue on our way. It crosses my mind to drop gentle hints about last night and perhaps find out a little bit more about Gillian. Then I have a sudden fear of what I might learn and decide to leave it to chance.

As we walk around, I nod to an art journalist I know and don't particularly like, and hurry off somewhere else with Shona and Archie. As casually as possible, I chat to them about nothing in particular, and Shona asks me bluntly, "What did you think of Gillian?"

"She's nice," I say without thinking. It now begins to dawn on me that I was never going to get away with the subtle hint scheme, as Bonnie probably told them her fix-up plans in advance. Bugger!

Archie laughs. "*Nice!* If I told her you said that, she would batter you."

My turn to laugh now. "Well, perhaps *nice* isn't the word for her, but, well…"

"Well what?" Shona asks with a smile. "She's single, you're single. What are you waiting for?"

"Oh God, how long have you got?" Panicking, I wish that I could be somewhere else, as this conversation is getting wildly out of control.

"Gerry told me about Jack," Archie adds, "but sometimes you need to see the whole picture, mate." Whatever I was expecting, it wasn't that, and I don't say anything for a moment. I really like Archie, and the reason I do is that he's very honest. However, his last statement nettles me a little; had it come from anyone else I would be raging, but coming from Archie it requires some thought. He looks at me and he's obviously worried that he has upset me so I rush to assuage him.

"Don't worry, mate, I'm not upset." I'm only half lying here, but because it's Archie, I don't want to make him feel any worse than he already does. Confused by all this, I say the first thing that comes into my head. "It's just I need to focus on Jack at the moment and I haven't got the emotional energy for a new relationship."

Shona jumps in. "Look, you're not marrying her. It's just that you obviously got on well with her."

Recalling Gillian's face last night, I smile and then I remember what a great time I had. The thought of her conversation and easy manner starts to flood back, and I have to hold myself in check as I realise I don't have that much of a poker face. Wanly, I come back with, "She seems very good company." Pathetic, really.

Shona gets a bit impatient, as she probably has a better idea of what's going on in my head than I'm comfortable with. Looking me in the eye, she snaps, "Well then, give her your play to read, and at least you can gain another friend—someone to laugh at your terrible jokes!"

Reluctantly, I begin to sense that although I'm being fenced in, there's real wisdom in what Shona has said. "OK, and I suppose you have her number handy, just in case."

Shona smiles. "Better than that: she's meeting us here. Jim and Bonnie are picking her up."

"Bastards! Bloody bastards!" I laugh, and Archie puts his arm around me and steers me towards a waiter knocking out some rubbish New World claret.

Chapter Sixteen
Goodbye Girl

Gillian should have walked in at that moment and added a dramatic end to that conversation. Instead she didn't come for another twenty minutes, allowing me to go through a variety of emotions, mostly terror. The only feeling I have that comes close to blocking that out is curiosity, and I desperately need to know the answers to the following questions:
  Is she coming because I'm here?
  Does she fancy me?
  Did she enjoy last night?
  Does she fancy me?
  Is she coming to make friends, or something else?
  Does she fancy me?
  Of course, I am too nervous to ask Shona and Archie any of the real questions, so I resort to talking designed to hide the feelings I'm experiencing. You know the sort of nonsense, particularly if it has been a long time since your last functioning relationship. It sort of revolves around feeling completely inadequate and wondering what on earth is wrong with you, and then the other side of that is total overconfidence.
  Last year, I had a go at Internet dating, and it was a complete disaster. It began when I looked at a few sites and

found one that I liked. Then I put a photo and a modest profile on. Suddenly and quite frighteningly, I was deluged with women who fell in love with me before even meeting me. That was bad enough, but any woman I contacted outside this group either ignored me or treated me like a sex pest in waiting. It was a nightmare and I wasted huge amounts of time on it. Many people find love this way, but it wasn't for me. Gerry laughed like a drain when I told him about this, reckoned that I would meet a bunny-boiler, and offered to come with me to each date as a minder.

Then there was the time that I actually sent him an urgent text in the toilet of a pub, as I needed him to ring me and pretend to be in a crisis, so I could get out of a date from hell. I had corresponded with a woman who seemed sexy and cool and when I arrived at the pub, I was faced with Mrs. Grady, Old Lady, who had put a fifteen-year-old photo on her profile.

Gerry, the bastard, waited twenty-five minutes before calling me though. *twenty-five minutes!* He laughed fit to burst and I went home and deleted my profile at once. I've pretty much been single ever since.

However long those twenty-five minutes seemed, waiting for Gerry to call, the twenty minutes I have to wait for Gillian are infinitely worse. They are full of stuff like, "Do I look OK?" and "What does she see in me?" Alternatively I start fretting about whether my teeth are clean, and then thinking, "Oh fuck it, I don't want to go out with her anyway." In short, in the twenty minutes between Shona telling me she's coming and her actual arrival, I've turned into an emotional basket case.

Then she comes in, wearing an outfit that makes her seem like an elegant waif. It's obvious that this is a woman with an understanding of how to dress discreetly but sexily. On seeing her, my first and only thought is that I want to rush to the toilet. Seriously, I need to pee just as she arrives. This is priceless, completely priceless, and as Gerry accompanies her over to us she says, "Hi!" and all I can say is, "You'll have to excuse me; I need to go to the bathroom."

Gerry just bursts out laughing and Shona looks mortified, but Archie catches Gerry's infectious laugh and that catches Gillian. Like a dog with its tail between its legs, I slope off to the toilet, horrified at myself. Oh God, what an idiot I must look! Then, standing at the urinal, I realise that because of my nerves I cannot go. This is rapidly turning into a nightmare and I start to look for a window to climb out of. Luckily, the automatic flush comes on and the sound of running water overcomes my nerves so I can at last pee.

The situation is awful and as I wash my hands, my mind, or whatever's left of it, can only focus on not trying to spill water on my crotch, so at least I don't look as if I've wet myself. Unbelievably, I manage this task, and try to compose myself by the dryer. The next few minutes are spent knowing that I need to get a grip on myself and remember that I am, after all, not butt ugly and not that much of a dullard either. Above all, what is going through my mind is Shona's observation that "at least you can have another friend", and with that in mind I go back into the gallery.

I rejoin the group and Gillian comes straight over.

"Are you OK?" If only she knew.

"I'm fine; too much Coke with Jack this afternoon." It's a lame excuse, but at the moment it's the best I can come up with.

She looks at me gently and says, "Is that your little boy?"

"Yes, he is my angel. I have him every Saturday."

The warmth of my reply clearly impresses her and she looks me in the eye and says straightaway: "He is a lucky boy, having you as a dad." Blushing immediately, I can't think of an answer; I'm literally speechless.

She ploughs on: "Shona told me you are having some issues with your ex."

"Oh God, yes. I won't bore you with it." Relaxing, I'm at least making some noise worthy of being called conversation, though I'm not keen to discuss the Ex for obvious reasons. I change the subject quickly: "Have you seen Jenny's art before?"

She smiles, and that's lovely, and I feel a warmth from just being near her. She replies, "I've seen the oil painting at Shona's, but that's all."

"OK then, you're in for a treat; let's get a walking tour from Gerry."

We call him over, and he walks from the other side of the gallery where he was talking to the owner. He fusses over Gillian and really gets us into the pictures, giving us an insight into a lot of what Jenny's trying to say. He's great at this, and I secretly wish I had this level of insight into other artists' work. To be truthful, he trails us around and takes a load of pressure off me, which prevents me talking and making an arse of myself. Gillian looks interested and I love that, because I adore Jenny's work and the passion on the canvas. Suddenly I remember that I've pretty much ignored Bonnie and Jim since they arrived. Spotting them taking to Jenny, I wave and the three of them walk over.

Apologising for not speaking sooner, I hug Bonnie and Jim and in the end that turns into a group hug with Gerry, Gillian and Jenny. It's been a great night and Jenny is thanking us all, practically in tears of joy. I know those tears well and they are the result of laying your soul out on display artistically. That knowledge comes from experience, as I had similar feelings on the last night of my play, and I'd dearly love to shed those tears again.

Gerry holds her hand, and she starts to cry properly, as the emotion of the evening really gets the better of her. There is a lot of clucking and Jenny soon smiles again, and we're all talking about the show and the various highlights, and sharing drinks. At this point Archie and Shona reappear and we all agree to retire to a tapas bar that I love near the Bullring.

Chapter Seventeen
It Had to be You

We make our way up to Digbeth and walk towards the Bullring. This is where the old industrialised Birmingham is swept away by the commercialism of the newly refurbished city centre. As we walk up the road we're still buzzing from the reception that Jenny's work has received. The gallery owner has managed to sell four paintings already, and Jenny is beside herself.

We go into the tapas bar and order a load of dishes and wine, and the chat is as hot as the food. My friends organise themselves so that I have to sit next to Gillian and soon we're talking like old mates. She is gentle and funny, kind and in short really considerate. I gradually lose my remaining nerves and look at Gerry, and he smiles.

Then she does something that really pleases me. The level of attention she's giving me is unbelievably flattering but when she starts to talk about my playwriting again it makes me feel like I'm twenty years old. Then I look at her whilst she's chatting to Shona and I think that maybe, just maybe, I could start to dream about asking her out for the safe lunch before jumping into the nervous dinner and the awkward silence as I drop her off and fret about being asked in for coffee. The fretting, of course, would be evenly split between fear of her not asking me in and the equally scary thought of her inviting me inside. Weird or what?

The evening ends in the usual coffee and mints, and Gerry gets up to say a few words. The bar is empty apart from us, and he taps his coffee cup with mock solemnity. Jenny laughs along with the rest of us. "My friends, let us make a toast to the following: good friends, both old and new." At this point he waves his glass at Gillian and we all bang the table to acknowledge the newest addition to our group. He continues his monologue. "Obviously I want to pay homage to my brilliant wife and her fantastic exhibition." Again he has to pause to allow us to bang the table and register our approval. "Lastly I just want to say to Jenny, I love you and always will."

Cue "awww"s and applause in equal measure, and we start drinking the dregs of our drinks and the remnants of our coffee. At this point Gerry tells me that Jenny is driving him home and, without thinking, I offer Gillian a ride back to hers in my DS.

With the faint hint of half a smile she looks at me and accepts, and I offer my arm like in the movies; she gently grasps it as we leave the tapas bar with the others. Archie and Shona go the opposite way to the cab rank, whilst Bonnie and Jim walk on ahead and Gerry and Jenny linger behind, leaving Gillian and me together. The conversation becomes very clipped as I am now shorn of the comfort blanket of my friends, and I fight down the rising panic and attempt to relax.

We're just small talking, and I really want to be like Woody Allen in *Annie Hall* where he kisses Diane Keaton on their first date. He tells her that the first kiss always makes him really nervous and if they get it out of the way they can enjoy the rest of their evening. However, I just know I haven't got the *savoir faire* for that, and try to focus on not making an idiot of myself. For God's sake, I am forty-two years old and I'm as nervous as a teenager. It would be funny if it weren't so pathetic. To emphasise that point, my next thought is, "Oh God, please don't make her laugh at my car; I don't think I could bear the disappointment." It makes me wonder why anybody listens to me, really.

After what seems an hour but in reality is ten minutes, we reach the DS and I look at her and she looks at me. "I'm sorry about the car, but I have a weakness for old Citroëns." She smiles, and I open her side of the car and let her in. For some reason she's stopped talking and I start to get worried and hope that I haven't made a *faux pas*.

Walking behind the car, I'm shaking, but eventually I get in and after I make myself comfortable, she says, "What a great car. I really love it!"

"Thank you. It's a bit dented and..."

Suddenly she says sharply, "Stop apologising for yourself!" and reaches over and gives me a kiss. We break apart and she looks at me, waiting for me to speak.

"That's nice!" is my line. At the moment I'm very surprised, but in a good way.

"Yes, very nice!" she says. "I'm glad we got that out of the way. There's a line in a Woody Allen film; he says to his date, 'We'll kiss now, prevent all that nervous tension.' I've always wanted to do that."

"Oh my God: *Annie Hall*. I love that film!" We both burst out laughing, and the evening is just beginning for both of us.

Chapter Eighteen
Plan Nine from Outer Space

It's Sunday evening, and a gentleman never tells! Suffice to say that Gillian needed to be somewhere this morning, and I kissed her goodbye as she left my flat to get in a cab. Instinctively I know this is much too early, but we do have a lot in common and I need to sort out some stuff before getting really excited. You can rest assured that I didn't do the typical male "I'll call you!" nonsense. She left with my mobile, landline and email; I even made another date on Tuesday for dinner.

All this is very cool, but I'm now in the grip of a bit of a crisis. The whole new relationship thing is getting in the way of me concentrating on Jack, and that's making me feel guilty. Of course all of that is feeding my paranoia about being a crap Saturday Burger Bar Dad. It's not as if I don't have experience of this stuff. My dad didn't even do the burger bar thing, as I only saw him once a fortnight, and if I was lucky we would go for a drive and end up in a Little Chef on the A303. The conversation was as stilted as the food was greasy. At least I ring Jack every day and we have a relationship that is relaxed and he's able to share stuff with me. It's strange, but however much I look at it, I find it pointless to think about comparing my relationship with my dad and my relationship with Jack. It was a different time, and although people began to talk about the "new man" in the eighties, it wasn't a concept in our house.

My dad was an office worker for the Council—had been for thirty years. He grew up in the stultifying boredom of local government and I believe he was bored rigid by it. The truth is that he hardly ever talked about it, and certainly not to me. Say what you like about the Ex, he sees me every Saturday and once during the week, and if I want to, I can usually have more contact. My mum was bitter, and with some reason, when he came home one day and announced he was leaving to live with a female colleague. There was lots of unpleasantness and she used my sister and me as a stick to punish him with, while at the same time trying to convince us that it was his fault.

There was no doubt that Dad leaving was a bolt out of the blue, but there was also no doubt he was unhappy for a long time before that. Maybe it was his job or his relationship with Mum. Of course it was impossible for that to be discussed with us kids in those days. Mum just rasped on about betrayal and abandonment and was never able to see a rounded picture, which is completely understandable. After all, is my picture of Ex any more reliable? OK, I can talk about stuff but is my role in our divorce as clear as it should be?

Later, I did get to spend time with Dad before he died. We shared our thoughts on politics, life and other unimportant stuff. He even tried to give me career guidance after my A-levels. None of that made up for the fact that I missed the kite-flying, trips to the zoo and the other stuff that even I, as a Burger Bad Dad, get to do with Jack.

As part of my youth work with Gerry I did a psychology course, and we talked about perception and attribution. The lecturer used an example of watching someone trip over a stone, then everyone thinking they were clumsy. We laughed and then she asked us to be the person tripping over the stone, and then it was a matter of "blaming the person who left the stone there". The point of all this psychobabble is that there is a tendency to blame other people for your predicaments rather than your own actions.

In my case, the Ex is an easy target, with her career taking precedence, her temper and her unfailing ability to undermine everything I did. My "problem" is that I can see the other side of her, and I can see aspects of my personality that must have driven her mad. The trouble, then, with this type of retrospective is that you can go too far the other way. You start seeing your faults a lot more clearly than you can see your good stuff, the stuff that made you attractive in the first place.

My phone rings, and it's Gerry. I pick up and he just says, "Well?"

I play dumb: "Well what?"

He laughs, and I can hear him shouting at Jenny: "He says 'well what?'" Then I can hear Jenny laughing too.

"Bugger off, the pair of you!" Obviously there's some mirth involved here, and I'm at the end of Gerry's tickling stick. It's not a comfortable place to be.

He's practically beside himself. "Well, Paul, you can't blame us! You were mooning over her and you gave Archie such a look when they offered her a cab ride home. They're still laughing about that, by the way."

I'm mortified. I've already mentioned my lack of a poker face, and now I've turned into Michael Corleone after being hit by "the Thunderbolt". I feel compelled to say, "Oh God, was I that obvious?"

Gerry's laughter gives me my answer, and he doesn't really need to add, "Well…yes, really."

There's a sensation of myself reddening; I'm really embarrassed, and Gerry's laughter isn't helping that much. "Oh God! I'll ring Archie and apologise."

"For fuck's sake, don't do that! It's the best laugh they've had in ages." He's off again, laughing, and despite my shock at being so obvious, it's hard not to join in.

"Have you just rung to gloat?" I eventually manage to get out.

"If anyone should be gloating, it's you!" he replies, and he's laughing so much at this point he has to hand the phone over to Jenny.

After a shout at Gerry to behave himself, we do the usual pleasantries, and she says, "Honestly, Paul, we're happy for you."

I reply, "Honestly, I don't know who's worse: she only spent the night. We're not engaged or anything." She then breaks up and tells Gerry what I've said and he comes back on the phone.

"We know, we know, but when were you that into a girl that you talked to her and then didn't come to me with fourteen reasons why it isn't the right time to go out with her?" Deciding to leave that question hanging in the air, I reel from his level of perception. He then gets it together enough to ask me over. "Anyway, you want to have a glass of wine at ours? Jenny wants you to meet a director she knows."

I'm ambivalent: it's been an awesome weekend, and I just want to chill and prepare for my meeting with the Ex and John. "Well, to be honest, I'd rather not. I need to spend some time working things out for tomorrow."

He's quite blunt: "Look, actually we're not taking no for an answer. I'll help you about tomorrow, so get your arse over here." He says this in such a way that it's difficult to refuse: it's the command from a brother who needs you to feel loved. Looking at the clock, I find it's 6.30, and an evening with Gerry and Jenny is beginning to exert quite a pull. There are no blockages to that, as I have clothes for work tomorrow and the flat is tidy.

Thinking about the trial ahead tomorrow, I suddenly make up my mind to go, mostly because I can foresee a sleepless night of worry. "OK, I'll be over in an hour."

Gerry bellows, "Great! Bring a manuscript of your play." Clearly he's happy to be doing this, and for me the meeting with the director does sound interesting.

I reply with an enthusiastic, "OK, mate. See you soon!"

We hang up, and instead of worrying about meeting my Ex tomorrow, I'm meeting a director. But what I'm wondering is: could I be lucky twice in one weekend?

Chapter Nineteen
An Offer I Can't Refuse

The drive from my flat in Sutton Coldfield to Gerry's in Moseley isn't very long. He loves thinking of himself as a Brummie, but he's actually from Solihull: a very posh part of the West Midlands, which, if you believe 99.9% of its residents, is wholly unconnected with Birmingham.

Moseley, on the other hand, is right in the heart of the city and is a mixture of shabby chic and student life; it's as Bohemian as Brum gets. The perfect sort of place, in fact, to find a youth worker and his artist partner. As I'm parking the car, my mobile chirrups, announcing a text. I take a look, and it's from Gerry telling me to meet him in the Patrick Kavanagh on the corner.

It's easy to love the Pat Kav, as it's known locally, and tonight, drinking in a pub dedicated to an Irish writer little-known in England seems very appropriate.

Gerry, Jenny and presumably the mystery director are sitting at a table near the stage, which is empty.

Gerry sees me, gets up to walk over, gives me a hug, and just says, "Beck's?"

"Yeah, thanks, mate! How's it going?" I nod to the table where the other two are sitting.

"It's going brilliant; how's you?" It's not just a polite request for information, but a question about whether I'm ready to meet a guy who could be very useful to me.

Looking at him with a smile, I say in all honesty, "My best weekend for a very long time. I'm pretty much ready for anything."

He laughs. "You spoken to her today?" Gerry's like the brother I never had, and I've never kept anything from him.

"Yes, just before I left, and a couple of texts through the day. We're meeting on Tuesday for dinner." Almost unconsciously, I can feel myself puffing with pride as I'm saying this. Yes, despite the fact I'm a bit of a twat, I'm seeing a girl three times in the same week!

"Fantastic! We're thrilled."

"So am I. Very thrilled." I pause for a moment. "Who's the mystery director?"

"To be honest, he is a friend of Jenny's from uni, whom she's kept in touch with. He worked in London but has moved up to Brum to head up a theatre company and he is looking for new writers."

"OK, that's a good start. Let's see what he's saying."

We go over and Jenny introduces me to Trevor, who it turns out acted in some TV stuff I've seen and is glad to be recognised. We chat about some stuff and he's just a cool guy and very knowledgeable about the theatre. He comes to the point quite quickly: "Jenny has told me about your writing and the profound nature of your plays. I've been employed by the theatre to sort out a few things and one of those tasks is to showcase new and emerging writers. Jenny's judgment is one that I trust, so can I read your work with a view to putting it on?"

My heart skips a beat and I don't think about the implications until much later, in my rush to accept his offer. We talk about percentages and a very small upfront fee, and about working with emerging actors. Frankly I'm delirious—and then it's over. Trevor's partner arrives—a delicate and dark young man with a hint of melancholy about him—and they head off for a late supper.

Jenny smiles and says, "Well, that seemed easy!"

Released from the tension of the meeting with Trevor, I roar with laughter. "Too easy! Have you been badgering the poor bloke?"

Gerry laughs too.

"Well..." she replies. "Let's just say he had been aware of your work for some time."

We are all smiling, and I'm profuse in my thanks as Gerry moves to get more drinks. He looks at my glass and I say, "I can't have more alcohol; I'm driving." This a genuine wish, as despite my fear of being awake all night, I do want to sleep in my own bed. There's also a part of me that wants some time alone talking to Gillian.

Jenny says, "Why don't you stay? Then we can talk about Jack." With those magic words, it doesn't take long for them to persuade me to stop over and Gerry gets me another Beck's. We call it a night at about 10 p.m. and the chatter is about the last night's exhibition and Trevor's offer to showcase my play. I also notice that they are discreetly not mentioning Gillian.

We pile into their house, and after drinks are served, Gerry says, "So what's the story?"

"With Jack?"

"Yeah, we want to help you, but we are really concerned about all of this and we need you to be clear about what you're doing."

"Hold on." I try to rally against this assault on my competence. "You're assuming that I can't deal with this."

"No..." Jenny joins the fray, "but you are too nice and we're terrified that in your attempt to be conciliatory, you won't get what you want and, more importantly, what Jack needs."

"Look, I don't even know what she is proposing." Quickly, I settle down. Jenny very rarely gets involved in my issues with Ex, but when she does she always brings a calm eye to the proceedings.

Gerry pipes up, sensing I'm not hostile. "Have you got a list of stuff you want to ask her?"

At this point I hesitate: with Gillian and the trip out with Jack this weekend, I have no real strategy for my meeting with the Ex tomorrow. "Not really; I was going to do it tonight," I say weakly, almost like a schoolboy admitting that he hasn't done his homework.

He pulls out a pen and looks me in the eye. "Right, let's get this done together—and the one thing I want you to remember is to make sure that she understands is that nothing can be done without your consent."

Jenny then puts a killer sentence together, which encompasses an essential dilemma for me. "She can only hurt you if you allow her to. You need to ensure that you are fighting for Jack's interests." She smiles in an almost sisterly kind of way. "Gerry and I know how much Jack means to you and what's more how much you mean to Jack."

Acknowledging the truth of this, we sit down to write a list of questions and strategies that may help to stop the plans of the Ex and John. At least it could allow us to throw a large enough spanner into the works to slow this process down and permit Jack's wishes to be heard. That is, if I can find the balls.

Chapter Twenty
D-Day

From the alarm sounding to me walking to the wine bar in Sutton, where we've agreed to meet, seems but the passage of a moment. Monday truly has gone by in a flash of nervous excitement.

Luckily, I've been incredibly busy today and I haven't had a lot of time to think about the meeting with Ex. There was a phone conversation with Gillian, but to be frank it was unsatisfactory as she was in the staffroom and I was in the newsroom. However, we say goodbye and express our joint pleasure at the thought of meeting on Tuesday.

As I'm walking to the wine bar, Gerry rings to wish me luck and reminds me to stick to the list of questions that we came up with the previous evening. In addition to that, we also compiled a list of demands that I must make. He repeats his offer, made drunkenly last night, to come and help me out. Again I refuse, saying that it will only make the Ex harder. Needing a moment to collect myself, I stop before I go into the bar. Then I think about having a smoke, decide that it will be ages before I can get a chance, and light one up. It's what I call a habit fag and I don't enjoy it at all, though I continue to drag on it.

The smoking does give me a little time to think about what's ahead, and I decide to think only of Jack, and make a conscious decision to cowboy up and get on with it. With that thought, I stub out the cigarette and walk in.

John and Ex are already there and, as predicted, they have a sheaf of papers, including a number of glossy brochures. The usual greetings are exchanged and I offer a round of drinks, which they refuse, before I go to the bar and get a mineral water.

So we get down to business, presaged by a pause; an awkward silence that each side knows bears bad tidings. Ex decides to open the batting and her first shot is a lusty blow to my ego: "I'm Jack's main carer and I feel that I have a right to make most of the decisions that relate to his welfare. His school appears unconcerned about the dip in his performance and I want him to have extra tuition, and we want to start choosing his next school now. We have agreed that a private school would give him a really good start in life."

Trying to disguise my disquiet at her one-sided view of this, I look at her; holding down my anger at her presumptions, I get my list out of my pocket. There's a weird noise when I clear my throat to speak, but I carry on. "I feel I need to say that I came here only because I have Jack's interests at heart, and I want to make sure that we make the right decisions for him." There are nods all round, so I feel that we are at least here for the right reasons. I crack on: "Most importantly, I want any decisions we make to be subject to Jack's wishes, and I also have a list of things that frankly are pre-conditions for me before I will agree to any change in the plans for his education." Ex tries to interrupt but I plough on. "Please let me finish. I want to go through these questions and leave them with you, because I'm sure you will want to bear them in mind when you are discussing this between yourselves." Pausing, I take a drink, allowing this to sink in.

Slowly I put down my glass, and they're looking at the paper; as I have their attention, I decide to be more forceful. "I don't expect answers to these questions today, and frankly some of them might be impossible to answer, but I would like to be able to look Jack in the eye and say to him that we have looked into everything."

"What do you want to know?" Ex asks, in a semi-hostile fashion.

"Here are the questions I have put down." I hand them the paper and they look at the questions that Gerry and I came up with last night. I then proceed to read them, from a copy I made at work.

"Are you anticipating a change of educational provision to impact on my ability to see Jack, contrary to the agreement we made in court? Are you going to bear the full costs of sending Jack to a fee-paying school yourselves? How much choice will Jack get into where he will go to school? Would you consider a non-residential fee-paying option? Are you looking for schools locally or are you stretching the net wider? Will I have a veto on any change in his education? If he does attend a residential school, where will he stay at holiday times? What will happen if he does not like his new school or performs poorly? Who will pay the extra costs of uniform and equipment?"

There's a pause after I've finished reading, and I take it from this that they weren't expecting such a list. There's a definite hesitation, and I decide to pile on the pressure. "That list is by no means the end of my concerns and I think that as Jack's dad, I'm entitled to have some answers."

Ex seems to be quite angry and John answers in his posh West Midlands drawl: "Well, Paul, you have given this a lot of thought. We obviously need some time to reflect on your questions." Ex nods and I look her in the eye. From the look of her it's clear she thought this would be a walk in the park.

Thanks to Gerry, I've put a cramp in her evening. What a fucking bonus!

John starts up again. "Paul, we've got some brochures from different schools. We would like you to see what Jack could gain from these places."

She hands them over and says, "We want to discuss something else with you." I nod, wondering what might come up. "John is in line for a promotion and he may have to move to London if he gets it. I have been told I can transfer if that happens. Therefore the decision on his schooling is quite urgent."

This is a shock, and I'm reeling from this news; not wanting to lose it completely, I take a drink of water, which frankly does not help much. Somehow, I manage to make a sensible comment.

"I can't see the urgency. In Jack's interests, I don't want to make a quick decision just because it fits your plans. The emotional wellbeing of our son is at stake here."

Ex is obviously seeing red and starting to get agitated. "Typical! By the time you make up your mind, the best schools will be full and Jack will have to attend another crappy school."

Angrily, I bite back: "I'm still not sure why you want this, anyway. Jack is happy where he is and as far as I am concerned until last Tuesday you were too. Why, all of a sudden, do we need to change all the plans for him moving on to secondary school, without even discussing it with him?"

"He's ten; he doesn't know what is good for him." Ex says this as if it's the most reasonable thing in the world.

This isn't getting us anywhere and I decide to put my foot down.

"Look, the one thing I will not do is rush this. In the end I may agree to a change, but not with a gun at my head." My face must mirror my determination, as there is a very pregnant pause.

John, sensing danger, nips in: "Paul, we want to assure you that no one will do that." Weirdly, I look at him, and despite his plummy voice I'm starting to like him. He looks at Ex and continues. "We all want the best for Jack and we know you have misgivings about this type of education for him. All we want is for you to explore some alternatives with us."

"That's very interesting, but this isn't about what I want; it's about what Jack wants." They're both silent as frankly that point is unanswerable. Then I point to my list: "I want you to look at those questions and I'll promise to look at your brochures with an open mind. However, I want to make this very clear..." Stopping for effect, I eventually continue: "I will not agree to him attending private school because it is convenient for your careers." This is very strange, and I can't quite believe it: I'm on fire.

Ex also appears to be on fire for quite different reasons. "How bloody dare you! At least I've got a career." John reaches over and puts his hand on hers, at which point she unbelievably shuts up. Who is this wonder man, I ask myself?

As usual, I let her rudeness slide and John says, "Well, I think we know where we all stand. Why don't we have a drink and then we can go away and read what we have here and get back in touch?"

With some speed, I agree to the second proposal but not the first, as I can't wait to be out of the place. Very soon after I make my excuses and walk back to the car park, for the first time really proud of myself for facing up to the Ex. In football terms I've got a useful away point; it might not be a cup final win but it is better than what I usually get.

Chapter Twenty-One
Take a Deep Breath

The elation of my away point lasts most of the evening, during which I have been instructed to telephone Gerry and recount the conversation.

Both he and Jenny are thrilled about my performance, especially when I tell them about my assertion that I won't make any decisions with a "gun to my head".

Gerry is fulsome in his praise: "That showed her, my old son. I'm proud of you. Did you give them the old guff about being open-minded?"

"Yes, and I think I got away with it!"

"Top man, Paul. Top man."

And so it goes on, backwards and forwards, with Gerry stopping every so often to say, "Jenny! Guess what Paul said?"

All brilliant for the ego, I think you'll agree, but when the phone goes down, I start the process of reflection and the strangeness of John's effect on Ex's temper begins to bother me. It wasn't that she appears to be cowed by his authority; it just seems that they have an understanding about not upsetting me. Is that it? Is there an elaborate plot going on here to ensure my compliance? Ruminating, I get myself a coffee and leaf through the brochures that I've been given. They're awful. The schools all seem to be in old Georgian country houses and have pictures of healthy chaps playing cricket and rugger. Most have a page on their alumni and feature quotes like "the lessons I learned from my time at Snotyard School have made me the man I am today". Not a woman or a non-white person to be seen.

Angrily, I have visions of Jack in twenty-five years' time as a solicitor with cauliflower ears attending an Old Snotyardians' black-tie dinner and being invited to join the Masons. Ghastly, just bloody ghastly.

The funny thing is that there are millions of parents out there that would love that idea: their son a solicitor and all that. It's not as if I live an alternative lifestyle or am a particularly brooding class warrior. It's just…oh God, I don't know. I just don't want him to be in this sausage machine churning out middle-class drones who know the cost of everything and the value of nothing. Suddenly, in the face of this middle-class PR bollocks, my real-life lack of achievement comes back to haunt me and I begin to have doubts. Particularly as I'm looking at possible redundancy and I live in a pokey flat in Sutton Coldfield, which I will have to sell if I lose my job. Bollocks.

The phone rings and it's Gillian; she seems really happy, which at the moment is just the tonic I need. We talk about my meeting with the director, which right now seems like an eternity ago. Halfway through the conversation, as she pauses in her description of her day, a thought strikes me. Apart from the intensity of this weekend, I really don't know much about this woman at all. Yes, she's gorgeous, but I don't even know her surname. Immediately I confess my ignorance, ask her and she says, "Black. Gillian Black."

"Sounds lovely" is my reply.

She laughs and then says, "You mean you didn't ring Archie and Shona and find out all about me?"

It's my turn to laugh now and I say, "I'm sorry, it's just that I'm a bit rusty at the dating thing!" as though this is a proper explanation.

"Well," she says, "I'll see you tomorrow and we can both fill in all the blanks. OK?"

"Sounds perfect!" is my cheesy yet truthful response. That call lifts me and I get a cosy feeling that I try hard to cling onto. Obviously I'm keen for it to last, in order to prevent the previous negativity engulfing me again.

Whilst doing that, I have a thought that strikes me hard—one that chills me a little. What if Jack really fancies this sort of education? The brochures look great and most of them are all adventure and jolly hockey sticks, not forgetting that a ten-year-old isn't likely to see that nonsense the way I see it. That would test me and it would also be a difficult task to focus him on a school career at a bog standard comprehensive. Oh God, I wish I didn't have the ability to see both sides of an argument! Somehow I rein that thought in and look at the bright side: whatever happens, Jack is going to be part of my life. The other thing is that I'm determined to ensure is that Jack is happy too. However this school business shakes out, I decide to focus on that. If it's in my power, I will make sure that Jack is as happy as possible.

With that thought I move to my laptop and check my emails. There are two that strike my eye. The first is from Ex and the second from Gillian. I save hers till last, as I don't anticipate that the Ex has anything nice to say. I open it with trepidation and my prediction is confirmed.

> Paul
> *Thank you for meeting us and being open-minded. We would like to answer your questions as quickly as possible,*

but we cannot answer them with certainty unless we talk to Jack about our plans in the weeks to come. We would like your patience and help in this matter. We need to tell Jack about our career plans and at that point we want to discuss possible options for his school and all the other stuff that moving down south involves. This is obviously going to upset him and we would ask you to be as supportive as possible. In return we are committed to maintaining your relationship with Jack. The view that we have is that Jack needs to feel settled and we feel that could be achieved at a boarding school near us. It will also assist his education, as we are determined to ensure he achieves his potential.

This, as you can imagine, is a huge shock. I'm staggered, and my suspicion about the two of them conspiring to keep me sweet in order to sort their careers isn't at all mollified. It's clear I need time to ponder this and I decide to leave it for tonight, as it is so far beyond Ex's usual behaviour that it makes my head hurt. The fact that Jack's new school won't just be private, that it's likely to be far away, chills me to the marrow. A physical as well as an emotional distance is on the cards and I need to focus on something else quickly, before I'm subsumed in despair.

So after that nonsense, I turn to Gillian's email, hoping it will cheer me up. As expected, it's a real tonic.

Hi Paul,
Just thought you'd like to know I found this.
Love,
Gillian

She has attached a link to an article from the *Birmingham Mail:* **"Local Playwright Hits the Spot."**

It has a fulsome tribute to my play, and I blush. The review is one that I had obviously read when it first came out. However it's the fact that she took the effort to look it up that really amazes me. It's a goodish end to a really difficult day, and it strikes me that having Gillian in my life, however tenuously, is a really great thing.

Chapter Twenty-Two
The Day of Our Proper First Date

There are times that I can be a bit of a dick, and this is one of those days when it's very apparent. This morning I wake up with a smile on my face, but by the time I've found my car keys I'm scowling at myself and completely at sea. The reason for this self-loathing is a complete panic attack at the thought of my date tonight. Yes, a panic attack: a surge of feelings that revolves around a lack of confidence in myself. Consider this: I've already made love to this woman. We have spent the weekend chatting to one another, and what is more, she's shown interest in me and my work, This is the real killer: it's clear that she really likes me, and I'm still thinking about making a good impression. Like I said, what a knob I really am!

Well there you have it, my self-confidence problem: the old self-deprecation that prepares me for rejection before my first date. The other thing I need to learn to do is take a risk on my life. Unusually, I know I'm only coming this way once and I need to get on with it. Yet, and this is a real problem for me, there's the terror of feeling rejected. If I were a psychologist, then I would probably understand all this nonsense.

You can just imagine it; some Freud-like beardy with a roll top sweater, pontificating in a German accent: "Oh yes, Mr. Castle, your parents' divorce has planted in you a fear of abandonment. Hence you cannot bear rejection; the two themes are closely linked, I think."

Anyhow, I manage to get out of the door and get in the Citroën. The car floats me towards the paper's office and the start of another day in front of the Beak. On the journey down, I start to cheer up as the car wafts me onwards. The hydro-pneumatic suspension on the Citroën really feels like gliding on a cushion of air, and whilst it's stupid for a car to impact on your mood, this one just does.

It was literally the first thing I bought when I got a job; Ex and I had planned to live together, but she had to move to Birmingham for her work, and I stayed in London making tea in a local rag in Ealing. The car was bought for the trek to Brum at the weekend about the time John Major beat Neil Kinnock. After a couple of years I got this job and we got a house together. The Citroën wasn't cheap to run, wasn't cheap to buy and is still a constant worry because of its propensity to break down. However, when it does work, it's great, and looking down the long bonnet and seeing the black contoured shape in the windows of shops just makes me feel, well, different.

The car is, above all things, a statement about who I am as an individual. Ex hated it and as she went higher up the corporate ladder, her car moved from VW to Audi to BMW; I think she's on a 5 series at the moment. It's £50,000 worth of Teutonic engineering excellence, and from where I sit, without a speck of human feeling. It feels to me that it's designed by a robot and made by a robot for a bunch of corporate robots. Nasty. Don't get me wrong: it's a fine car, but where's the soul? Where is the sparkle? Where is the joy? A bit like my marriage, really.

With all this pointless thinking about cars, in no time I'm parking and hotfooting it past the smokers as I nod, knowing I'll be joining them as soon as I've read my work emails.

Walking through the newsroom, I find that everyone has their head down. It's amazing what the threat of redundancy can do to productivity! Doug, the editor, is hovering over my desk, and instinctively looks at his watch. Knowing I'm on time, I start mentally strapping on my armour for a row. It's not a coincidence that the redundancy memo had somehow emboldened this previously spineless editor, and I decide not to let this pass.

"Doug, what's up and why are you looking at your watch? I hope you are not checking on my timekeeping?"

He looks abashed and doesn't answer that, but carries on with what was previously on his mind. "I need you to do me a favour," he asks in a tone that doesn't suggest a favour at all.

"OK, what's that?" I ask in a tone that registers he's avoided my question.

"Steve will cover the court today as I need you to cover the cuts meeting at the Council and get some opinions from the politicos."

"OK, that sounds cool. What time?" I'm actually thrilled to get out of court duty and start getting my stuff together.

Doug replies in a worried tone, "Two o'clock. I need the copy quickly, though."

I'm intrigued by this and ask, "What's the hurry? Deadline isn't until the usual time, is it?"

"No reason, but I might need to make some room elsewhere as it could be a developing story. The Unions are meeting tomorrow as a response to any cuts the Council might bring in." At heart I feel something is wrong, but in my excitement to do a bit of proper journalism I resolve to deal with that later. I finish with, "OK. I'll work on it as soon as I can, and it'll be on your desk right after that."

He turns to go, murmuring, "Thanks, Paul."

However I decide to be assertive again, realising that this is becoming a habit. "Any more news on the memo?"

He turns round and gives me a "rabbit in the headlights" look. There's a frozen thought stuck in his head, and if he had the balls he'd tell me to get stuffed and mind my own business. Typically, he bottles it: "No, but you guys will probably know before me!" With that, he scuttles off to bully the tea lady.

Looking at him go, I shrug my shoulders and nod at Steve as he packs up his bag for court. Before I leave, I sit down at my desk and look at my watch. Knowing I have a few hours before the meeting, I call a few Council contacts and ask some pertinent questions. The Councillors are gloomy and that crosses all parties, although some of the Tories are up for the cuts and talk about council tax payers and a fat-cat bureaucracy.

Birmingham has had a lot of issues lately and top of that list is the abject performance of its Social Services Department. Recently I did a great piece from the point of view of the workers, which got some good feedback. The reality is that Birmingham is huge and it's hard to make any difference across the entire city. In London, every borough has similar issues, but they're smaller and the size of Brum just magnifies every problem.

That being said, the proposed cuts are rumoured to be savage. This meeting is a preliminary discussion on economies to be made. When I arrive, the Councillors have a resigned air, particularly the Labour members who go through the motions of talking about resisting but are out of power both locally and nationally. Birmingham is run by a Conservative-

Liberal coalition, and many believe it's a model for the current government. This meeting is a prelude to the Full Council next week, and it's about last-minute posturing as the Cabinet hasn't finalised the figures. Those with particular interests are trying to make special pleas to prevent cuts.

One Labour stalwart sums it up in a conversation after the meeting has finished: "We just have to wait till the cuts bite and then maybe we can do something at the elections." Obviously that wasn't for publication.

One thing's for sure: this will put all useless speculation about my self-worth into its proper place. I'll need to focus on this story and that will make the day go much quicker and prevent me fretting about my date with Gillian tonight.

Chapter Twenty-Three
Tuesday on the Balti Mile

It's seven o'clock and I have an hour to get into town and meet Gillian. It took me a lot longer than I thought writing my story, as the Councillors at the meeting were their usual finger-pointing selves. The posturing is fairly pitiful, as we all know that the real decisions are made in Westminster and the local boys and girls just get to administer the cuts, especially since the ability to raise council tax to make up the difference has been taken away from them.

At the meeting Labour's position was just to rant but I got the impression that when it comes to it they're glad that someone else has to put their names to the cuts. Fantastic! Welcome to the party of Milibland, fighting hard to get to the middle. The left is dead: it went out with a whimper, not a bang, and my dad will be turning in his grave. Obviously that's for the Comment page and I have to keep all of that stuff to myself.

When I'd got my article down on paper, I knew I'd done a good job, but it will be interesting to see what the idiot editor does with it.

Doug actually used to be a great reporter. There was a time when it wasn't hard to remember him breaking a really good story on a local firm breaking waste dumping regulations, and lots of other really sound stuff. Since getting his arse on the editor's chair though, he's become cautious and is forever fretting. If this keeps up, I'll be sent to do weddings and the WI next.

After I file my copy, get showered and start getting ready, Gerry rings and laughingly shouts, "Got your condoms, mate?"

In a mock rage I tell him to "fuck off!" and we settle down into a quick bit of badinage before he wishes me luck and I get my keys.

Gillian is meeting me in Moseley; we're going for a curry as I've a favourite place there. It's friendly and serves really great food. This seemed like a good idea when I chose it, as I wanted something informal since I thought I might freeze if it was too posh. As you can see, my fretting begins quite early. An additional pressure is that I always like to be on time for stuff like this, and before long I'm looking at my watch and panicking.

So in order to deal with that stress, I decide to drive to Moseley and fret there rather than worry feebly at home. The drive down is easy at this time of night and I listen to some sixties soul to calm myself down. Driving down to the Balti mile, singing my head off to Otis Redding, is a great tonic for my nerves, and I start feeling really optimistic about the evening ahead.

However, I still need a cigarette when I park the car, and smoke that whilst looking at myself in the rearview mirror to check that I haven't any spinach or anything else on my teeth.

Looking at my watch, it's only 7.45, and I decide to wait outside the restaurant. Nervously, I look at myself in the restaurant window: I'm wearing a white cotton shirt with a button-down collar, a blue tie, a pair of black trousers and some fairly cool shoes that finish the ensemble. So I look fairly good and have to say that after my inspection in the window feel reasonably OK about myself. I've lifted a packet of Gauloises from the car and light one, realising I'm going to be here for what will seem like ages and might as well look nonchalant. Two cigarettes are smoked whilst the clock creeps round to eight, and by that time I'm as nervous as a schoolboy waiting for the Head after being caught doing something naughty behind the bike sheds.

Then as the clock reaches one minute past, she arrives and takes my breath away. Gillian really knows how to dress, and tonight she looks like a vision. She's wearing a knee-length black dress—low-cut but not too revealing—which has a velvet sheen, whilst a shawl covers her shoulders. Gillian, in short, looks fabulous; completely fabulous.

We kiss, and her eyes sparkle as she smiles. Naturally, I stammer that she looks lovely and with a charm impossible to describe she whispers in my ear, "Thank you; so do you." Practically shaking by now, I open the door for her and follow her into the restaurant.

The meal begins with the usual poppadoms and ends with the coffee and mints. In between those courses, we talk and laugh. I nearly forget that I'm nervous and remember that I can be interesting and funny. During the meal I find out that Gillian is forty-one and has a daughter, Geraldine, at university. This, she says, was a catalyst for her to change jobs and do some teaching again. We talk for ages, gently take the mick out of each other, and discuss politics. She was a leftie, then moved to the centre and is now moving left again in response to Cameron and Clegg's "nice" version of Thatcherism.

We explore our likes and dislikes, and apart from our shared love of *Annie Hall* we have a passion for Powell and Pressburger movies, Beethoven and the novels of HE Bates. To top it off, she loves Elvis Costello, a man I view as a musical god. We differ on a couple of things including modern poetry, and she loves Madonna and hates The Clash, but you can't have everything. At the end of the evening, I pay the bill, and she makes a strong attempt to go Dutch but I refuse point-blank to countenance this.

At this point, even I'm bound to confess that I've had a great night. Realising it was really lovely, I'm nervous about what to do now and I decide to ask how she got here.

"Oh, I got a cab" is her reply, which gives me the perfect opportunity to offer to drive her back.

"Would you like a lift home?" Even as the words are coming out of my mouth, I realise that my question is loaded with implications and I'm setting myself up to get really anxious. Issues include whether I should come in for coffee, who makes the first move if we want to kiss, and of course the whole bedroom etiquette. However, help is at hand, and she never gives me time to work through my neurosis.

"I would love that," she says, "unless you want me to stay at yours again?"

I'm speechless, and can only nod with a silly grin on my face as she reaches out and touches my hand. Somehow I manage to stand up and we walk arm in arm out into the street. I'm convinced that tonight I'm the luckiest guy in the world.

Chapter Twenty-Four
Black Coffee in Bed

We arrive back at the flat and kiss as soon as I've closed the door. Our lovemaking on Saturday was fantastic: slow, tender and, dare I say it, considerate. Tonight it's about passion and urgency, and in a different way just as fabulous.

Gillian is wearing beautiful, sexy lingerie, and we make love to do it justice. We finish and somehow, I don't know how, we've moved from the hallway to my bed. We lie in each other's arms and just kiss, and when that is over she just puts her head on my chest and murmurs, "So would you like a coffee, then?" We both giggle: a tinkle at first, then this silly witticism has us both laughing like drains.

On and on we laugh, settling down eventually, and then she gets up and says, "Mr. Paul Castle, I want to make you a coffee."

We laugh again and she picks up my shirt and puts it on. She is wearing nothing else, and it's breathtaking. She disappears and returns in a couple of minutes with two mugs of coffee. The sight of her in nothing but my shirt produces an erection and, giggling, she says, "You don't really want this coffee, then?"

Putting the coffee down, she climbs on top of me and we make love again. This time we take it slowly, and it is different as we explore each other and end up finishing together as she collapses on top of me after a long, passionate kiss.

"That was beautiful, Gillian!" is about all I can say afterwards, and even that's a struggle as I manfully try to regain my composure.

There's a giggle, and before I can work out what's going on she says, "What? You never tasted the coffee!"

Again we laugh and she kisses me, and after a short time we get into bed and fall into a fitful sleep. All night we sleep, kiss, make love and do the things that lovers do: reach out and stroke hair, place gentle hands on delicate places, hold each other like we never want to let go. Eventually she falls deeply asleep and the only sound in the flat is her gentle breathing.

That beautiful sound is the last thing I remember until the violent bawling of my alarm wakes me at 7 a.m.

Trying hard to resist the temptation to smash the clock, I reach out and I find she's not there. My heart lurches with the fear that she's gone and that I won't see her again. The room smells of her, and I'm devastated that she isn't next to me. I sit up and stop panicking, as her clothes are on the back of the chair. There's a rush of relief that makes me feel ashamed of doubting her, and I call her name.

"Hi! Good morning!" she answers, in a lovely, welcoming tone that fills me with joy.

"Where are you?" I ask eagerly, and I'm rewarded with an immediate response.

"Kitchen!" she shouts, and I get up, put on clean boxers and walk through.

"You look fantastic!" is my opening line; I kiss her and then we hug. She is again in my shirt, and I feel a stirring in my pants but try to damp that down as we both have to work this morning.

"You look fantastic yourself." She really knows how to make

me happy and I just melt as she says this. As I kiss her again, she playfully smacks my arse.

"Now then, Mr. Naughty, we have to work and I have to get home soon, as I can't go to work in your shirt."

"It would certainly provoke some conversation in the staffroom!" We both fall about and I feel incredibly content.

"Yes, it would," she laughs. "Now drink your coffee and I'll ring for a cab."

"You will not," I rasp. "I'm driving your home!" I stick my chin out in a gesture that brooks no defiance.

"You'll be late, silly" is her reply, said in a way that indicates that she's flattered by my attention.

"No, I'm OK. I filed my copy last night and have some time this morning." This has the virtue of being true, but she still protests before eventually giving in. Sipping my coffee, I watch her make toast and we chat the usual small talk. All of a sudden I blurt out. "You're gorgeous, Gillian. Just bloody gorgeous."

She stops and looks me in the eye. "I'm just me, Paul." It has a wistful quality.

"Well, from where I am sitting, that's gorgeous!" This is said in a voice that I hope suggests sincerity.

"Thank you, and may I say that you look gorgeous too." For once, I take the compliment and she follows it up with another. "You're a very special person, Paul. Very, very special."

"I sense a 'but' coming here." It hasn't taken long for my lack of self-confidence to reassert itself.

"No," she says. "No buts."

That brings another smile as I think that I've found someone who might be able to make me feel good about myself. She hugs me again and pops a piece of toast in my mouth and says, "Now have a shower while I get dressed, and then you can take me home."

Chapter Twenty-Five
Feeding the Mortgage Monster

The morning has left me in a daze, and as I'm driving Gillian leaves me in no doubt that she wants to see me again very soon. I drop her off at her beautiful flat, which is part of a posh town house in Harborne; she says that she adores it.

Part of the beauty of last night was the "getting to know you" bit, and I told her all about Jack and my troubles with the Ex while she told me about her previous life. Gillian was widowed ten years ago and whilst she hasn't been deliberately hiding herself away, it's taken her till this time to have the emotional energy to get involved with someone. There was a lot to talk about, and she was genuinely warm and in many ways perfect for me. Not too young; interested in art and literature; very sexy and emotionally very open. We kiss at the roadside, as she says she will call me later. Then I watch her walk to the door and she turns to wave and blow me a kiss, before I drive to work in raptures.

Sadly my day that began so well does not continue in the same way. As I walk to my desk, Doug appears.

"Can we talk, Paul?" is his opening gambit, and I nod as

we walk to his office. His opening salvo says a lot about him and the current direction of the paper. "I read your copy, Paul. Good stuff, but there's not much analysis of the national angle."

"What are you saying?" I'm still in a bit of a Gillian-inspired daze and have to work hard to be as angry as I should be.

"Well, I want some Birmingham-doing-its-bit copy" is his answer, and I'm not really sure what he's on about.

"Birmingham doing its bit?" It's sounds like a bad headline from 1940, even in a provincial rag like ours. My tone indicates how crap I think it is.

He continues regardless: "Yes, you know the thing: Brum pulls its weight in a crisis." Doug hasn't got the wit to understand my meaning, even from the exaggerated tone in my voice, and that says a lot about where his head is at the moment.

More than anything, I'm angry at his inability to understand my nuances. In addition, I'm also a bit pissed-off that he's ruined my "morning after the night before" good mood. Therefore, I decide to give him both barrels of my humour-injected invective. "I know: I could write a piece that everyone in Brum wants to lose their schools and hospitals to help Cameron and his chums in the City. At the same time, there's been a spontaneous outburst of 'There'll be Bluebirds Over the Pound Shops of Small Heath' up and down the Coventry Road."

"Very funny!" he says, in such a downbeat way that it's clear he's a bit surprised by my assertiveness; that's something we have in common.

Deciding I'm on a roll, I crack on: "Look, you're the editor and I accept that, but you wanted a piece on cuts and I'm not doing a rah-rah piece for the Tories."

"Don't forget that Birmingham is the model for the coalition at the moment."

Oh God, is that the best he can come up with? If Doug is supposed to be the finest writer on the paper, as intimated by his status as editor, we're all in trouble.

Genuinely, I start to lose it; my post-Gillian morning mood is wearing off and that's exposing my lack of sleep. "So fucking what? Look, are you after a Knighthood or something?"

"Paul, I'm just looking for balance: the public mood is for cuts in waste." Well, at least you can say he's trying.

"OK, I'll write a nice piece on all the money we're wasting on schools, hospitals and social services, and how much the bankers deserve all those bonuses for all the good that they're doing." I'm practically screaming at this point, and Doug appears genuinely shocked. The whole office outside has gone quiet.

Realising his point isn't getting through, Doug spinelessly backs down. "Look, I think that I'll write what I want in an op-ed piece, but could you look at yours to make sure it's balanced?"

Right now, I give him a look that suggests he'll be lucky. Deciding he's too stupid to read body language, I spell it out for him. "My copy's filed; you're the editor, so edit. I'm off to court."

As I'm walking away, I suddenly realise that I'm shaking. Reaching my desk, I sit at and try to compose myself; not very successfully, as it happens. Suddenly I need a cigarette, and stomp off to feed my addiction and try to resist the temptation to have a meltdown. As I storm out of the newsroom, I get a few looks and nods, and one of the sports hacks mumbles "nice one!" as I pass.

As I'm walking down the steps, my mobile chirrups, announcing a text, and I read it on my way out of the door. It's from Gillian, and my anger begins to evaporate.

Hi,
Had the best time last night! Would you like dinner on Friday?
Love, G x

Reading her text completes the process of spinning my bad mood on its head, and my mind is full of Friday night. Without even thinking, I text back an enthusiastic acceptance and join the smokers.

By the time I have sparked up, I've been joined by a couple of lags from the newsroom. It's clear that my colleagues have come down to discuss my outburst, so having me there is like a bonus for them. One comes over and says, "Nice one, Paul."

Without starting another rant, I nod at the compliment and, not wanting to acknowledge the fact that I'm still shaking, keep quiet. We chat about something inconsequential and I stub out my fag and say goodbye and walk over to court.

That gives me time for reflection, and I conclude that this situation has been brewing for ages. Doug was the senior reporter under the last editor, Bob Freeman. When he retired, Doug applied and got the job, never replacing the senior reporter's job. Instead he began employing a couple of interns to take up the slack. What followed was that he allocated stories to whoever was quickest to brown-nose him the most, and as I didn't play that game I got the perennial gig at court. But what Doug knows as well as I do is that I'm a much better writer and journalist than him, just with much blunter elbows.

In my mind's eye, Doug is the male equivalent of Ex: single-minded and career focused. On the rare occasions that we've socialised together, work's always been the only thing that he can talk about. I don't really mention this to disparage him, but the newsroom is full of intelligent writers; he treats them not with respect but with ill-concealed fear. This obviously inspires contempt in return from his workforce.

In fact, in many ways I don't dislike him. We started on the paper together, and when I returned full-time after my separation he helped me a great deal with contacts and stories to follow up. We always got on OK, but with the recession and the new government, he's turned into a management toady: more Gus Hedges than Woodward and Bernstein.

My situation is such that—and it makes me mad to admit this—I need this job to pay the mortgage. That leaves me with the knowledge that my first non-court piece in a long time is going to be butchered, and there isn't much I can do about it. So much for freedom of the press.

Chapter Twenty-Six
Wednesday's Dad is Full of Woe

Putting my boy to bed on our Wednesday evenings together is a task I love. If I were to put a handle on the one activity I miss the most from my marriage, it's reading to Jack and tucking him in at bedtime. So after a long day slaving over a hot pen in the Magistrates' Court, I relish my evening with Jack and love the fact that I'm reading him a few chapters of Roald Dahl's *Matilda*.

We've played some Xbox games tonight and I won a couple, for once. After picking him up from school, we talked about lessons and I asked him about what he liked, gently probing for any signs that Ex had let slip her plans for his education. However, it seems that Ex is as good as her word and keeping quiet about the future. All this reminds me that I need to answer her email from the other night.

So after finishing off a chapter about Miss Honey, I kiss him and tuck him in and switch off the light at the same time as saying, "I love you." Moving into the lounge, I potter about; after lifting the lid on my laptop, I think about the text I got from Gillian at four o'clock.

> Hi Paul,
> Have been thinking about you all day. Can't wait till Friday.
> Speak tonight.
> G x

That's lovely, just lovely, and I think of her in my shirt and can almost smell her next to me. The intro music for Windows interrupts me, and I remember the Ex needs answering, but decide to call Gillian first. Sighing with anticipation, I ring her mobile and there's hardly a pause before she answers.

"Hi! I was hoping that would be you." Almost every word she says is brilliant for my ego. It's like she is the secretary of the Paul Castle Fan Club.

"I can't chat enough to you!" is my rather weak response, and she giggles. If she only knew the power of that musical laugh!

"So how's Jack?" I'm touched by the thought she gives to my boy.

My answer is full of enthusiasm: "Great! We had a lovely time. I've put him to bed. Listen, you don't mind me spending time…" There's a voice in my head that tells me I already know the answer, but it comes anyway.

"Don't be silly. The fact that you love him so much…well, it makes you more attractive, frankly." The effect this sentence has is just awesome.

"Does it?" I reply innocently.

"Of course. Do you think that I would go out with anyone who would abandon their child?" Of course I know the answer to that too.

"No, obviously not." There's part of me that knows Gillian is different to my Ex; that she won't treat my gentle side as a character flaw.

"You're a special man, Paul Castle."

Again this makes me feel fantastic. There's a pause as I digest this assault on my insecurity, and I answer with interest. "Well, my dear Gillian Black, you're special too."

"I don't know about that." It's clear, of course, that it's been a long time since she's heard words like these, and it's no surprise that she's coy.

"Well, that isn't fair!" I shoot back, pretending to be affronted. "How can I be special when you aren't?"

And we go on and on. Sadly, I tell her that I want to meet tomorrow but have a shift at Gerry's youth club and she tells me that she's teaching a class at the Tech. So we have to wait, and both of us express our frustration at the delay.

After a long call with much laughter and joy, we sign off, agreeing to chat later before we go to bed. At this point I have to settle down to some emailing to try to appease the Ex. Before starting that, I look at my inbox and there is another email from her.

Paul,

It's been two days since I last emailed you and we cannot wait for you to gaze at your navel.

Please let us know what you are going to do and ensure that we can make plans for Jack and have all of this settled. Time is passing and the chances of a good school are draining away while you twiddle your thumbs hoping this will all go away.

Well, welcome back to the old Ex! Anyway, at least I don't have to worry about her turning over a new leaf. Deciding to abandon the email, I make up my mind to call her, as I want her to tell me a lot more than she has so far. I'm going to use the tip

Gerry gave me right at the start of this process, and write down my thoughts in order to keep control of the conversation.

There needs to be a delay, though, as I want to let Jack get right off to sleep first, since a call to his mum can lead to raised voices. To take my mind off this, I make coffee and fire off a romantic text to Gillian and send a few emails to friends. Just as I am doing this, Trevor the director emails, and he wants to meet me on Thursday afternoon. I look at my diary and offer him lunchtime or after 4 p.m.

He fires back that 4.30 is cool and he wants to know whether I have any more plays to hand. I've written about six plays apart from the one that he has, although I think only three are really fit to be seen. He quickly sends back a reply for me to bring them tomorrow if I can, and he adds, "It was great to meet you and I really am looking forward to chatting to you about your work."

This all sounds very promising but, and it's a really big but, I have been here before, with lots of interest and promises of options before the rug's pulled from under me. Or directors going back on the promise of a certain gig, leaving me defeated and deflated after another rejection. The play that Gerry saw, used to cement my credentials as a writer at Bonnie's dinner party, was the exception. It was picked up by another director friend of Jenny's, and it got a short run at a playhouse workshop space. It was really well received and did good numbers, but the director got another gig in London, and down went my hopes of another crack at making it.

All of this reminiscence doesn't put me in the correct frame of mind to phone Ex, so I decide to get a coffee and listen to the Clash on my iPod. There's nothing better than them to get you in the mood for a row. So, starting with "I Fought The Law", I jot down a few things I want to say and questions needing some answers. It's hard to get on top of, but I think about this for a few minutes and by the end of "Should I Stay Or Should I Go?" I've enough questions to ask and enough backbone to ask them. Joe Strummer: fucking priceless!

Picking the phone up, I dial the number and John answers. "Hi, Paul! Nice to hear from you."

A good start, at least, and I decide to try and keep it that way. "Hi, John! Have you a speakerphone? It would be good to talk to both of you."

There's a bit of chat between them and then some clicking; then the voice of my Ex booms over the phone.

"Hi, can you hear that?"

"Yeah, loud and clear. Can you both hear me?"

"Yes. What's up? Is Jack OK?" I'm touched by her concern and irritated that she thinks I'm an incompetent carer.

Biting my lip, I carry on. "Yeah, he's fine," I answer, and brace myself. "Listen: I got your email and I'm not trying to be difficult, but I think that you're asking a lot."

Ex is obviously upset and snaps back, "What on earth do you mean by that?"

I'm determined, despite the Clash's best efforts, to keep this civil. "Well, for my benefit I need to know when you plan to leave for London and when Jack will be leaving. It would also be handy to know what schools you are thinking about and all the other questions that I left you with on Monday." Not bad, if I say so myself. A classic example of assertion, not aggression, with the added bonus that they can't see me breaking into a cold sweat!

Surprisingly it's John who answers. "Paul, we don't know a lot of the answers just yet, but we can tell you some rough plans we have. Would that help you?"

"Yes, it would." My word, he's got assertiveness in bucket loads.

As Paul Weller says, all that rugby puts hairs on your chest!

"Well, I'm looking to move down to London in a month or so; certainly by the end of May."

"OK," I say in a noncommittal way. "Are you selling the house?" This question suddenly occurs to me, but for the moment I can't think why.

"No, we are letting it out. Why are you asking?" Ex is the personification of hostility. That's probably driven by suspicion that I'm after her money, which I'm most definitely not.

"It's just that Jack might notice the 'For Sale' sign, that's all." There's a silence after this, which I fill with my next question: "When will your transfer be finalised?"

Ex answers in a much less hostile way. "I've been given a verbal 'yes' and I am expecting to move at the end of June."

"Which would explain why you're keen to get sorted." Everything is falling into place now, and I'm angry that they didn't admit this at the start of the process. Bizarrely, I find myself angrier about her treatment of the school than about anything else. Sometimes I think I'm just potty.

"I'm glad you understand, Paul. Can we just say that we are committed to ensuring that you see Jack as much as possible."

Digesting that, I try to not sound harsh when I need more clarification, "I sense that you guys are going to add a rider to that." I feel I'm getting down to the nitty-gritty of this now.

"Both of our jobs will require a good deal of foreign travel, often at short notice. We're hoping to get a good boarding school for Jack so that we can work secure in the knowledge that he will be looked after if we are called away."

"I see." The tone of my voice reflects the fact that I'm starting to get really peeved. It seems Jack is being shunted to Snotyard School for the Emotionally Retarded to facilitate their jet-set life style.

Ex decides at this point to chip in.

"Look, we want Jack to have the best education we can give him."

I bite back, "Why can't he live with me and see you at the weekends?"

"The court gave me residency and you know it!" She starts bellowing down the phone.

However unhappy I am, I refuse to let her have the satisfaction of making me lose my temper. "Look, it's an option you can consider. You want stability for him and I can give him that, and that will allow you to work wherever without worrying about him." Talk about Mr. Reasonable!

There's a lot of whispering going on, none of which I can hear properly, and then John pops up. "Paul, we will certainly consider that, but we are keen to have Jack near us so that he can be closer to his mum and gran."

My hopes of having Jack during the week start to recede, and rather than continue to rile the Ex, I make a gesture. "OK, I think we need to move on, and I have a suggestion to make."

"Go on." John's reply is full of wariness. It's almost as if he cannot understand why I'm not rolling over as Ex no doubt predicted.

My suggestion is to the point. "I want to be with you when you tell Jack that you are moving down to London. I want to be there because he has to know I'm not going to abandon him."

"That's an interesting idea" is the lukewarm response, which is followed by more whispering.

Ignoring this, I decide to make a dignified exit. "Furthermore, I'm telling you that I am not going to use Jack as an emotional football and I only want to support him as best I can and get this right for him." I feel I have to say this, as I don't want my kid to feel that he is in the middle of a fight in which he alone will be the loser. As angry as I am with the Ex, I refuse to use Jack to get what I want.

"That's fine, Paul."

"Hold on, John. I haven't finished yet." I'm really unhappy now and I need to get this stuff off my chest.

"Sorry, Paul: please continue." He seems a little intimidated, which makes me feel, unbelievably, a touch uncomfortable.

"I want to keep this as amicable as possible, but if I feel that Jack is being dragooned into something he doesn't want to do, I'll be getting legal advice."

"Paul, let me assure you that we only want the best for Jack." On the surface, this appears to be a sincere response. Ex is very quiet and a vision comes into my head of John sitting on top of her with a hand over her mouth as she desperately tries to scream and shout at me. To think I once called this man a "private school prick"!

Emotionally drained, I want to leave it there, but he continues. "With your permission, can we tell Jack after you bring him home on Saturday?"

"That will be fine, John. I'm glad we've had this chance to talk."

There's a pause. "OK. Goodnight, Paul."

"Goodnight. See you Saturday."

The phone goes down, and I sense that whatever happens Jack is going to be moving down south. For the first time, the pain of it begins to overwhelm me as I feel my boy slipping away from me.

Chapter Twenty-Seven
Sleepless in Sutton Coldfield

Sweating, I wake at 4 o'clock in the morning, still struggling to get a grip on what's happening. After talking to Ex and John, I'd phoned Gillian, who was a complete star and settled me down. We arranged to discuss everything on Friday. It was magnificent to feel that I had someone there for me, and she was so cool about all my nonsense and even offered to "give me some space", which I refused point-blank. The relief in her voice following my refusal was palpable, and I was delighted by that and told her so.

Turning over and over in bed, I've tried to think of solutions or escape routes. The problem is that I've got very little to work with. Jack is technically required to live with his mother unless we both agree otherwise. Anything else requires a visit to the legal firm of Youscrewme and I'llscrewyou, then to the judge, and I still might get nothing. My only hope lies in what Jack wants, and that is a terrible thing to do to him. He has to choose which parent to hurt and it is going to be hard for him. The Ex is unlikely to give up without a fight and I'm reluctant to start one because of the risk of him getting caught in the crossfire.

It's five before I get off to sleep and when the alarm goes off, no amount of snooze button pushes will recover the sleep I've lost.

Eventually I wake up and rush around getting Jack ready, and we both arrive bleary-eyed at school. He's cool enough to want me to stay in the car and walk into the playground on his own. That gives me the chance to look at him disappearing through the gate and my tiredness and emotional state bring me nearly to tears. Somehow I just manage to get a grip on myself.

Opening the window I light a cigarette, something I rarely do in the Citroën but for once see it properly as only a car. Shaking my head, I resolve to get myself sorted and start the DS, saying "Thunderbirds are GO!" in my head. The day is going to be an emotional one, I fear.

By midmorning, that's true is so many ways. Up till now Gillian and I have been texting like a couple of sixteen-year-olds. Today is different, as hers are all about caring for me and the language is that of a lover in distress at my predicament. As you already know, this is something I'm very much unused to. Responding with all I have emotionally, I make sure she knows that I'm never going to forget the care she is showing. I use the words "much love" at end of each text and I really want to say "I love you". Somehow, I'm just too scared to make that little change in wording.

Now most women and some men would tut here and say horrible things about me being a commitment-phobe. In my defence, it has to be said that my reluctance to say "I love you" is purely based on my fear that I'll scare her away. All that being said, I'm getting close to believing that Gillian is the nearest thing to a soulmate I'm ever likely to come across.

Typically, it's just with Jack, redundancy and my self-confidence, the timing's a bit off. My problems, if you can call them that, are the Freudian, beardy fear of rejection and abandonment. Everything that's happened to me before Gillian is a slightly different version of watching my dad walking out of the front door carrying his suitcase, on the way to live with his secretary.

That's kind of hard to get your head around. After all, loads of people are shitloads worse off than me. However, everyone measures their own pain, and every rejection letter from a theatre company or book publisher, the hard words and departure of the Ex, the unsatisfying journalism job, are all just versions of my dad leaving. Just diluted versions of the first time I ever knew what distressed really meant.

As I begin a new text to Gillian, there's a shadow across the desk announcing the arrival of Doug. "Busy, are we?" He asks this in a vaguely sarcastic way, and I decide that I'll have my head cut off before I'll tell him about Gillian.

"Just a contact in the unions, telling me some news about the cuts meeting."

His face lights up—the newspaperman surfacing at last. "Anything that can go in the paper?" It takes all of my energy not to slap him on the back, welcoming his return to the world of the reporter.

However, I still need to cover up my outrageous lie, and say the first thing that comes into my head. "I need another source; you want me to follow it up?" That might buy me some time.

"Yes, go ahead and run with it; Steve can cover court. Just don't come back with a story of the winter of discontent when it's just the summer of hot air."

I laugh, not at his joke but at the fact that I've got away with texting Gillian at work and now have another assignment. Bonus! Still, I need to make sure he understands I'm taking no nonsense.

"Nice line, Doug. Did you edit my Council piece?"

"Not too much. It was OK, as I said. I'll use an op-ed piece." He says this as if he's trying to be authoritative, but really he just looks like a pompous prat. It's impossible for me not to grimace as he smugly smiles. "Deadline's at the normal time for the first edition but I can make more space if you can get something really substantial."

He saunters back to his office, and I've got myself on a proper story. My rant at him the other day must have done some good, but I don't have time to reflect on that as I had blagged about the text. The stinger on that is I've hardly any contacts in the unions and not much to go on.

However, it's good to have friends, and Gerry knows a couple of people in the local UNISON branch. Quickly, I text him and ask if we can talk. He fires back a reply and we arrange to go for a coffee. With fifteen minutes to burn, I ring around the few contacts I have and come up short until I chat to one guy who remembers me from a pretty pro-union piece I wrote that got massacred by Spineless Doug. His reaction to the cuts is sullen acceptance. It seems that most of the more bellicose statements are posturing that will frighten nobody. He adds that the job cuts are being got out of the way now and that the first casualties will be casual and temporary workers. Elections are a few years away and it's dole today and hopefully bread tomorrow, even if there isn't any jam.

Not knowing the intricacies of Council employment policies, I foolishly say that these cuts don't sound that drastic. He just lets go, and angrily explains the impact of the cuts and gives some numbers. He's really clear-sighted about their impact, and it doesn't take long for me to work out that he is definitely not a man to upset. Even as I bridle at his attempt to label me as a member of the right-wing media, we hunker down to talk about whether the cuts will be seriously opposed.

His feeling is no, and I ask whether I can quote him, at which point he laughs. We agree on the attribution of "senior union official". At the end of the conversation we say goodbye and I thank him profusely, then shoot off to see Gerry.

When we meet, for the first five minutes I have to listen to his constant ranting about the variety of concoctions served in the modern coffee shop. As always, he talks about going to a proper café in his youth, and having a choice of tea or coffee. Now, he rants on, you have twenty-five choices just for the coffee. The only problem with this is that he orders a large skinny latte with hazelnut syrup, which kind of undermines his argument. Pondering that, I realise that I should have asked him why he's on skinny lattes.

He just looks at me and, guessing what I'm thinking, says, "Keep this to yourself, but I've started worrying about my health."

"Oh God! You're not ill, are you?" That answer is filled with genuine concern.

He laughs and says, "No, don't be soft! Did you think I'm at death's door?"

Quickly, I crack back at him, "Well if you die, can I have your CDs?" We both break out in laughter and when that dies down, I ask in all seriousness, "Mate, are you OK?"

"Too much lard and beer; need to lose a few stone and get my blood pressure down."

As soon as he says this, I'm alarmed. "Blood pressure?"

"Yeah, I've got to get it down." Typically, I can't think of anything else to say after that, and the thoughts running round my head are trite and simply not what two old friends say to one another.

In the end I look at him and say, "Just let me know if you

need anything." He makes a face that says "yeah, OK", and we talk about a couple of guys we know in UNISON as a diversion from speaking about things that matter.

He calls them, and we have a three-way on the speakerphone, then the story is pretty much written. A couple of hours later, I file and I'm pretty pleased with myself, although depressed as the title sums up what's wrong with this country.

Union Leaders Pessimistic Over Ability to Fight Cuts
by Paul Castle
The vanguard of the working-class, ha bloody ha!

My copy filed, I shoot out to a late lunch, calling Gerry on the way to a sandwich place we both use. He agrees to me buying him lunch as part-payment for sorting me out with the story. We meet and order some food and Gerry turns his nose up at a salad I choose, which kind of worries me a little, given our previous conversation about his health. We then chat and get round to the subject of Jack, and I tell him about the nice email, followed by the nasty email and then the phone call.

He says, "Never!" and "What a cow!" in the appropriate places, and I give him the stinger about the Ex's move down south, which drives him to a four-letter frenzy. The next ten minutes were taken up with his ranting and his shouts of "Go and get legal advice!" and me batting that back as I am worried about the implications for Jack. His parting shot was to make sure that I have as much to say as possible about contact and access.

"Don't let her walk all over you, and most definitely make sure that Jack knows that you're going to be seeing him as often as possible." He pauses as if to reinforce the importance of his next statement. "Make sure you discuss this with Gillian. All of it."

"Yeah, she knows most of it." I say this with an emphasis that suggests this is an automatic thing, her sharing my life.

"Good." We've both finished eating, and he gets up to leave and I follow suit. He reaches across and hugs me, very, very hard. "Listen to me: Jenny and I are behind you 100%. Make sure you go the distance."

"OK! Let go now—people are starting to stare!" I say in a funny voice, as both of us probably couldn't give a damn what people think.

He laughs and then adds as an afterthought, "Oh bugger! I forgot to tell you that Trevor's looking for you."

Laughing, I theatrically slap my forehead. "Oh, thank God you said that! In all the excitement, I forgot I'm meeting him at 4.30."

We walk to the door and he says with a laugh, "Good luck with that, and don't be late for the youth club tonight."

After that, it's back to the office to get some other stuff together, but my heart isn't really in it. The only thing I'm thinking about is losing my son and the possibility of having my play staged.

Chapter Twenty-Eight
When One Door Closes…

Later, Doug calls me into the office and goes through my copy; every sentence is read with a frown. However, he doesn't wield his blue pencil and I get two bylines in one edition.

It's getting near the time, so I say goodbye to everyone and leave at 4.10. The theatre is only a five-minute walk, but I have this thing about being early.

The place is practically empty and it has the usual glass-and-wood atrium of the modern provincial theatre, littered with display boards and leaflets advertising the coming programme.

Feeling really nervous, I ask at the Box Office but they don't know about my meeting and ask me to sit down and wait while they find Trevor.

Having settled myself in the futuristic armchair, I flick through the theatre's coming attractions, mentally choosing which I'd like to take Gillian to see. There are a couple of good bands coming as well as a few bits-and-bobs that wipe my cultural nose. Finally I spot an advert for a rhythm and blues band fronted by Paul Jones; that really floats my boat and read about it till Trevor turns up.

"Ah, Paul! See anything you like?" he asks with a grin.

"Actually, loads, Trevor!" There's no harm in flattering the guy.

"That's great! Jenny says you love the theatre." All true, and not doing me any harm either.

Without a hint of ingratiation I say, "I love this theatre; it's a great place to come." I'm actually telling the truth here and I think that Trevor knows that, as I can imagine he can smell bullshit a mile away.

"Yeah, Jenny said that," he says, confirming my suspicion. "Look, come to my office and we can talk."

I follow him to his workspace, and it's a poky hole compared to the atrium we've just left. For the next fifteen minutes, he talks about my focus as a writer and my narrative strengths and then asks me what else I have.

Naturally, I start to gush my thanks but soon settle down to say, "I've another three complete plays and another couple that need a polish."

"That sounds great, Paul. One of my strengths in my previous jobs was to encourage new writing, and the board here have given me a specific remit to do that."

"OK, that sounds very good to me, Trevor." I hold back on the gushing as I sense he wants to talk numbers. So it turns out.

He looks me in the eye. "I want to commission the play you gave me on Sunday, and I want to put it on in our workshop space with a young director we're keen on. This will be a model for future work with you and other new writers, actors and directors."

"Brilliant!" It's all I can say, really; but like the man run over by a train, I'm chuffed to bits.

Trevor makes a stern face as he adds a caveat: "However, there is hardly any money for the budget and I want decent actors to give this programme a kick-start, so your fee will be quite small. But if it works well, I want you to write lots for me and I'm hoping that I can pay you more in the future.

I want your other scripts as soon as possible, as I'm keen to get started."

"Trevor, that's great! It'll be a real pleasure!" At least I have the power of speech now, and I'm feeling fantastic. With a smile, I hand him the three scripts I have in my bag and he accepts them with obvious relish; I resolve to get to work on my other plays.

However, he's quick to warn me: "You won't be saying that soon, when I and the director are after you for rewrites and all of that!"

Being a journalist, I know the pressure of deadlines, but resist the temptation of bigging myself up so I settle for more thanks. "Trevor, you know I can't thank you enough."

It's all small talk from then on, and I can't wait to call Gillian and tell her the news. Trevor's all smiles, and he promises to call me next week to organise dates for meeting the director and an actor he's lined up for an audition.

Gillian, two bylines, and a play potentially produced: what a great week that would be in normal circumstances! All of that is shrouded, of course, by the whole Jack thing. However, I have no time to process that as my shift at the youth club is looming. Feeling peckish, I grab a quick bite at a curry house I know that does early evening light meals, and try to relax a little. Whilst doing this, I text everyone I know about the play being produced, and I'm flattered by the amount of people who seem genuinely thrilled at my achievement.

After finishing my meal, I sit back and try to use that positive energy from the texts to gee me up for the shift at the youth club. The kids there are pretty full-on and you have to be pretty focused to keep up. That's going to be hard as I'm now feeling the results of my late, late nights with Gillian and my broken sleep last night after the call with the Ex.

Also, I have to try hard not to be affected by the spectre of the conversation and tears that await me on Saturday. Usually I'm a glass-half-full kind of guy, but it's hard to see telling Jack about his mother leaving Birmingham through anything other than a half-empty glass.

Chapter Twenty-Nine
Whim of Iron

Working with Gerry is a true honour. He's a superb youth worker, and the kids love him. More importantly, they respect him, and even when stuff gets a bit out of hand it never seems like he has anything other than total control. The shift goes like clockwork, and I run a pool competition, having a blast in the process. We shut up shop at 9.00 and Gerry asks me for a pint, which I reluctantly refuse. My resolve to work on Trevor's stuff kicks in, and I need to get a grip on the scripts, plus I want to talk at length with Gillian. He understands my head is still in another place, so he lets me go without too much abuse, which is a relief.

Driving to my door takes only a couple of minutes, and I'm excited by the prospect of chatting to Gillian. After letting myself in and doing the male thing with the post—bin, bin, ignore, ignore, bin, ignore—I call her.

"Hi! It's lovely to hear your voice." She sounds delighted to hear from me.

"Well, I've missed you: two whole hours without a call or a text!"

After this opening, she laughs, and we chat like this for what seems like ages; I eventually cough up my need to start getting scripts together and she lets me go on the promise that I will call her when I finish.

Without a pause, I look at some of my older writing on my computer. One of the plays requires only a bit of polish, and it reminds me that every writer has to rewrite and I'm no different. However, I'm generally a procrastinator and my reluctance to show this stuff beyond my social circle has up to now been put down to the need to "finish it properly". Well, sometimes you have to say "enough is enough" and risk something.

Maybe now is the time. The whole Gillian thing has taken me by surprise. In my ignorance, I thought that the emotional turmoil of being in a relationship would be distracting and disorientating, but actually it's the reverse. It's liberating: a kind of understanding of what's possible when you have self-belief.

As I sit here, very calmly, editing, the thoughts that start invading my head concern a long-term future with a woman I've known for just six days. Thinking about rushing too far into a very uncertain future is a bit like a wild guessing game. Foolishly, I sit and imagine a scenario where I express my plans and emotions to Gillian and she says, "Don't be silly; we're having a bit of fun." Slowly this becomes a dominant thought and I have to force myself to focus on something else as I was never that good at multitasking.

The tiredness begins to bite and I decide to have coffee to allow me some space to call Gerry. I very rarely ask his opinion, but at this point it seems like a sensible thing to do, or my previous thoughts will start to drive me mad.

He picks up the call, and he sounds a little unlike his normal self.

"Gerry, mate, how are you?"

He comes back with, "Same as when you left me a couple of hours ago. What's up?"

"Oh, you know!" I'm sincerely hoping he does know.

"Nope!" We both laugh, and he adds, "You sound like a teenager."

"Oh God, do I?" This is pathetic, I know, but I'm completely out of practice with people professing that they like me.

"You know you do." He pauses and then lets me have it: "I love you and you're like a brother to me. I know that right now you are finding all sorts of blockages to pursuing a relationship with Gillian, aren't you?"

"Yes, but the whole Jack thing...." I leave that thought hanging there.

"Listen, Gillian is great and you are great. We have a very strong feeling that you will be great together." Gerry is getting a little frustrated at this point.

"But I've only known her for a week!"

Now Gerry does something very unusual: he loses his temper.

"Listen: you're forty-two, not nineteen. You haven't got time to go out with people, screw around, and see if it will work out. You are accommodating and conciliatory and so is she; you both have similar views on art, life and politics. You're attractive and so is she. She wants you and you want her. Your only problem is that the Wicked Witch of NatWest has robbed you of your confidence. Gillian is perfect for you—now fucking get on with it!"

He lets that sink in, and I'm speechless. Then suddenly I'm crying like a baby, thanking him and telling him how important he and Jenny are to me. All the emotion and tiredness of the last few days is getting the better of me and I sound completely pathetic.

He lets me finish and says, "We love you too. Now fuck off and ring Gillian and let me get back to making love to Jenny!"

There's a high-pitched sound in the background, which

I suspect is Jenny protesting at his last remark, and I've a terrible feeling it's true. Bursting out laughing, I know I'll be hearing an awful lot more about our phone call if it is: Gerry will be telling everyone he had a night of passion ruined by my blubbing. Quickly, I ring off and try to work out a plan of what to say to Gillian.

Taking my time, I plan this with military precision. Methodically I write down all the reasons I love her, and all the reasons why she might not want to go to the next stage. In addition, I think about all the arguments she might advance for it being too soon and I how I'm going to convince her of our compatibility and how strong my feelings are.

Feeling very unconfident, I pick up the phone with some trepidation and dial the number; she picks up almost at once.

"Hi Paul! Listen, I'm desperate to see you. Can I come over?"

"Yes," I say automatically.

"Can I stay?" There's real hope in her voice; desperation even.

"Of course." What else can I say?

"See you in fifteen minutes, then."

"I can't wait!" is my answer, and you know what? I can't.

"Neither can I." And with that she puts the phone down, leaving me thirty minutes to get a shower and wash up.

Chapter Thirty
It Takes Two

Gillian actually takes twenty-three minutes to arrive, and we spend a lovely few moments kissing and then we make love on my couch. It's a wonderful, tender, but very sexy coming together of two people expressing their feelings for each other in a very physical way.

There's a brief hiatus when we finish, and we hold each other tightly. It takes a few minutes for us to get our breath back, and then I kiss her gently and lovingly.

She looks into my eyes and…I'll never get over what she says: "It would be very easy to fall in love with you, Mr. Paul Castle."

I'm taken aback; speechless.

She looks a little frightened and hastily starts to explain. "I'm sorry. I don't want to scare you; it's just that Archie said you were wonderful and…"

I butt in, not out of rudeness but to reassure her.

"I'm not scared by that in the slightest. In fact I feel the same way you do." There's a deafening silence.

The whole thing about her coming over has left me groping for words to express my feelings. As a writer, I'm fairly upset that that's happened.

Finally, I try to marshal my thoughts, and say very quietly, "I think at this stage…" I pause: she is looking in my eyes, and I can even feel her heart beating. "I want to…sort of…ask permission to fall in love with you."

"Ask permission?" She looks a little confused. I can't really blame her for this.

"Well…" I grope for a reply, very conscious that I'm making this up as I go along. "There's no doubt I feel very happy to be with you; the feelings I have for you are love, I know it. That being said, we've only known each other for six days and I don't want to scare you away by going too fast."

There's a pause, and she looks at me with a face full of joy. "Mr. Paul Castle, would you do me the honour of falling in love with me?"

A smile breaks out on her face and I answer in a very formal tone, "In that case, Gillian Black, will you allow me to express my sincerest feelings of tenderness, affection and desire, and inform you that I'm madly in love with you?" The writer in me has returned. Hoo-bloody-rah!

Gillian quietly kisses me passionately and says, voice trembling, "I love you."

And this is what we say, pretty much, for the rest of the evening. We make love, make coffee, make toast and make love again. It's all about expressing a love born out of more than just desire, but mutual understanding and respect.

We eventually get to bed about 3.30, make love again then fall asleep in each other's arms.

The alarm clock, screeching at 7.00, wakes me and I groggily sit up, still half-asleep, and again have the shock of waking up alone.

I hear the shower and stealthily slip into the bathroom where she jumps with shock when she turns round and spies me. We both laugh and, turning the tap off, she wraps a towel around herself and we kiss.

"Good morning, darling," I say with an exaggerated formality.

"Paul, you monster! Sneaking up on me!"

"You look gorgeous, darling." My formal tone is still intact and we keep laughing.

She blushes and answers, "So do you. Bad man!"

Reaching out, I hold her, and I'm conscious of her holding me just as tightly. I want to make love to her almost urgently, right here on the bathroom floor, and she comically frowns when I tell her that: "No, you bad boy, that floor will be freezing." And then she leads me to the bedroom and we make love there.

Eventually the two of us have to stop this romancing and get ready for work, laughing and kissing and savouring the moments before her cab arrives. Pretty soon she's speeding towards work and leaving me at home desperate to see her and begrudging everything that conspires to keep us apart.

As I'm about to leave, my mobile bleeps and I read the text from her, which simply says:

I love you. G. x

Happily, for once I have no words to express the emotions that text produces.

Chapter Thirty-One
Welcome to the Working Week

Somehow, I'm not sure how, I manage to get myself focused for work and get to the car. The Citroën rises on its suspension and I begin the drive to work and to deal with the implications of being properly in love for the first time since the Ex.

The feeling isn't one of unalloyed joy; it's one of joy masking great pain. Still needing to get a grip on the situation with Jack, I can see with great clarity how upset he will be at how much his life is going to change. As I ponder this, I begin to look at a life with Gillian but without the regular contact with Jack. The tragedy is that Jack could have a great life with me, but the Ex has the residence order and without forcing the issue in court, I can do nothing.

All of a sudden it's all a bit much, and just before I arrive at work, the Elvis Costello song "Alison" comes on and I'm crying like an over-emotional idiot. My long nights with Gillian and the excitement of the last week have made me a bit of a tired and emotional basket case—a very, *very* tired one at that.

Pulling in to the side of the road, I try to get myself together. The mixture of emotions and feelings—elation and despair, joy and sadness, victory and defeat—is encapsulated in those beautiful lyrics. Reluctantly, I face up to the reality that I'm an emotional mess: happy and sad existing in the same space. Apparently some people can compartmentalise that sort of stuff, but I can't, and so I sit there trying to get some perspective and sense into my life.

Somewhere in the background behind the music and the contradictory thoughts going on in my head, I hear a mobile phone ringing. Suddenly I have no idea what time it is or how long the phone's been going off, and I pull it out of my pocket and answer it, still in a bit of a daze. The voice on the other end sounds strange to me, like I'm talking underwater.

"Paul...Paul! Where the fuck are you?" It's Doug. The Spineless One.

Eventually, I answer as I begin to get myself together. "Hi, Doug! What can I do for you?"

"It's madness here, and I need you in right away. A couple of stories are breaking and I want you on them, and the union story is going tits up."

Suddenly I'm back in focus again. "OK, I'm on my way; got stuck in traffic." Switching off the phone I start getting my head together. In the time I've been sitting here the CD has restarted and Elvis is thumping out "Welcome to the Working Week". That's as good a way as any to get me to focus on the day ahead, and I start the car and get to work to find Doug in a state of advanced mental meltdown.

"Paul! Come in the office." His tone isn't friendly.

We walk in together, and he looks at me in what I can only describe as an imploring way. "Brian is off sick—'stress'—and everyone else is sorted or just not *bothered enough!*" He shouts the last line at the open door of his office and then turns to me. "I need a reporter up at City Hall; the Council staff are voting on strike action." He is practically tearing his hair out.

"What the hell has prompted that?"

"Somebody leaked an interim report detailing the cuts, and they're apparently savage." Doug is spitting these words out in an unbelievably agitated way.

"That's crap, Doug: the UNISON boys are saying there's no stomach for it." I'm regurgitating what I've been told, and it occurs to me that either I've been had or they've been taken by surprise. Either way, it makes me look a bit of an idiot.

"Well, that's not what I'm hearing. There's an emergency meeting at lunchtime. I need the story and want to know if you've been played by the Union boys." He's obviously cottoned on, and that isn't looking good for me.

Cursing under my breath, all I want to do is find out what's happening as I'm angry and my reputation is on the line. I'm sure I haven't been played but I also have a front-page byline in the paper with "Union leaders pessimistic over ability to fight cuts". Bollocks.

The phone's ringing red-hot and Doug just looks like a heart attack waiting to happen, so I slip out of the office while he answers it. My first thought is to ring Gerry, and I walk across the road to a greasy spoon café we all use when we need some peace and to fiddle our expenses. There is the thought looming that I've a lot riding on this, and when Gerry answers my call, I sound stressed as I explain to him what's going on.

"Paul, I heard them tell you there wasn't any heart for industrial action." This is music to my ears but won't cut much ice with Doug and the suits upstairs.

"Unfortunately that isn't going to help me with the Spineless Wonder when he needs a scapegoat. He's stressed now and I think he's lining me up in his sights." Gerry murmurs assent at my reading of the situation.

When all's said and done, my best friend's great and, after a moment's pause, he says in a voice that oozes calm, "OK, mate, I'll make a few calls and I'll call you back on your mobile. Go and have a cigarette and calm down."

The wait's interminable, made only slightly bearable by some romantic texting with Gillian. That at least makes the delay for news a little easier to bear, but in the back of my mind I'm racing over the possibilities if today goes horribly wrong.

Gerry eventually calls back, breaking my little burst of texting, saying he can't get hold of our contact. All I can do is manage a groan, and he tries hard to cheer me up. "Don't, mate; it's no problem. I've left messages for him. What's the panic? You're nowhere near your deadline, are you?"

"Yeah, but Doug's coming under a load of heat and that pressure will be diverted my way."

"OK, I'll go higher up the UNISON ladder, I know our man's boss; he's met Jenny and I'll use that to get me an in."

"Thanks, mate. See you soon." Scarcely feeling better, I put the phone down and try to read something.

Feeling fairly useless, I decide to ring Doug, to try and stress to him that I'm working on the case and attempt to put his mind at rest.

Knowing that I need to sound unfazed, I sit down and try to sound measured and unflustered. Doug doesn't sound in any way unfazed, measured or unflustered: "Paul, what's going on? The board are going mad upstairs and some Councillors are up in arms. Apparently, the staff at City Hall are in a revolutionary mood."

"Look, we report the news, and yesterday we wrote a measured, well-sourced piece."

His panic is evident. "And today that story's been blown to bits after less than twenty-four hours."

Holding it together, I maintain my poise. "Doug, you don't know that as the meeting hasn't happened yet. It could all be a storm in a teacup."

"You don't seem to realise that we, and that really means you, have dropped the ball, and with your story last night we look like a load of Union stooges." He's put the worst-case scenario together but in essence that could all be true.

Fighting my own rising sense of panic, I try to get some hard facts out of him in order to rescue something from this nonsense. "Listen, what does the leaked document say?"

He sounds far, far beyond the end of his tether. "No one fucking knows—don't you listen?" He's conveniently ignored the fact that he hadn't told me this.

At that moment, I get a text from Gerry. It just says "Call me", and I hang up on Doug, promising to ring him back.

Gerry cheers me with some very good news. "Listen, the UNISON office is in a worse panic than Doug. The leaked document is the Finance Committee's proposed cuts for the Full Council next week, and this has gone round the email system in next to no time and the atmosphere is febrile. The members are also angry that the leadership essentially called them apathetic yesterday in your article. They want to talk to you, and I've a copy of the leaked document going to your iPhone."

"You're a lifesaver!" I mange to say, and he laughs at my evident sense of relief.

He replies, in an older brother-like way, "It's because you needed a break. Call Martin at UNISON on 496 0721. He's waiting for your call. Keep in touch with how things are going."

"You work for the Council; you'll know as quickly as I will," I reply, wondering what he's on about.

"Idiot! I mean about Gillian."

His humour is infectious, and I respond in kind. His care for me is evident and I joke, "OK, call you in a couple of years—see if I can move to the next stage." I need time, lots of time, to tell him about last night.

"Bugger off! I'll call you later!" He hangs up, still laughing.

It takes me a couple of minutes to compose some questions, then I ring Martin and he basically gives me what Gerry has already told me. He allows me to give attribution to the story, which is really cool. Then I ask to go to the meeting, and on the strength of some former pieces and Gerry and Jenny's friendship he agrees. Relaxing, I drink the rest of my coffee reading the leaked memo, satisfied that despite Doug's flapping I can pull another good story out of the bag and sort out the mess into the bargain.

Chapter Thirty-Two
The People's Flag

My blood is up as I read the memo very quickly and assess its implications for jobs and services. As I reach the end, Gerry texts me with the time and place of the emergency Union meeting; he obviously knew that Martin would let me in. He wants me to meet him in Victoria Square. Usually this is my favourite place in Brum, but today I've no time to take it in. When I have some leisure, it's an impressive public space, littered with really good art including a piece by Anthony Gormley, who designed the Angel of the North.

It takes me fifteen minutes to get all my stuff together, and we hug as meet and I mutter my thanks as he's bailed me out big-time today. He just says "bollocks!" and we leave it at that as we make our way there.

Gerry and I arrive at the meeting, and my press pass gets me admittance. It's being held in the Council Chamber: this in itself is unusual, but it appears that more than five hundred people are there already. The whole thing is organised chaos and the Union leadership are clearly unprepared and have to get themselves together to work out how to use the PA.

It's an angry yet dignified protest and a real bottom-up demand for leadership. There are at least half a dozen contributions from the crowd. One woman bursts into tears, and I take down her speech for a quote in the paper:

"I've seen my team cut from six to three people, so we have to work twice as hard, and we have more and more elderly people waiting for a service—just to assess them for home helps and other care packages. Elderly people don't like asking for help, and when they do it is usually 100% genuine and long overdue. I used to love working with them, helping them stay in their homes with the dignity they so richly deserve. Now, thanks to the cuts already in place, I have to tell them they can't have an assessment for at least four months, and even if they meet the criteria I don't know if they will get a service. That's the situation now, and the leaked document says more cuts are planned and I don't think I can take any more. It's not the issue of working harder; it will be having to see deserving elderly people struggle to get the services they are entitled to and that they've paid for all their lives. The look of resignation, the acceptance of more struggle and pain…"

It's very powerful stuff, made stronger by her inability to finish her sentence as she breaks down in tears. Her descent from the podium is greeted with thunderous applause and, after more speeches, there's a motion for a ballot on strike action, which is passed with a great roar. The meeting ends, and you can sense a feeling of solidarity and togetherness as everyone troops from the chamber. At that point my phone rings, and Doug's spitting blood at the other end. "I need you! I need you here! What the fuck is happening?"

"Doug, I'm on my way; get the kettle on." I walk with Gerry out of the building and through the square, and we both laugh at Doug's inability to keep his knickers on.

"So, what's the story about yesterday's piece?" I ask him. He shrugs. From anyone else I would be upset, but I know he wouldn't stitch me.

"You heard the call; the Union guys are just as surprised as anyone."

They hadn't looked at all comfortable speaking to the crowd, and my piece did get mentioned a couple of times.

"You don't think they were using the paper to put a bomb under the membership's arse, do you?"

Gerry shrugs. "Those Union boys are not that sophisticated, mate. Most of the lads are romantics: lovers of an idealised working-class or jaded careerists trying to get a gig in the Labour party."

Wryly, I comment, "Bloody worked, though! They would have been out today if the law allowed it."

Gerry's smiling. "Yeah, it's good to see a bit of positive action one way or another."

"I'm too old for that bollocks." I don't know why I'm saying that; I really don't. The meeting was a moving event, seeing a group fighting for their jobs and most importantly their services and their community. Yet it's funny: I'm in my professional role as detached observer and cynical hack, and I don't want Gerry to see how moved I was by it.

The other thing that's on my mind is my emotional outburst in the car this morning. I'm generally pretty good at keeping everything together but with Gillian and the Jack situation hitting me simultaneously, and work in a state of flux, I need a more professional mask, for work if not for Gerry.

Of course he's already seen through that. "You're fooling nobody with that hard-boiled hack shite; you work for the local rag, not *The Times*."

We both fall about and, laughing, I tell him, "OK, you know me too well." By that time we've reached the office, and we hug to say goodbye. We've made a loose agreement to meet at some point over the weekend. He troops off and I've ninety minutes to the deadline, and rather than panic I decide to have a cigarette and text Gillian:

Hi baby!
Can't wait to see you tonight.
Love you, Paul xxxx

There is real joy at that thought, and I cannot help smiling as the text is processed and sent. With my thoughts running to our proposed romantic dinner, I light my cigarette and make the appropriate noises to my smoker colleagues. The phone rings and my mobile screen says "Doug"—probably in an advanced state of meltdown. I ignore this and finish my fag in peace. Each long intake of smoke is made doubly satisfying as it probably mirrors the smoke coming out of his ears. Eventually the tobacco becomes ash and I slowly trudge up the stairs to what I imagine will be a maelstrom.

Walking through the door, it appears just like any other day and I conclude it was merely Doug having a breakdown.

"Thank fuck you're back! Where have you been?" is his charming greeting.

Smiling, I decide not to get involved in his posturing. "At the meeting, where you told me to be. It finished 10 minutes ago with them burning down City Hall, and I think they're planning to take over the BRMB and announce martial law."

"Ha ha! Very funny, I don't think."

It's clear that he's not stopped behaving like a headless chicken, and I walk to my desk and start singing, "You don't get me—I'm part of the Union!", much to the mirth of a couple of my colleagues. "You'll have one thousand words in twenty-five minutes, Doug!" I shout at him, and with that he waves back at me and stomps back into his office.

Ben at the next desk says, *sotto voce*, "Why do we have to put up with that prick?"

That's a question I don't have time to answer as I rip through a story, and whilst it's emotional it does have the virtue of being a pretty straight record of the meeting. Recalling some of the more memorable contributions, I use the team leader's account of assessing elderly people for home care as the human interest, and add the unanimous vote for a ballot on strike action. Then I make sure there are copious references to the membership's view of their leadership, which gets me off the hook regarding yesterday's article.

It's a good piece, and I file it and wait for Doug to start flapping and demanding a "Britain can take it" rewrite. You know the sort of thing: "Council vows to resist Union blackmail" or maybe "Council tax payers' anger at strike threat" or whatever right-wing tosh he's spouting this week. Grabbing a coffee, I look at my emails and see one from the Union official I spoke to yesterday.

Dear Paul

Got the message from Gerry and can only say sorry. I imagine you're quite upset, but believe me no one is as surprised as me about the events of today.

I'm just digesting that when Doug casts his shadow over my desk.

"Yeah, that's fine; just get me some political reaction from the parties and we're done." He's really calm after his impression of a man on the edge of a nervous breakdown just a half an hour ago.

"OK, Doug. You're sure you're OK with that?"

"Just get me the political stuff," he says in a cool voice.

I wouldn't have minded "thanks for all your hard work". However, I'm sitting in wonder with the change that's come over him. Ringing round, I get the fairly predictable comments from the local parties, which is all good knockabout stuff, and then I find I'm finished.

Satisfied, I lean back in the chair and then the adrenaline runs out and I'm knocked sideways by how tired I am. Not the greatest preparation for my night out with Gillian.

Chapter Thirty-Three
Friday Night at Home

After the excitement of the day I'm not in the greatest shape, but I want to make an impression on Gillian, and the thought of dinner is looming. Rushing home, I get back at about 4.30, just missing the Friday night nonsense of rush hour.

Opening my door, I'm struck with the thought of her kissing me on the doorstep just over seven hours ago, and walking into the corridor of the flat,

I can still smell her perfume. The lightness of it defines her: it's subtle and delicate, yet hints at a deep passion burning underneath. This morning I loved it, and after the day I've had it's awoken memories of passionate embraces, miles away from the hurly-burly of industrial action and newspaper deadlines.

Even though I'm bone-weary, I have an overwhelming urge to hear her voice, and I reach for the phone: "Hi, baby!"

She giggles at my greeting and I get goose bumps.

"How are you?" she asks.

"Very well now that I'm speaking to you." We talk and share the memories of our days: hers hectic, mine likewise. We both say how tired we are and she surprises me again.

"Can you cook?"

I hate false modesty in others, but for me it's a definite position, so despite being a bit of an *artiste* in the kitchen, I answer, "OK, I guess."

"Lets blow out the restaurant idea, and I'll come over and you can make me beans on toast and a mug of tea, and we can relax and just talk."

"You know what?" I say with relish. "That sounds just perfect!"

So we say a quick goodbye and I get to work in the kitchen. After looking round for a few minutes, I start to prepare a few enchiladas using some recipe a friend sent me. They are not fiery hot but rely on a tangy salsa for the taste, one that I'm very good at making. I decide on this dish in honour of our first kiss when leaving the tapas bar. What a romantic!

Remembering that I always keep some nachos for Gerry, I get those ready as well, while heating up some refried beans as a side dish. It's a tasty, informal meal, so I change into some jeans and a T-shirt.

Gillian arrives at about seven o'clock, and she sits in my kitchen/diner and watches me finish the cooking. In fact, she's a perfect guest, helping set the table, and she seems perfectly at home in my flat. We talk about our day, and it strikes me that this is one of the first times we've done this. I mean, of course we've talked, but it was the excitement of finding out about someone. That was the big stuff: Who are you? What moves you? What are your values? That stuff. This is different; this is the little bitty my-day-was-great/good/OK/rubbish/complete garbage kind of conversation between two people who really care about one another.

We eat the dinner I've prepared, and we talk about the stuff at the union meeting and how it might pan out. There's a little bit of a pause here, then she says in quite a blunt change of conversation, "Paul, we need to talk about Jack. Look, I'm sorry, but I spoke to

Archie, and this situation is making you unhappy, isn't it?"

"Yes it is, but I'm someone who doesn't like to share my unhappiness around."

She smiles and takes my hand. "I hope you don't mind, but I want to tell you something."

At this point she gets up off her chair and walks over to me, straddles me in a very erotic way and gives me a long, lingering, passionate kiss. "Yes," she says, "I know you want to make everybody around you feel good, but last night you gave me permission to be in love with you."

My heart races when she says that and I reply, "It's a fantastic feeling, hearing you say that."

"Well, then." She looks into my eyes. "I want to be able to give you help when you need it and be a support for you. It seems to me that you're great at helping others but not good at accepting help; you can recognise the good things in other people but not yourself; and you allow people to make decisions that suit them, but you don't extend the same courtesy to yourself."

Not many people have explained those things to me so lovingly but so bluntly.

"I don't know what to do sometimes; I just don't like upsetting people."

She kisses me again, and it's a loving, beautiful kiss. "Well, I can understand that, but Jack is part of you and I have always been impressed by the way that you care for him."

"You know a lot about me, Gillian!" I laugh as I say that.

"You've no idea!" At this point, I'm very interested in how she knows all about me. However, before I can ask and deal with any of that, I get kissed again. Gillian is straddled across me and it isn't very conductive to intelligent thought, so I give up the struggle.

Her face is very close to mine, and she whispers very gently, "Paul, I just want you to know that I have not loved a man since Ray died." Nodding, I hold her tightly: an unspoken acknowledgement of how glad I am that she's chosen me. She continues, and I'm too insensible to talk. "You're a very special person, and whatever you decide to do about Jack, I'll be there for you."

There's a little pause and I manage to say, "Thank you. I don't know what to say, except I love you. I couldn't love anyone who didn't understand my feelings about Jack."

"Yes," she says, "I do understand them, so we have to sort of talk about tomorrow and why I can't be a consideration."

"What do you mean?" I'm flabbergasted by this, and to tell the truth a bit concerned. She starts running her hands through my hair: a gesture that tests my ability to focus to the extreme.

"Paul, you must, and I mean *must*, do what is right for Jack. The situation with us will sort itself out, and I'm here for the long haul. I've been waiting for Mr. Right, not Mr. Right Now, and you're most definitely Mr. Right. So let me give you the promise that whatever you decide, as long as it's right for Jack and you, I will fit around it."

"Thank you, thank you!" and I kiss her with passion. It's a passion based on the knowledge that, for once, I'm in love with someone who knows that love is about sharing.

Our lips part, and she looks me straight in the eyes. "Now, Mr. Castle, take me to your bed."

Chapter Thirty-Four
D-Day Again

It's Saturday evening, and the Citroën is making its way to Jack's house; today we've christened it "Thunderbird 7". He saw the *Thunderbird 6* film on DVD the other day, and he thought that the DS deserved a new name. Deliberately, I haven't told him that DS pronounced in French is déesse, which translates into English as goddess; that's for later.

During the day, I told Jack that I was seeing someone special called Gillian. He responded to this with a very interesting comment: "That's good, Dad! You need someone to make you smile." He's a ten-year-old with the insight of Clare Rayner. I didn't dwell on this topic as I wanted to present it in a matter-of-fact way, ensuring he knew that it wouldn't impact on our relationship.

At that point he became obsessed with the film we were off to see, and that was that. It was a cartoon about monsters, and I think he liked it. I wasn't that impressed, but we talked about it excitedly all the way to McDonald's.

We did the usual thing and near the end of the meal he said to me, "Mum says we're having a chat later."

"That's right, about school and stuff."

"I'm doing much better since my report, Dad." That's a

heartbreaker, the way that he seems to think that he has to justify himself to me.

"It's not that, Jack. Your mum wants to chat to you about stuff after school and I'm sure she's as pleased as me that you're doing well." This is said really quickly, as I want to dispel the idea that he has anything to fear about his report and any more of that nonsense.

"OK, Dad!" he said, now confident in the knowledge that the "chat" this evening would not result in a telling-off. After that, it was "Thunderbirds are GO!" and the drive home, and if I had allayed his fears, it was only the beginning of mine.

After what seems a very short journey, I nervously pull into Ex's drive and we're here: ready to face some unpleasant (at least for me) music.

Jack scoots across, as he usually does, to hug me, and I hold him very tightly. Gillian said this morning that she wasn't going to give me advice, except to make sure that Jack knows that I love him. This was, as you can imagine, brilliant guidance.

"OK, Jack! Let's go in—it's cold!" As I am saying this, he hugs me hard and lets go.

In no time he's hugging his mum, and we go into the dining room. It always was a formal sort of room, Ex's taste being severe and her relationship with John not having mellowed that. The table's clear except for a pile of papers in the middle, and John is hovering in the kitchen making drinks.

"Hi, Paul! Would you like something?" He's friendly and I reply in kind, and put in a request for a coffee.

Ex is quiet and reserved, and she asks me to sit down and tells Jack to go and change. He runs upstairs, and she immediately opens the conversation.

"Paul, I want to tell you that I've got my transfer. Basically I can move at any time in the next three months. Time is now a factor, and we would like you to consider all the options, and if you have any ideas of your own they would be very welcome." Hesitantly, I nod, and am very relieved when John comes in and takes Ex's order for drinks, as it gives me a chance to hold down the thought ringing round my head: "you made your bed; now lie in it!"

Eventually that thought leaves, and I'm trying hard not to get emotional. "What does Jack know at this stage; what have you told him?"

"Only that we're chatting about school." She seems really distracted, really distant.

"OK, we need to tell him because he was asking me stuff today that I didn't have answers to, and I don't want to lie to him."

She nods and John adds his agreement when he arrives with the drinks. At that point, Jack comes in with a big smile and practically jumps on a chair next to me. John asks him what he wants for a drink and after that is fetched, there's an awkwardness that is filled with Jack telling his mum what he and I have done that afternoon.

After that conversation has run its course, Jack looks at his mother and, with a directness only a ten-year-old can get away with, says, "Mum, why is Dad here?"

Chapter Thirty-Five
Not a Hogwarts Letter

All in all, this is a very good question: what am I doing?

Is the answer to endorse the Ex's terrible decision to educate Jack privately? Perhaps I'm being harsh, because the next words out of her mouth are a total surprise: "Jack, both Daddy and I love you very much and even though we aren't married any more we'll never stop loving you."

"I know that, Mummy." Jack is quiet but very attentive now, and I would hazard a guess that he knows he is about to hear something important.

She looks at John, and starts again. "John and Mummy… well, we love each other too. You understand that?"

"Yes, Mum." Jack says this in a "do get on with it" sort of voice.

"John is very clever and he has got a promotion, and he is going to work in London." The silence is deafening. Jack's just looking around at the rest of us. "I want to be with John and you, so we are moving to be near him."

Jack decides to speak, and it's the cry of all children who don't like change. "But I want to stay here, Mum."

Jack's pleas go unanswered, as the Ex blunders on. "John and I have very difficult jobs, and we want you to be settled and very happy." She pauses; I think, to let Jack take all this in. "We thought that you might like to go to a school like Hogwarts, not a magic school but a school that you can live at and have long holidays and all that." Jack says nothing, I think it's a bit too much.

John fills the awkward pause. "There will be loads of things to do and you'll make a lot of friends, and you will see your dad very often."

"Every week?" he asks, with a lump in his throat, desperate for something that's unchanging in his life.

"Well, we don't know at the moment because we need you to think about what school you want."

Jack's lip is trembling and he says, "I don't know." Then the dam bursts and he's sobbing into his arms on the table.

"Jack, darling!" Ex tries to console him, and it's clear that this isn't the reaction she is expecting. It's like this for ten minutes, and he just can't stop crying; he's unreachable.

Then all of a sudden he says something that makes the Ex freeze. "Why can't I stay with Dad?"

The atmosphere could be cut with a knife, and I don't say a word; this is the Ex's call and she can bloody well make it. "Well, you live with John and me, and we're going to London and your dad is staying in Birmingham."

"Why do I have to go to a boarding school? Why can't I go to a normal school?" is his next brilliant, awkward question.

"Well, John and I will have to work abroad sometimes and that means it will be difficult for us to look after you. Besides, we think you will enjoy it." This goes on and on, and my contributions are limited to promises to see Jack as often as I can. He's clearly not with the programme and ninety minutes of chat later, that hasn't changed.

John comes up with a great suggestion: "Jack, all of this is a lot for you to take in. I think we need to stop now and let it sink in for a bit. Your mum and I need to talk to your dad and I think you would be better off watching a DVD. What do you think?"

"Yes, that's great! Can I watch *Toy Story*?"

"Top movie!" I hear myself say in my head. Very appropriate.

"Of course, Jack." John, to my surprise, takes his hand and leads him off to the living room, whilst I look at Ex, who is clearly struggling.

"That was hard."

She takes time to answer, clearly trying to collect herself. "Yes. Thanks for your help."

However I leave that unanswered, mainly because I'm not here to help her; I'm here for Jack. John returns and goes straight to the drinks cabinet and pours himself a stiff Scotch, asking absentmindedly whether anyone else wants to join him.

"A wine for me," Ex says, raising an eyebrow for my request.

"Coffee for me." I pause. "Driving."

Nods all round, and after drinks are done, we discuss options and I lay my prejudices aside and make a few suggestions about schools and about whether I could see him on Saturdays as normal. All of that depends on the school selected, and that depends mainly on Jack's input.

We agree that Ex and John will take Jack through the brochures and that they will try to pick a school with good access from Birmingham. They also agree to try to find a home that likewise isn't difficult to commute to.

Eventually I leave, feeling unsatisfied as everything is still up in the air. The worst-case scenario is them sending Jack away to some school miles away from anywhere while I end up having him for a short periods during the holidays. Technically this is a breach of agreements made in court, but as I acceded to residence being mainly with her the court isn't likely to be too friendly to my asserting my parental rights now. Likewise, if I kick off about the educational arrangements, I have to have a better argument than my class prejudices and my memories of reading *Tom Brown's School Days*.

All of that presupposes that I could do that without hurting Jack and upsetting his relationship with the Ex. As I want the best for him, putting a wedge between him and his mother isn't going to achieve anything. With all of this whirring in my mind, I know I have to tell Gillian what's happened, and when I get back home I grab some of last night's Chianti and reach for the phone.

Chapter Thirty-Six
I'll Be There for You When the Rain Starts to Fall

I briefly spoke to Gillian on the mobile as I left the Ex's house, and just said I wanted to see her and would call when I got home. Surprisingly, when I call again there's no answer on her home number. Thinking she might be in the shower, I check my mobile for messages and am just about to ring her when a message pipes through:

I'll be at yours in 5 minutes. Love you G x

The woman is a mind reader! As I take a long drink from my glass, I send back a text saying:

Can't wait! Love you too! P xx

Waiting for Gillian, I indulge in a frantic texting session with Gerry, Bonnie and Archie to put them out of their suspense. Which is odd, really, as I don't have anything concrete to tell them except that Jack's just getting used to the idea of moving.

The news is received with grace and a "we're there for you" type of support, which makes this easier for me. The truth, and it's a hard one to face, is that if I pushed the issue and manipulated Jack I could get him to stay with me. He knows I would look after him and that he'd get to see his mother. All this idle speculation is OK, but I want him to make a decision that's right for him—to go to where he will be happy. This isn't about what I want at all.

Of course, I don't want him to do a *Catcher in the Rye*, but neither do I want him at Dogshit High School being battered by drug dealers for dinner money. I'm hanged if I choose one thing; throttled if I choose another. Wanting to hear his voice, I decide to call him, and Ex answers.

"Hi, Paul." This is delivered in a pleasant tone and I really appreciate the gesture.

"Hi. Is Jack about?" Responding in kind isn't a chore today.

"No, he's in bed. You want me to see if he's still awake?" Again it appears that she wants to be nice to me.

"No, I'll talk to him tomorrow. How was the rest of the evening?" I ask this with genuine concern for all three of them.

"OK. He was quiet and we made a list of the things he wanted to do at school."

Before I can stop myself, I laugh out loud. "Jack made a list!" And then she's laughing too. I want to say something, but don't really know how to phrase it, as it's not strictly business. "Look I need to tell you something, in case Jack mentions it."

Ex doesn't stop laughing. "What is it? The new girlfriend? We know already, and it's OK. The one thing I know about you, Paul, is that you wouldn't mention it to Jack if she wasn't a nice person."

"Thanks," I say, and I actually mean it.

"You're welcome! See you on Wednesday." And with that she hangs up.

Sitting down, I get about two and a half minutes to reflect on that, then the doorbell rings and I rush to open it. However, Instead of just Gillian, I have Gerry, Jenny, Archie, Shona, Bonnie and Jim as well. Speechless, I look at them shouting "Surprise!" and Gerry hugs me and soon they're all trampling through the door.

Gillian's last in, and she kisses me sweetly on the mouth and says, "It was Gerry's idea, and we all agreed that today would be tough so we all wanted to be here for you."

After what seems like ages, I hug her, putting in a lot of emotion and at that point whisper "Perfect!" to her.

Following everyone, I walk into the kitchen/diner, and Gerry's stuffing the fridge with alcohol and making disparaging remarks about its contents. "This is like a vegetarian accountant's fridge: no beer and nothing you can fry."

Jenny makes some weird disapproving noise, and I'm happy to see everyone. Gillian's in the middle of it all, pouring drinks, and I settle down to be looked after by my friends. They just knew that whatever the result, the meeting would have been hard for me.

Between all of them they get chapter and verse about what happened tonight. With the exception of Gerry and Bonnie, none of them really know the Ex that well and those two confirm my accounts of her to the others.

This is a great feeling for me, and maybe it's unfair on the Ex, but to have a group of people completely on my side gives a great sense of strength. That being said, Gerry is at his blokie worst. After slagging off the Ex, he gets to my cupboards and I get an ear-bashing: "Lentils and rice…holy shit! No wonder you're skinny!"

All of his laughter is fine, but I like to think of myself as a decent host. "Shall I make something?" I ask plaintively, which inspires another round of laughter. When this dies down, there's a ring on the doorbell and before I can get there Jim is away, coming back a couple of minutes later with four large pizza boxes that get plonked on the table. Suddenly plates appear, and a raucous evening begins.

At the height of this, Gerry staggers drunkenly to his feet. "I just want to say…" Everyone pipes down. "I just want to say that Paul is a great mate and we are here to say good luck in your fight with the Wicked Witch of NatWest and…" He waits for the cheers to die down. "And while we're here, all the love in the world to you and Gillian."

The roar of these six friends overwhelms us, and after they have left we have our own little toast to "friends and lovers". We make love with a lot of passion and sleep with lots of passion too. We wake the next morning knowing that whatever happens, we will always be able to say that we know that love comes in many forms.

Chapter Thirty-Seven
Easy Like Sunday Morning

That waking thought is accompanied by other musings on our own relationship. As this is happening, I stroke Gillian's hair and she makes a cooing sound that's truly beautiful. Then I kiss her on the cheek, and she reaches over and embraces me for what seems like a lifetime.

"I love you," are the first words out of her mouth, and I reciprocate and we kiss more urgently; pretty soon, we're making love again. The bedroom has blinds, and they're slightly ajar so we explore each other bathed in sunlight. It's perfect, and I feel closer to her than at any other time. Very quietly, I whisper "thank you!" to her when we have recovered our composure.

"What are you thanking me for?"

"Last night, and well…just making my life easy when it could be very hard."

She kisses me on the mouth and whispers, "I love you, and you've no idea what you've done for me." We kiss again and just lie there safe in the knowledge that, at least for now, contentment is an easier aspiration than usual. A cup of coffee appears five minutes shy of midday and it's followed by a kiss and a piece of toast.

We decide to spend a couple of hours lounging, then she will have to go home to get some clothes ready for work. Sadly, I have a lot of domestic chores to do before I can start working again on the plays for Trevor. There's a voice in my head that keeps nagging me, and I ask her a very forward question. Considering my previous reluctance to share my place, it's quite a surprise to hear it coming out of my mouth.

"Baby, do you want to leave some stuff over, so we can do this and not have to keep running backwards and forwards?"

Gillian holds my hand. "I would love to, if you don't mind. A girl needs clean knickers!" We both laugh, as she is normally very feminine and delicate about stuff like that.

Having broached the subject, I decide to push my luck: "I want to ask you to move in with me, but as we've only been going out a week and a bit, I guess that's premature?"

"A bit," she says, "but you can ask me in fifteen minutes; that would be OK."

When the laughter dies down, we sort out a brunch and after that we embark on what I consider a fabulous indulgence: we slip out to the newsagent on the corner and buy the Sunday papers: *The Observer* for her and *The Independent* for me. We then sit at each end of the sofa just reading, and the only sound is the rustling of papers and the occasional boiling of the kettle. It's just two people completely immersed in each other and so comfortable together that even the silence says "I love you". The papers are devoured and we decide to think about the rest of the day.

Sadly, for us that means parting company and sorting out some domestic and work stuff. The parting is overlong and full of "I wish I/you could stay".

However, she leaves with a passionate kiss and I walk her to her car and give her another kiss, which turns into several.

Waving her off, I feel bereft and after walking inside my flat I immediately begin to miss her terribly.

For the rest of the afternoon, I work through my domestic tasks like an automaton, and only just notice a dark sock in the white wash. Throwing it across the room, it brings back an uncomfortable memory of ruining a white wash of the Ex's with a similar stray sock. This despite having mastered my washing for the three years of college and my two years in London!

Eventually I complete a load of washing and get a batch of clothes together and ironed for work. It's a mechanical process and there is even less joy in it than usual. The thought of doing it with Gillian sometime in the future makes me smile, and I put that feeling in my emotional bank for later. That good thought leads to another, and I feel the need to speak to Jack, as I'm keen to touch base with him, make sure he's OK and see how he feels about last night.

The phone trills impatiently, with no relenting. They must have gone out. I send an email, which I know will get forwarded to her Blackberry. Realising I have to wait, I return to the scripts that I've to agreed to give to Trevor. By the time I've settled down and got my brain into gear, the phone rings, and it's Jack.

He sounds surprisingly great and he tells me about his day with John's mum and dad, who live in the country. Then I ask him how he's feeling and whether he's looked at the school brochures Mummy has for him. He just says "yeah" and that they all seem to play rugby and it looks too rough. One has a gigantic library, though, and an environmental centre. Wickedly, I have an idea that this is a posh name for a greenhouse, but think better of telling him.

Instead, I ask him where it is, and he doesn't know. I reply that it's OK and we chat about Wednesday, and I ask him whether he would like to go out with Gillian as well as me. He says that'll be great, but could we have a go on the ice rink? That's quickly sorted and he rings off saying, "Love you, Dad."

After this I feel that a return to my scripts is necessary, because I have the idea that my new status of "man in functional relationship" will happily rob me of time that I now take very much for granted. Therefore I resolve to be a bit more organised and use my diary, instead of using it to jot down notes, story ideas and phone numbers without the callers' names beside them.

By this time, it's seven o'clock, and my mobile rings. It's Gillian: a few short sentences are all that's needed and my newfound resolve to manage my time better is blown to bits.

She's on her way over.

Chapter Thirty-Eight
Class Struggle (Sort Of)

My Monday mornings are rarely, if ever, a source of happiness. However, waking up next to Gillian is a fantastic feeling, and thinking about that, I decide to make a suggestion to her.

"Darling, why don't you stay here forever?" She hugs me in an embrace that nearly moves me to tears. "Does that mean yes?" I ask, with a hopeful timbre in my voice.

"Yes..." She's gathering herself. "But you need to see to Jack first."

My look of disappointment is evident. She rushes to reassure me: "Darling, I love you and I want to be with you and wake up with you every day. However, I need you to be really happy with the Jack situation; there are so many unknowns."

Nodding, I know that this makes a lot of sense. Bugger!

"One thing that we both know, though..." she says, smiling, "is that I really love you."

With that, I kiss her passionately on the mouth, knowing that what she's said is both wise and prudent. This morning I don't feel particularly careful and my recklessness is evident, but she suggests something to make me feel a lot better.

"What I want most, though, is never to be away from you. I'm happy just to come over most nights and be with you."

This is definitely a great step forward.

"Fantastic! That's great!" My zeal for this proposal is evident in my voice.

She smiles at my enthusiasm, then adds, "But that isn't moving in!" I wait for the rest of the statement. "I need to talk to Geraldine first, and when we know where we are with Jack, we'll make all our formal decisions then."

Fixing her with a smile, I tell her, "That's very considerate, and you know that's making me love you even more—if that's possible."

She laughs and hits me with a pillow, which starts a fight, like the ones you see in the bed adverts. The laughter is joyous, and the rest of the morning flies by in a daze; for the time being, at least, I don't have to kid myself that waking up in an empty bed is OK.

We leave the flat together, and I love the fact that she will be coming home to me tonight with some clothes and stuff. I'm elated, and these feelings give me some protection against the nonsense that awaits me at work.

The whole Council story and Gillian have immunised me from the realisation that there are some redundancies on the cards. As I walk into the newsroom, it's clear that there are others who are not similarly inoculated.

Doug is having an animated discussion with Mike Samuels, who is a bit of a local legend as a sports reporter. He's frequently interviewed on the local TV stations, as he has the ear of a lot of the names at Villa, Wolves, City and the Albion.

Football has changed a lot, and Mike has been able to work around that and still operate at a high level. He never gets used to plant stories, and I often hear him on the phone saying, "I hope you're not looking for a puff piece here, because I don't do that."

He's also a straight shooter, calm in a crisis, and a sound guy who is basically unflappable. So it's surprising to see him angry; but then again, Doug can start an argument in an empty room.

Mike is screaming, and the whole newsroom is watching. "I cannot write with redundancy hanging over me!"

Doug is trying to move away from the wall that Mike has him verbally pinned against. "I see," Doug says weakly.

"No, you don't see, you spineless idiot!" Cruel but fair, I'm thinking, as Mike thunders on. "The whole basis of a newspaper is quality reporting to attract readership." He points his finger accusingly. "You spend too much time listening to accountants and ignoring reporters." Mike then trots out my favourite line: "You know the cost of everything and the value of nothing!"

Standing by my desk, I look at Ben, my workspace neighbour; he's not slow in offering an explanation. "Mike got stiffed on some of his expenses." Thankful for the heads-up, I nod whilst Mike continues his fusillade.

"I've worked for four editors; every one of them except you has valued my work and understood the necessity of having talented writers covering sport."

Doug attempts to rally: "Look, Mike, I understand, but you know it is a harsh climate out there."

At these words, Mike completely loses it. "You fucking moron! Do you expect me to eat the shit that you spoonfeed the office clerk? This paper has made a profit every year since it began printing. I've never known it make a loss. I have shares in the paper, for fuck's sake! Do you want me to go on local radio and tell them you won't pay legitimate expenses? I only have to pick up my mobile and you'll be a laughingstock in a matter of hours. Now pay my mileage, you prick!"

At this point, Doug is relieved to see that Mike has walked away. Sadly for him, though, each and every member of the newsroom has decided to give Mike a standing ovation. With that, he decides to skulk away back to his office, and it's clear that he's visibly shaken.

A bit shocked myself, I sit down to find a message on my computer from Ex, asking me to call her. However, I need a cigarette before I tackle that conversation, and time to digest and discuss the rumpus on the newsroom floor. I nod to Ben, a fellow smoker, and we go down to the front door to discuss the newsroom dust-up.

As we join the others, they're already turning over Doug-versus-Mike. The consensus of the Filterati chugging away on the doorstep is that Doug's a prat and Mike's lost it: not very profound, but probably as good as I can come up with today.

This leads me to reflect that everyone seems under pressure at the moment, and I think back to the team leader at the UNISON meeting. I mean, in here the Doug and Mike boxing match nonsense will be sorted in a couple of minutes and that will be that. However, we don't have to say no to old and vulnerable people without a proper voice. Say what you like about Council workers, most of us couldn't do the caring and working with the vulnerable. I knew a bloke once who worked with really hard-to-reach kids. He spent ages telling Gerry and me some of the horror stories that make up the lives of some of these youngsters: abuse on abuse and knockback after knockback. Oh God! I mean, Bonnie reaches for the gin when she maxes out her credit card, and I start to chain-smoke when Spurs are one-nil down at half time!

Thanking my lucky stars that I don't have to tell old people they can't get any care, I trudge back inside to get on with the business of making more profit for the paper.

All of that, and the fracas, is put to one side as I focus on the content of the Ex's email.

> *Paul,*
> *Jack is coming with us to London for a couple of days, firstly to look at some schools and secondly to look at houses in the London area.*
> *I want to take him out of school, and the best time for us and him is tomorrow, Wednesday and Thursday. I've cleared it with the Head, but do you mind swapping your evening with him to another day?*
> *Please call me and let me know if that is OK.*

"Well, she couldn't have been nicer" is my first thought. Ex appears to be really trying hard to keep me in the loop and I decide to be as positive as possible. Apart from anything else, I need to be in touch with everything and it is unlike me to be unpleasant, so I give her a call and say the appropriate things, then wish them a vaguely sincere "good luck".

As I ponder this, another fracas erupts in the office. The Father of the Chapel, our shop steward if you like, is at it hammer-and-tongs with Doug. The tone of the argument is not pleasant and they make no attempt to lower their voices. Mike the sports journo has obviously been to the Union and this is the result.

More doors are slammed and twenty minutes later word comes round that a memo is flying about concerning an emergency Union meeting. All jolly exciting, but my mind is fixed on Jack being driven round school after school, and hoping he isn't seduced by all the nonsense that is inevitably going to be spouted.

Sadly, I know that my antipathy is based on a bar stool preacher's view of private education. In essence I decide that if Jack wants this chance, I will have to be as supportive as I can and be there for him if it all goes wrong.

Absentmindedly I ask Ben, "Where did you go to school, mate?"

"Why?" he shoots back.

"Just asking. My ex wants to send my son to private school."

He makes a face and says cheekily, "I went to Ball Cruncher Comprehensive. Far as I know private school is all tuck, ruck and fuck."

"Thanks for that image, Ben. Now I'm really enthusiastic about supporting her educational choices."

He looks at me with a smile. "Glad I could help! Let me know when he's looking for a university place." We both laugh, and get our heads down as Doug is looking over, scowling.

Five minutes later, Ben pipes up: "Listen, Mental Mike…" —how soon you get a nickname in these places!—"went to a private school, so why don't you ask him?"

"Too scared at the moment!" I reply, laughing.

"Seriously, he doesn't go on about it." He thinks for a while and says, "Well, you wouldn't in here."

I laugh again. "Thanks, Ben. I'll try to get a chat with him later."

Surprised at this revelation, I wonder about this and it leads me to thinking that Mike, despite his outburst with Doug today, is a pretty good guy. Actually, he's a warm-hearted man of great wit and a really sound writer. In addition to his work for the paper, he's ghostwritten a couple of really good biographies.

Later on, I buttonhole him at his desk. "Mike, how are you?"

"Hi, Paul! What brings you over to the Sports Department? As if I didn't know." Clearly he's expecting to recount his clash with our spineless editor, blow by blow.

My mind's focused on private education, so I miss the

implication. "What? Oh yeah, sorry…no, I'm impressed with you standing up to Doug."

"Not everyone is. The City section have christened me Mental Mike." He rolls his eyes, and we laugh. The City section is a trio of spivs who go "yah, yah, yah" a lot and can barely spell their names, never mind understand post-neoclassical endogenous growth theory.

I decide to break some bad news to him. "Yeah, well, sorry Mike, but the News section started the christening party." We both smirk, and he rolls his eyes again.

"Thanks, Paul! That's done my ego the power of good." I'm not sure that I'm supposed to laugh at this particular remark, so I decide to button my lip.

"Listen, seriously, I've got a little bit of a personal matter to discuss with you. Can I buy you a coffee?"

Mike, who is obviously still in humorous mode, replies, "It's years since I've been asked out, Paul. I'm flattered and everything but I have to say no. I'm straight and married with two kids."

Laughing at his witticism, I pretend to be angry. "Can't anyone be serious in here?"

"Not since Doug got appointed editor!" is Mike's *sotto voce* reply. We both laugh, and then he goes all sensible. "What can I do for you?"

"Private education. You went to that sort of school, I hear?"

Whatever he's expecting, it wasn't that, but he recovers his equilibrium quickly. "Yeah, what do you want to know?"

Unthinkingly, I blurt out, "Oh, I don't know. It's my Ex. She wants to send my son to a posh school and my only argument is based on class prejudice and the fact that I'll lose him."

Mike rolls his eyes again and says, "Oh God, you do need some educating. Let's get a coffee and I'll fill you in." He gets up to go with me.

His colleague pipes up: "Mike, you've got a deadline at twelve and you still need to make that call to Villa."

"Well, that can bloody well wait. Fuckwit Doug has made a militant out of me. That, coupled with losing my child benefit, has turned me into Arthur Scargill. Come on, Paul, but you're buying the coffee."

So off we go, and he gives me chapter and verse about private education. This turns out to be a good laugh, reminiscing with Mike about his school days, and it's clear that he had a great time. He does, however, tell it to me straight, and the end of all of his banter he pauses and gives me a cracking piece of advice.

"The only way you'll lose your kid is if you let him go." The wisdom of that comes home to me and he follows it up with a one-two of some power. "The other thing is this: if he wants to go and you stop him, he will resent you holding him back. If he doesn't, then you've got a point. However, it has to be his choice. I was pretty much forced to go and I hated it for a couple of terms. However, I soon learned that if you get involved you get loads more out. Look, I still have loads of friends from school because it's an immersive process and we're not all stuck-up twats."

"Yeah, but..." is my insightful reply. Clearly I've given this some thought!

"No buts, Paul. Get with the programme and get involved. It sounds like it's happening anyway, so just make sure that he knows that you're always there for him."

Which, all in all, is sound advice: reasoned and based on experience that I don't have. I think about all this as I'm walking back to my desk, and I decide to call the Ex.

"Hi," I say, a bit sheepishly.

"Hi," she says. "You've phoned me twice in one day. You don't want to get married again, do you?" This is clearly a funny joke, and she spends the next fifteen seconds laughing like a drain. I'm so taken aback by the humour of this remark that I wait for her to stop cackling, and eventually she says, "You there, Paul?"

"Sorry. It's been a long time since I've heard you laugh."

"That's OK. What do you want, anyway?"

"Just to ask for a list of the schools you're taking Jack to see. I want to be prepared if he asks me anything or wants to know what I think."

Ex sounds surprised and flutters around getting the names of the schools and their locations. She then asks: "You're taking an interest; why the change?"

"Lots of reasons, really. Ultimately I just want the best for him." In addition to Mike's counsel, I actually think that a fight about it would be the worst thing I could do to Jack at the moment.

"OK. I'll email you some links to their websites, if you like."

"That's good. Speak soon!" I put the phone down, and I'm comforted that I can at least say I'm trying this on for size.

Chapter Thirty-Nine
It's Only a Job

Lunchtime arrives, and I go out to catch the spring sunshine, even though there is a chill in the air that reminds me strangely of autumn. The city is its usual bustling self and my thoughts are confused, mixing extreme pleasure and extreme pain. Gillian calls on the mobile and I answer with enthusiasm. Her mood is happy and she has some news.

"Paul, I've spoken to Geraldine, and she's delighted about us, apparently. She says I've been behaving so oddly lately that I either must have a man or be going bonkers."

"That's fantastic news, baby!" This tilts my general mood back to the right side of happy.

"Of course, I told her that just because I'm going out with you she shouldn't rule out the possibility that I'm bonkers."

We laugh together for a moment and it's fun again, and I tell her about Jack going away with the Ex and changing our plans to meet him on Wednesday, which is no bother for her.

"I think that most things are no bother for you!" I say, with warmth that expresses my admiration of her ability to manage difficulties with ease.

"When you lose a loved one, nothing is much bother after that, so don't you be worrying!"

My admiration, as you can imagine, is multiplied, and I sigh a little. "Thank you, anyway!" As if that comes anyway near expressing how I feel about what she's brought to my life.

After a pause, I tell her about Mike and his gunfight at the water cooler corral, and then wax lyrical about his advice for me to get on board. She approves and makes me promise again to look after Jack's needs first and not compromise because of her. "I'll try, but you're so great and I'm so happy and don't want to lose that."

There isn't even the hint of a pause before she gently but firmly comes back with, "Promise me that you will do the right thing for Jack, and you'll never lose me."

Reluctantly, I reply, "OK, but remember: whatever happens, I will always love you." It's a cliché but at the moment it's the best I can come up with. It's after one o'clock and I have to get back for a phone call, so we do the usual slushy stuff saying goodbye.

It's a short walk, and I quickly get back to the office. Greeting me there is a huddle of people outside in the street. Looking around, I see that it's not just the usual smokers. Ben, of course, is in the middle of the scrum, and I walk up and ask him what's going on.

"Its Mental Mike!" He looks across at the Health Correspondent, who is looking a bit disapproving at Mike's new epithet. "He's been suspended!"

"What! Has Doug gone mad?" My first though is that whatever Mike's done, it isn't worth a suspension.

Ben brings me up to speed with all that's happened.

"We all got a memo; as soon as filed his copy, he was shot out the door." He says this excitedly, and it's clear he loves having the skinny on this story.

I think about this, and all I can come up with is, "Doug's heading for a world of trouble!"

This is absolutely true, as I have the idea that the Union won't take this lying down.

Ben looks at me, frowning, and with an understandable level of self-interest says, "Yeah, but I'm not in the mood for a scrap at the moment. I need the cash. I can't afford to go on strike."

That is precisely the dilemma the Union will be facing if it tries to strong-arm the paper. As I'm rolling this around in my head, I just blurt out: "Yeah, same with me. When's the deadline for the voluntary redundancies, by the way?"

"For fuck's sake, Paul, is your head up your arse?" He laughs and then suddenly stops and says, "Oh God, you're serious, aren't you?"

"Yeah," I say sheepishly.

"A week today," he adds, with a sad look on his face.

We've both lit cigarettes, and we finish them in silence; as we get to the end, word comes down that we're being called to a Union meeting at two o'clock. Ben and I nod sagely at each other, stub out our fags and go inside. He begins to whistle "The Red Flag". Witty bastard.

The atmosphere in the newsroom is mutinous, but I file my copy on time. Doug is encamped in his office, a very strange look on his face. I have to see him before the meeting about another matter, and the conversation rapidly comes round to this morning.

"I'm the piggy in the middle, getting all the grief!" There's nothing to add to that and I add nothing. "This place is going to have to learn about the real world—it's really hard out there."

Again this doesn't seem a good place to comment. I just hope he isn't confusing my silence with tacit support. Quickly, I get my business out of the way and head for the door.

Doug calls me back. "Paul, you're a good writer and I'm bringing back the post of senior reporter. I want you to apply, OK?"

"Holy shit!" is my first thought. Where has this all come from?

"I'll give it some thought. I have a few personal issues I need to resolve, and now isn't the best time to be discussing career plans."

Doug shrugs. "Yeah, I understand. Anyway this will all be sorted soon, so bear it in mind, will you?"

I'm nodding as I leave his office; the idea of being senior reporter seems so ridiculous at the moment that I can barely keep myself from laughing as I go back into the newsroom.

At 1.55, I give Gillian a quick ring and we talk about the Union meeting and chat like excited schoolchildren who are going on an outing. Time's pressing, so I'm not able to tell her about Doug and the job offer before everyone starts filing out of the newsroom towards the canteen. I hastily say goodbye and tell her I love her to bits, then join the rest of my colleagues.

The meeting's nowhere near as dignified as the Council workers' assembly I saw in Victoria Square. It's an angry and volatile expression of frustration; a reaction to a company bearing down on its employees. In short, it's like a pressure cooker blowing off steam.

At the end of all the huffing and puffing, we agree to empower the committee to negotiate for Mike and report back in two days. In the meantime, we are to be balloted on strike action. The meeting breaks up and I head downstairs, and the newsroom is still up in arms about Mike and wants to walk out now.

The Father of the Chapel is trying to rein them in, whilst our editor is nowhere to be seen. In terms of usefulness to the paper, Mike has a national reputation and Doug isn't well known on his housing estate. The guys upstairs must be shitting themselves, particularly if Mike goes public, and I suspect it's the reason he isn't here at the moment.

It would of course be typical of this place for them to pull the rug from under him, but he hasn't really batted for his guys in the newsroom and that's why they're particularly militant. In all honesty, Mike was out of line and Doug, whilst not handling this very well, doesn't deserve the slagging he's getting at the moment. However, industrial relations are never noted for the fair-minded nature of their arguments. That isn't exactly profound but the reality is that since the eighties the nature of all public discourse has become coarser and more fractured. When it's not spin, deflection and obfuscation, it's screeching and incendiary. There is a part of me that blames the information overload twenty-four-hour culture that we have. Competing news organisations are so desperate to fill space that every argument is magnified and nuance is presented as division.

Nationally, I'd like to believe that it will all somehow come together and that the clashing ideologies of right and left could meet in the middle and constructively debate ideas to arrive at compromise. However given the current political situation—cuts, more cuts and VAT rises—the reality is that conversation is not measured unless it's in decibels. *The Sun* and the *Daily Mail* act like some right-wing propaganda militia, and any target from people on benefit to single mothers is grist for the mill.

All this nonsense isn't getting my work done and I get my jacket on to head off for court. Ben asks me where I'm going.

"Off to court; there's a double stabbing being tried."

His reply is class: "It'll be nice to see some honest villainy, not like round here."

"Exactly!" I start laughing and say goodbye, urging him not to get the sack while I'm gone.

Chapter Forty
Having Your Cake...

Court is a non-event with a load of guilty pleas and no trials to speak of. Obviously this impacts greatly on the main actors in these dramas but for the humble hack reporter in the gallery it's all pretty tame stuff. Reaching the pavement outside, I walk through the suburban hoodie-wearing teenage inhabitants of court who are trying to look tough and sadly becoming something of a parody. It's sad, and it just seems these kids are lost, their only status coming from how hard they look or what sentence they've got. When did Britain sign up for that?

The days of full employment seem a lifetime away, and certainly the prospects for these youngsters seem especially bleak. Where are their role models? What do they value? It just seems pathetic that a country that used to have a massive industrial base and a notion of pride in its manufacturing is now a prisoner to the fluctuations in the financial sector. It appears that bankers are more important than farmers; stockbrokers more valued than engineers. The result: a hideous mixture of wealth nestling alongside great need. My other concern is the cultural poverty that comes along with that: Generation *X Factor*.

The iPod nano–bearing, trainer-wearing yoof, permanently hard-wired to Facebook, live a virtual existence oblivious to the world around them. It's a nightmare of constant celebrity stimulation, of looking at Katie's latest boob job and Peter's tears on telly and forgetting the real people, struggling, living in the next street.

To think that Jack is heading for that is awful, but my other vision, of him growing up career-obsessed and seeing success as only materially based, is worse. My only hope for him, as I see it, is if I can point out to him some of the things money can't buy. Sadly, I suspect that my efforts will be marginal, and that leads me to the conclusion that I may have to consider the prospect of moving to be near him.

Deep down, I suspect that Gillian knows this, and that would explain her reluctance to move in with me. I'm confident that she wants to, but her feelings are those of someone unwilling to commit completely to something that might disappear in a few months.

After starting the Citroën, I drive home a little deflated and reach for the phone.

Gillian is, as ever, pleased to hear my voice. "Paul, I want to come over! I'm packing a bag, so we aren't going to have to go backwards and forwards every time I want clean knickers." I laugh, but she has a very serious voice on. "You must remember what I said about looking at Jack's needs first."

"Of course, darling, but…"

She cuts in straightaway: "There are no buts here, because I need to know, to absolutely *know*, that his needs will come first." The memory of my recent reflection bites deep. She adds hastily, "I know that you love me; rest assured that this will work out all right. Let's get Jack settled and then we can make plans together."

"OK." It's the only thing I'm confident about saying without getting too messed up.

Her gentle reassurance asserts itself again. "Paul, trust me. Things will be all right."

"Of course I trust you. It's my Ex I don't trust."

The effect of those words brings some sharpness to her tone, and it pulls me up short.

"Paul, you must trust, my love. Believe me when I tell you that I'm willing to work with you on this. The only way she can hurt you and me is if we let her. So stop all that, and focus just for now on Jack." Finally, if only temporarily, I begin to believe, and we chat about work before she rings off with a promise to be over in an hour.

Whilst I'm waiting for her, I call Jack and he is full of excitement knowing he is bunking off school tomorrow. He tells me about some of the schools he's going to visit and the fact that he will help his mother and John choose their next house.

Later, I talk to him about missing him on Wednesday and ask whether he still wants to go ice skating some time. He says that he would rather watch a video, and asks if Gillian will be there when we meet. Making a promise on her behalf, I say yes, but tell him that we will need to talk about that when he's back in Birmingham. He seems very cool about the whole Gillian thing, which is a great start for both of us. He rings off promising to tell me about all the places he's visited, and what he likes about them.

"Love you, Dad."

"Love you, Jack." I have a momentary compulsion, wanting their week to be a complete disaster and for Jack to hate every one of their school choices and loathe every house they look at. That's childish, but I really feel that I have the right to be silly at this stage, safe in the knowledge that it will last until

Gillian comes round and insists on me being mature. To add to this outburst of sensibleness, I will also have Mental Mike's words ringing in my ears. But for now, I want to indulge myself and feel a little bit silly and a little bit sorry for myself.

Chapter Forty-One
Reflections, Part Two

The time between me saying goodbye to Jack and Gillian arriving seems like an eternity, and I have to hold myself back from ringing her. As always, I'm fretting about fuck-all as it is really only forty-five minutes, but when she arrives I gather her up in my arms and kiss her passionately.

When we eventually settle down, she asks me about Jack and how I'm feeling. The answer is that I'm conflicted because, being honest, I don't want her to see how much Jack's going away is hurting me, so I settle for an unenthusiastic "OK".

Gillian, of course, sees right through that bollocks and is very gentle with me. "Paul, you don't have to hide how much you'll miss Jack."

I'm of course stunned by both her perspicacity and her empathy. There's something else too. It's an understanding that my gentleness, my nature, isn't something to sneer at; the opposite is what I'm used to, and when Gillian responds in a completely different way to the Ex it catches me completely off guard.

I splutter some old guff about how much I love him and her, and in a gentle way she cuts me dead.

"Listen to me. You're fretting about this. We will make decisions that will be the best for all of us. That means we have to wait until they have made their decision before we make ours."

"But what happens if his school is miles away and..."

"Look, I have a suggestion." She says this gently, patiently. "We cannot go round in circles; when we know everything, then we will spend as much time as we like talking and making plans. In the meantime, we have to talk about how much I love you, Paul Castle."

My dam bursts as I look her in the eyes and I then actually start to cry. It's weird, because I never thought that I could be this happy and that this would be the only way I can express it. It doesn't take her long to dry my eyes.

Then we talk about the romantic stuff cherished by new lovers, and just chat nonsense. Somehow we get to the subject of work and Mike, redundancies and the various bouts of nonsense.

At this point, she fixes me with a stare: "Are you happy at work?"

"Sort of." It's a pretty weak response, but one that reflects my ambivalence. "I love writing, but it isn't much of a challenge. My heart is really set on the idea that we could get some plays done. I'm really hoping that Trevor's plan comes off."

Gillian gently probes the answer for more information: "What would happen if it did take off? Would you give up work?"

"I might; it would depend on money and other stuff, how we end up and what else is happening." After saying that, I smile and shrug my shoulders, and reach over and kiss her. "I'm not that worried about all that. It's you and Jack first. The rest will work itself out."

"Well there you are. We'll sort it out together." It seems a good note on which to end that part of the conversation and concentrate on food. We opt for a Chinese takeaway and a DVD, and we settle down to relax in each other's company.

Chapter Forty-Two
Tears Before Bedtime, Part Two

Gillian and I spend the rest of the evening together, watching a French movie that we have discovered we both like. It's *Cyrano de Bergerac*, and its warmth and passion are a perfect fillip for me, although Gillian is very quiet. A couple of years ago, I tried to adapt *Cyrano* for a modern audience and failed miserably. Truthfully, I wasn't able to do it justice, particularly as Steve Martin had done it before with a great deal of wit and charm. The movie he made, *Roxanne*, is a guilty pleasure of mine. Ex disapproved of it, in the process describing it as silly tosh, which of course it is—completely. However, I sometimes need silly tosh, and I have a sneaky feeling that most other people do too. What's the betting that, apart from the seriously anally retentive, most couples will have a couple of dodgy DVDs in their cabinet? Mostly they'll be indifferent, silly rom-coms that have touched them somehow, even if it's only that they went to see them at the cinema together.

Cyrano is very long, and by the time it's finished we're sleepy and reluctant to stir. Gillian is very clingy, which I like, and I'd happily stay there except for a bout of pins and needles that wakes me from my half-doze. Slowly, we get up from the sofa and make our way to get ready for bed.

Whilst I'm brushing my teeth in the bathroom, Gillian comes in and wraps me in a huge hug, and it's clear she's gently weeping. Confused, I want to comfort her, and in reply to my requests for the reason behind her tears, I just get, "I'm being silly."

She refuses to elucidate and I decide to push it a little because I'm worried that I've unconsciously upset her. This is typical of me: if something goes wrong, I will be the one who agonises about it and say sorry, even if I've nothing to apologise for. You know the type already: the sort of bloke who, when you bump into him in the supermarket, says sorry for your terrible trolley-driving that gave him a dead leg.

She smiles when I tell her that, but that suddenly seems to bring on a fresh bout of tears and she hastens to reassure me. "Oh no, darling, it's just so silly." I hug her and try to comfort her, which appears to have the opposite effect. Instead of just leaving this alone, I get all masculine and, in a fairly gentle way, demand to know the reason for her tears; after all, the steel in her voice is quite an effective tool to get my attention when I'm stressed.

This has the effect that I want, and she starts to explain. "It's so silly, just so silly, and I don't want you to misunderstand."

I start to get very nervous, and this is a most discomfiting feeling, so I brace myself for some bad news. In fact I begin to get a feeling of impatience, because if this is going to be painful I want it over with, so convinced am I that her tears are a precursor of bad news for me. She gets a tissue from the box by the sink and blows her nose, and then leads me gently to the bedroom. I'm trying not to panic and shout "get on with it, woman!"

Of course, I realise that I'm very insecure, and the only thought in my head is the beardy psychologist lecturing me on my fear of rejection. There's a distinct pause, which isn't, as you can imagine, doing anything for my nerves. She looks at me, kisses me on the lips, and then with a barely audible voice, slowly begins to talk.

"You must promise me that you will not take this the wrong way." She waits for an answer. All that I'm thinking about at this stage is all *the times* I have been turned over by women. It usually starts with "it's not about you; it's me" or "you're lovely, but…" or some other such line that really means it is about me.

Suddenly, I realise I'm expected to speak at this point, and say something like "yes, but…", at which point she tenderly puts a finger to my lips as if she realises I'm thinking the worst—which of course I am.

"Promise me, Paul." I nod, and my stomach is in my boots as I'm waiting for disaster in her next sentence. She can see I'm not convinced and I think that inspires her to an explanation to calm me down a bit.

"Tomorrow's Ray's birthday, and he loved French movies and, well, you know…" A fresh tear runs down her cheek and I begin to see, at last, what an utter selfish arse I've been.

I blurt out: "I'm so sorry; I didn't know."

She grabs my hand and says in barely a whisper, "There's no reason for you to apologise." She holds my hand up to her mouth and kisses it in a gesture I find very tender. "I'm being silly and I need to say this and try and help you to understand."

She pauses and kisses my hand again; in this context it's a demand for patience, and I readily accede and allow her to continue. "Ray was my best friend, my lover, Geraldine's father and a lovely man. I loved him and lost him to cancer, which was terrible, as you can imagine."

I nod at this, as words seem absolutely pointless.

"After he died, I never thought I would go out of the house again, let alone find someone whom I could love as much as him." She stops again; it's as if she is choosing each word with the greatest of care. I cannot even begin to say anything vaguely sensible, so I let her continue.

"Then after a long time, I allowed my friends and family to help me get on my feet and then, after a lot more time, I started living my life again That's because in my heart I knew Ray would not want me to spend the rest of my life in mourning. However, I never thought I would find such love again. The thing that makes this so silly is that I know in my heart, with absolute conviction, Ray would like you and he would be delighted about me being in love with you."

A tear falls down my cheek at this point and I just know that at the end of this monologue I am simply going to hold her in my arms and hug her. I know that because I can feel how much emotion and time she is putting into each word. This is just so I don't feel bad about myself and so wretched and ashamed about my previous musings.

She squeezes my hand and again my eyes tell her everything is all right.

"Then after all that time, I found you, Paul, and because I love you, I sometimes forget about the pain of losing him. Then suddenly, tonight, with the movie, it has come flooding back and I feel a mixture of guilt about him and relief that I have found someone who I can tell this stuff to. In my heart, I think you'll understand." I draw her to me in a gesture that I hope will tell her that she hasn't misplaced her trust.

Continuing to hold her very close, like I'm never going to let her go, I can only hope that it's a sign to her that expresses how clearly I understand, and how grateful I am that she's in my life.

We kiss passionately and the necessity of saying those things is rendered superfluous; her understanding of my feelings is made plain as she pushes me down on my bed and begins to make love to me.

Chapter Forty-Three
The Morning After Tears

Groggily, and after far too many presses of the snooze button, I wake to find her gently stroking my hair, and the feeling of wellbeing inside me contrasts sharply with the panicky sensations that filled me last night. It's so different, in fact, that it feels like a contentment that I've never experienced before. The nearest thing that I can compare it to is the gentle feelings of paternal love that would sometimes overwhelm me when Jack, as a small baby, fell asleep as he lay on my chest with his head resting on my shoulder.

Gillian looks me in the eye. "Paul, would you mind if I don't come over tonight?"

Remembering last night's tears and the significance of the day, I rush to reassure her. "Of course not. What will you do?"

"Geraldine and I always like to spend Ray's birthday together. She was very young when he died, and she likes to remember his birthday rather than any other anniversary."

This sounds like a lovely gesture, and I gently assure her of my understanding. "Today is a day you need to spend with your daughter. Don't worry about it at all."

She reaches over and kisses me. "Thank you, lovely man. Geraldine is dying to meet you, by the way."

Looking in her eyes, there is an almost childlike enthusiasm, which I want to get to the bottom of. "Oh God, what have you told her about me?"

She gently chuckles, and just says, "Only the truth."

I put on a mock-*Dad's Army* Private Frazer accent, and say, "I'm doomed!"

We both roll about with laughter, and after a few cuddles we settle down in bed and make love again. She is very assertive this morning, in a similar way to last night, and the gesture is not lost on me. I surrender to her tender forcefulness and her kisses have a passionate nature that conveys deep emotional connection rather than our usual urgency. It is like a gesture expressing how much she loves me. I think that I have never felt so close to anyone in my life.

We shower together, an activity I always find intensely stimulating, and had we not just already done it I would definitely have tried to make love to her there and then. After this, we get dressed and potter about, listening to the fairly gloomy news on the TV while sorting out toast and coffee for breakfast.

Watching her, she looks at home, and it makes me feel very cool about the prospect of sharing my life with her. I feel warm and sorted and just want to blurt out protestations of love and all that stuff—all of which has been said, but which I want to say to her again and again.

At this point, her phone rings and she answers. It's her daughter, and they make arrangements to meet and plan their evening. When she puts down the phone, there is a certain look in her eye; she seems to be searching for approval or reassurance.

"It's OK! I understand completely." I'm trying not to say anything crass here, and find that a difficult trick to pull off. Nothing sounds quite right in my head: either too mawkish or too trite. My mind goes blank and I simply settle for, "Say 'hi' to Geraldine and tell her I'm thinking about her."

She just beams at me, trying to express without words that she's happy I can understand what today has in store and why I can't, for now, be part of it.

When I wave goodbye, after the kisses and hugs on the doorstep, I begin to muse on the depths of this remarkable, sexy woman who has arrived in my life and in many ways turned it on its head. Compared to the stuff she's gone through, my travails all seem fairly routine.

However, I'm a firm believer in each person measuring his or her own pain, and I'm cute enough to allow some perspective to fall on that. Mike's words come back to me with some power: "You will only lose your son if you let that happen." Trying to seek some solace from all of this is still bloody hard, and I'm still hurting from the thought that even now Jack might be driving to a place that will mean he is many miles from me.

This leaves me with a forlorn hope that Jack will hate London and every school he visits, and insist that he wants to stay up here with me.

This isn't much of a hope, I grant you, but I'm clinging to this metaphorical lifeboat. Until I hear differently, you'll have to prise my fingers off it with a blowtorch and a crowbar. That being said, I may, at some point, listen to the people who are saying that I have to be sensitive to Jack's wishes.

This sounds reasonable and very child-centred, and yet sometimes all I want to do is stamp my feet and shout. "What about me?"

Whatever happens, I appear to be completely shafted and I have very little room for manoeuvre. The only option is using a legal process that will be painful and could very well be counterproductive.

This painful set of feelings follows me around as I mechanically prepare for work and hopefully a much more peaceful day with my colleagues than yesterday.

Chapter Forty-Four
Desperation

Work was weird, and arriving home all I can really remember, apart from the usual court reports and being shouted out by a sub-editor for filing late, were the meetings Doug was having. He seemed to be holed up in his office with the Suits from upstairs. There was a definite "do not disturb" atmosphere about them, and the sub-editors were taking up the slack. Subs, on the whole, are nasty, vicious bastards, generally getting in the way between journos and a piece on the front page, and today was no different. The only exception was that they had real power, as opposed to the imaginary power they usually have. This is, as I'm sure you've gleaned, purely a hack's point of view, and without the subs nothing would function: the paper would be unreadable; that is, if it didn't close from all the lawsuits it would be defending. Today they're keeping it together as Doug and the Suits chatter for all they are worth.

Getting out of the car, I have time to wonder about how Gillian and Geraldine are getting on with their day, and how Jack is doing in the hunt for his new school. My flat seems very empty compared to this morning, and the gloom which followed me round after Gillian left could easily return if I let it. Starting with eating some leftovers and drinking some coffee, I end up doing humdrum stuff that reflects my lack of focus. I've got used to the nearness of Gillian and the anticipation of seeing her, and I miss her, especially as I know she won't be coming over.

The phone rings, and it's Jack, but lovely as it is to hear him, his news is terrible. He starts and ends the conversation waxing lyrical about a school he's seen, and it's clear he just adores it. In fact, the whole call is about what he's seen and the teachers and other kids he's met, all of whom have made him feel very welcome. This is a huge blow, and my last hope of Jack hating everything in front of him is laid to rest. Luckily Jack is unable to detect my feeling of despair from the tone of my voice. By the end of the call he's run out of superlatives for this new school, and before saying goodbye says, "Mum wants a word—see you soon!"

Ex comes on, and there is a definite hesitancy about her tone. "Jack has seen a school he likes very much."

Groaning, I mumble disconsolately, "So I've been hearing." My voice probably reflects my mood, as I feel that I can lay some of this on her since she is definitely the author of this situation.

She ploughs on: "They are very keen, if not insistent, about involving all the family in the life of the school, and that would mean that they would like to talk to you to see whether you are supportive of the arrangements."

There's a pause, and it's a pause that comes from a very independent individual, forced to ask for help and hoping something will prevent that from happening. She is obviously expecting me to roll over, and I petulantly want to say "fuck off and die", but the thought of upsetting Jack is obviously holding me back. By the same token, I want to make her sweat but cannot be sure that that isn't going to backfire on me or my son. So I go along, but my voice should tell her that I am very reluctant to do anything other than assist Jack. "Can I speak to the Head on the phone, or does he want to meet me?"

There is a little pause, and it is clear she is being quite guarded. "Well, I asked them, and they would prefer to see you personally. I don't want to press…" I barely suppress a grunt of disbelief at this point. "However, they will not offer him a place until they talk to you."

Again there's a pregnant pause, and she is waiting for me to dive in and make her life easier: a temptation I manfully resist. I do feel a bit childishly petulant but, hey, I'm not perfect. I decide, eventually, to think about Jack and ask when they want to see me.

"As soon as possible." The relief in her voice is palpable. "Unfortunately, they are as usual oversubscribed, and I don't like to ask as I know that you are busy at the moment…"

"That's OK. I will talk to the guy tomorrow if you give me a number, and hopefully get down there the day after."

"Thanks, Paul!"

My next question is one that I am not looking forward to asking. "Where is this place?" My stomach clenches, and I'm conscious that if it's a bad answer, my life is going to change in ways I can't imagine.

"It's near Godalming in Surrey. Jack liked it more than any of the others he saw." It's a hammer-blow, and the impact of having my son over 130 miles from me is appalling. Suddenly the good feelings I have about all of this fall away, as my stomach turns into a knot and all sorts of bad thoughts run through my head.

My only response is a clipped "That's a long way from Birmingham." I say this in a voice that doesn't hide my disappointment at the direction this is going.

Ex answers in a cool voice that indicates a desire not to upset me. "John and I know that, but Jack really likes it, and we felt that because this is a big move for him, his views are very important. We also feel strongly that you should know everything and be involved as much as possible."

By now I'm desperately trying to see that, and I know that this thing is very close to happening and that I have no idea how this will impact on my relationship with Jack. I'm mixed up and need time to think. "I have to go, as I am obviously a bit upset and have to let all this sink in, and I may want to talk to you later. Are you available to talk?"

"Yes, we are on this number all night." She says this with a small note of concern in her voice, which I'm trying hard not to acknowledge, as it doesn't fit my "Wicked Witch of NatWest" narrative.

I ring off without any pleasantries, and at this point panic starts to get into my head. The idea of a minimum drive of two and a half hours to see Jack twice a week is soul-destroying. Of course, that will be no deterrent to me seeing him, but it means a restriction: a massive mental and physical distance. Then I begin to imagine all sorts, and an overwhelming sense of bereavement begins to sink in. This manifests itself in an almost physical feeling of despair and it acts like a fog blotting out my senses for a few minutes; when I come to, I find that I'm gently weeping for the loss of contact, even for our unsatisfactory Wednesday nights and Burger Bar Saturdays.

It's hard, and although I try to be positive, I find it difficult to see practical solutions. The sadness becomes overwhelming as I accept that I'll have to struggle to maintain any meaningful contact with Jack, unless I decide to move nearer to this school. Even with that, I cannot be sure that my contact with him will survive the change in his circumstances and that of Ex and John. Now I really need the reassurance that Gillian could bring, but I'm loath to disturb her time with her daughter, especially today of all days. In any case, I want to look at solutions, and at the moment I'm just panicking about things and getting myself into a state of advanced neurosis, from which I'll eventually have to emerge.

Of course, if Gillian were here she would be telling me to focus on Jack and how everything else would work itself out. Right now I can't begin to see how that will happen. It's hard for me to admit to myself that I've not one clue how I can maintain my relationship with Jack in Surrey and build my life with Gillian in Birmingham. Very quickly I start to get agitated, and it all begins to go round and round in my head.

Knowing that I need to get a grip on myself, I decide upon a chat with Gerry and call him straightaway. He is bullish, of course, and his first suggestion is hiring a sniper. Under other circumstances that would be funny, but he quickly realises that I'm not in the mood for this. He senses that I'm very upset, which after all is why I like him, and he offers to come over.

Nice as that offer is, all I can see is a drunken descent into Ex-bashing, and I don't need that right now. He asks if Gillian is coming over and a little white lie is indicated, because if he knew she wasn't, he'd insist on meeting up.

"That's OK, then," he says. "She'll sort you out." Immediately I feel bad about lying to him, but I need the space, particularly in my head.

To divert him away from my little white lie, I decide to confide to him that her "everything is going to be all right" philosophy is not working for me at the moment.

He laughs and gets all older-brotherly. "Listen, mate, the one thing I am sure of is that she knows what she is talking about. Listen to her and things will be fine."

Having acknowledged my disquiet at what could be seen as Gillian's over-optimistic view of this, I plough on and reveal the crux of my concerns. "Mate, it's like this. My feeling is that if I want to maintain any sort of relationship with Jack, it means me moving down south. That means giving up the job, the flat and the potential of working on my plays with Trevor. That's not a problem, obviously, but, well, the whole Gillian thing...well, you know."

Gerry bursts out laughing. "Why don't you say you love her, idiot?"

It's annoying that he knows me well enough to spot this stuff straightaway. "OK, I love her, and this is the most inappropriate time for this to happen. The paper, the theatre, Jack...it's all driving me mental."

Gerry becomes very calm and says, "Paul, you are a great mate and I know you will get your head around this." This seems a bit optimistic but I let that ride as, after all, I trust Gerry.

The rest of the conversation is just like this: my doubts and his reassurance, and round and round we go. Eventually he decides to be firm, and at this point I'm given a stern lecture that amounts to "be patient, trust Gillian, and stop fucking panicking".

Chapter Forty-Five
...Because I've Been There Before

"Stop panicking" is a great motif for my life at the moment, and directly after the phone goes down I vow to take Gerry's advice. Within minutes, though, panic grips me again and, shaking, I reach for a Scotch. The temptation to drown my sorrows is nearly overwhelming but something holds me back and I stick to the one glass. Looking around at my flat, I just want to cry, as everywhere I glance there is Jack or Gillian. I give vent to some anger as Ex's decision has put me in the situation of having to choose a long-distance relationship with either one or the other. The soothing balm of Gillian not being available, I try hard to catch myself and not descend into a spiral of negative thoughts.

This lasts for about another five minutes, and I decide to do something positive and go to the Internet to look at the school's website. Groaning to myself, I have to say that it looks good and I can see why Jack likes it. It doesn't address itself to the socially mobile rugger-buggers like so many of the others; for instance, the sporting side of it is very much underplayed. There is also a nod to academia, but it's mostly about the immersive experience that Mike talked about. It looks a really cool place, and bearing in mind my prejudices about private school, that's fulsome praise. Fuck. One slick web page and I'm a purring class traitor.

At the end of all this, there is a ring on the doorbell, which is a surprise as I'm not expecting anyone. Opening the door, I'm staggered to find Gerry. Instantly I grab him and he kind of bear-hugs me, and for some reason this gesture makes me cry.

We sit in the lounge, and I try to apologise for my white lie, but he just shrugs his shoulders at me.

"Gillian told me she wasn't coming over today, and asked me to keep an eye on you. She must have had a sixth sense about Jack finding a good school or something."

Inwardly marvelling at the woman's intuition, I again try to say sorry, which once again is waved off. He's carrying a nice wine, which, in other circumstances, I would have cracked into, but I decide on a Coke as I take it off him and uncork it to let it breathe.

He is full of questions about my conversations with Ex and Jack, and I point him to my laptop as the school's website is still open. Gerry goes over and works away, and all I can hear is the tapping of his fingers on the keyboard. It's alarming to hear him so quiet, and after getting the drinks sorted I ask him what he thinks.

"It looks great, and I can see why Jack likes it. I've just emailed them, warning them about your Ex and her penchant for committing fraud and stealing ornate silver; I hope you don't mind." I laugh, halfway through a sip of Coke, which promptly goes up my nose. Having him here is already a fantastic tonic, and once again the value of really good friends is made very clear to me.

Seeing me laugh is the permission he needs, and he spends ages taking the piss out of the Ex with lines like "if you'd have killed her on your honeymoon, you'd be out now", which make me howl like a teenager.

Just then, Gillian rings, and I look at the clock and realise it's nearly 11 p.m. Excusing myself, I take the call in the bedroom, which again makes me feel like a teenager. She seems concerned, and admits that Gerry phoned her with my news and that she was going to ask him to go over before realising he already had his coat on. There is a sense of anxiety in her voice that leads me to suspect that she feels I might be upset.

Her next question rather confirms this: "I hope you don't mind me mentioning things to Gerry; I thought that you might need someone to talk to."

Some people might find all this an unbearable intrusion, but I'm not one of them. It crosses my mind to reassure her. Suddenly I remember why she isn't here and ask her how her day has gone.

"Oh, we have had a good day laughing at the happy memories and a sad day thinking of the unhappy ones. The same as usual, and we talked about you and how happy Geraldine is that I have found someone."

In the background, I hear a girl's voice saying "Hooray!'" and I ask the obvious question: "Is that Geraldine?"

"Yes, we've been drinking some wine and sorting out the world." She chuckles, with her usual musical tinkle that makes me miss her so much. At this point, I get a bit melancholy and start blubbing about Jack and all of my issues. Gillian is reassuring as usual, and she tells me that we will have a talk very soon after I get back from visiting the school. We ring off with the usual protestations of devotion, which at the start of every relationship is charming and touching and which couples in more jaded relationships drop. Sadly that's usually the signal that the rest is downhill for them.

It is a comforting thought, being in love, and if I could ever get my head round the idea that not everyone is going to walk out on me, I would be a much happier person. I keep going back, of course, to the memory of Dad holding his suitcase on his way out of the door to live somewhere else. Most times, that fear of abandonment is focused inwardly but sometimes it's focused outwards. Today, I'm trying to hold onto the thought that despite Jack's obvious desire to go to that school, he will miss me and our times together if they become less regular. The most important thing is that I don't want him to feel like I did: looking for a role-model dad who wasn't always there for me.

By the same token, I'm conflicted, because if I decide to make the move near London I risk my relationship with Gillian. I've had a long-distance relationship; it was when I was young and ardent, and there was always the sweetener that we knew it was only for a couple of years. At the time it was cool for me having two lives, especially as I was in my early twenties. Then there was the whole living-in-London thing, if you know what I mean.

Compare that with now, and I have to move south with no job and nowhere to live, leaving behind a mass of stuff that money can never buy. That isn't even factoring in Gillian. Or even the Trevor thing, which, for a writer, even a jaded hack like me, is very exciting. The thought of doing that work long-arm isn't brilliant and I can predict it won't appeal to Trevor.

None of this increases my emotional wellbeing, and all I can see is a very fretful long night ahead.

So I decide to do a typically male thing, and get pissed with Gerry and talk about something else instead.

Chapter Forty-Six
Sorting

It's Wednesday morning, and I have a massive hangover, which in my current state of mind isn't the most convenient way to start the day. This is followed by a text message from the Ex asking why I didn't call her last night and requesting me to sort out the meeting with the Head of Jack's new school. It's a very terse message and as usual makes no allowances for my feelings; certainly not what I need right now. Last night's displacement activity, a.k.a. getting pissed, apart from giving me a hangover hasn't gone any way to sorting out my feelings about the whole school business.

The phone rings, and it's Jenny; I give it to Gerry, who, despite my entreaties for him to stay in Jack's room, decided to crash on the sofa. He grunts a bit at her, and I leave them to it and head for a very welcome shower. As I step into the water, I'm filled with a feeling of painful loss, and it begins to sink in that I very soon have to make some horrible decisions that will affect me profoundly. Normally I love the shower, especially when, like today, I'm feeling grotty, and it doesn't take long for it to work its magic. By the time I get out I have at least shaken off the ringing in my ears and the headache. I need to sort out a load of stuff and I have to get my head right.

After taking the usual paracetamol and coffee (the breakfast of champions!), I decide to get going.

First, I ring work and ask for Doug, and am informed that he isn't available. This is puzzling, but I haven't the time or energy to worry about that. Asking for one of the subs, I tell him that I will be late in and he just grunts as we agree a time for my arrival; this gives me time to sort out some stuff.

Gerry, meanwhile, is bumbling about and trying to cheer me up before beginning to sort out his breakfast. My next move is to reach for the phone and ring Jack's potential new school to be put through to the Head Teacher. There is a bit of banter with the office staff and then the usual electronic rendition of *Greensleeves*.

This aural torture didn't last long, and all of a sudden I hear my name: "Mr. Castle?"

"Hello, is that Mr. Jardine?"

"Yes. Are you ringing to make an appointment regarding Jack?"

This takes me back. I'm impressed that he is savvy enough to know why I am calling. Also, he appears genuinely interested and has a welcoming, inclusive voice, which puts me at a disadvantage. After all, I'm clutching to my prejudices and he has no business being friendly and warm.

"Well, if you can make it down tomorrow, I can fit you in any time after lunch. I hate to press but we have a time issue here, which I hope that you are aware of."

A little annoyed, I leave that hanging for a second or two and then say, in my most reasonable voice, "I'll come down tomorrow and be with you about two o'clock, if that's OK?"

"Yes. That will be great. I look forward to meeting you."

With that, we say our goodbyes, and that's my second job completed. My third and final task is to ring the Ex and tell her that I've completed my mission, then try to get some details about where she will be living. This will help me make some decisions about my future as well as Jack's.

Ex picks up the phone and I say, "Hi!" It seems the only thing to do, as I'm not in the mood to be garrulous.

"Hi, Paul." There's an awkward pause and she continues: "You got my text message?"

"Yes, I've spoken to the Head and we are meeting tomorrow. I want to chat to you and John when I've finished with him."

"What about?" There is an obvious tension in her voice, and I suspect that is anxiety as I reckon she's feeling very insecure about my ability to put a large spanner in the works.

"Well, for one thing I want to tell you face to face what transpired at the meeting and I'd like to discuss ways we can make this work." Knowing this is going to happen has made me aware that I have to get on board and sort it out for Jack.

There's a pause, the kind that happens when someone is looking for a fight and finds that no one's turned up to oblige them.

"Oh, OK. There is a little restaurant place down the road from the school. We'll meet you there. Text me when you leave the school—we're staying about fifteen minutes away, at John's parents.'" At this point I would love to say how convenient all of that is, but I decide to button my lip, if only for the sake of good relations in the coming days.

"OK, I will call you as soon as I've cleared the school. Text me the address of the restaurant."

I put the phone down, take a deep breath and inwardly congratulate myself for not losing it, as well as for making her wait for me for a change. After half an hour plodding round the flat, tidying, I get ready for work and try, as far as possible, to focus on why Doug isn't there and why the subs are in charge. I have the idea that he has been sacked and that the triumph of Mental Mike will live in the newsroom for decades to come as the ultimate victory for journalism and free speech. Thinking that the management won't cave in that easily, I turn other ideas around, not least to try to blot out the fact that Gerry is some really making horrible noises in the bathroom.

When I get to work, the newsroom is a hive of inactivity and it's clear that something is up, creating one of those "water-cooler moments". Usually I hate American euphemisms, but this one is pretty appropriate. Everyone appears to be standing around in groups, and I obviously go to the group nearest my desk and start yakking.

Ben, of course, is at the forefront. "Doug has been moved out and the Suits are having a meeting with us in five minutes." It's hard, but I try to take this information in and, in all my confusion, ask some vaguely intelligent questions.

"How do you know he's gone?" I say, trying desperately to be concerned about Doug's loss, which frankly I'm not. In my defence, I do hope he hasn't got the complete elbow, but beyond that I've got too much going on in my life.

Ben is hopping about, desperate to tell me stuff and impart his superior information. "He came into the office early to clear his desk; he's off to Wolverhampton to run the paper there. Sideways move, he said. Wanker! The Suits are trying to patch something together to get us through the day."

I find myself relieved that he isn't being blown out completely; I nod and start for my desk, then sit down and try to get my head together. Given my hangover and emotional fragility, it isn't that easy.

Chapter Forty-Seven
An Offer I Can't Refuse?

My day is going pretty smoothly, and up to now has revolved around helping a couple of sub-editors drafted-in by the Suits upstairs to get a paper together. Whilst that's going on, there's an outbreak of undisguised joy announcing Mike's return. His reappearance gives a clue about Doug's departure and it seems that he has indeed had the rug pulled from underneath him. I consciously distance myself from the backslapping, and, whilst I am happy to see him back, treating him to a triumphant return strikes me as a bit unnecessary. After all, it was stupid he got suspended in the first place, but really the place needs him. If Doug hadn't been a complete idiot, he could have laughed it off and sorted it out another way. Then again, if hadn't been a complete idiot he would never have been made editor.

Noon arrives, and I've got through the morning and my head is beginning to feel OK-ish; the texts from Gillian have kept me sane. Deciding to reward myself, I walk to the coffee machine and I get myself a cappuccino and a biscuit. This allows me to think about how little I will miss this place if I do decide to move. Sure, it's an income, but it's also a drag on my other writing. Journalism and great literature are not often good bedfellows, and it's been a very long since I believed that the next Watergate is around the corner.

Having got my drink, I text Gillian and ask her to call me when she's free, for no other reason than that I want to hear the sound of her voice. Standing there, I slowly sip my coffee, and with all my emotional turmoil I have forgotten how much I used to like being here. After my marriage began to disintegrate, this place held me together. That sounds pretty pathetic, but I guess when your world is falling to bits latching on to something, even work, is a pretty good feeling. The banter and the camaraderie kept me sane, and with Gerry by my side I kept my shit together, more or less. Now with my world being disorientated in a different way, I feel that I need more than this place can give me at the moment.

Feeling a little better, I carry on drinking my coffee, and the sharpness of it reminds me that I've a lot to think about and a long journey tomorrow. The concept of a long drive to give my approval to handing over my son to the sort of shits that run this place fills me with a fresh dread.

Suddenly I'm aware that someone is talking to me. It's Brian, one of the subs.

"Paul! Wake up, you daft fucker!" He isn't very subtle today. I look at him, and, realising I must look like a dullard, come to attention.

"Hi, Brian! Sorry, lost in my thoughts," I say, as though this were some excuse.

He smiles and comes back, "Thoughts? Last time a journo had one of those, we had to fire him. So watch your step!"

I wasn't kidding about the subtlety. Laughing, I hang on to the thought that this guy is actually paid to be nasty, and when he's having a go at me then at least he's giving some other poor bastard some peace.

"What's up, Brian? Do you need me? Otherwise I'll have to go back to work."

This raises a smile, and the warmth of it surprises me. Come to think of it, I'm surprised by the whole conversation, as Brian generally barks at people and is only happy when the paper is put to bed. That's his cue to bugger off to the pub and sweatily leer over attractive women. I may be doing him a disservice here, but he's paid to be a shit, so what the hell?

"The MD wants you in his office," he says, with a kind of leery bonhomie that suggests I might not be in for a kicking.

Still in some trepidation, I ask the question, "What's he want?"

He shrugs. "Don't ask me! He just wants to have a chat with you."

I put my drink down and, after giving Ben a nod, gather up my jacket and head upstairs. My mind is racing with the idea that I'm going to get a bollocking, even though Brian didn't give that impression. The fuck-up with the Union story wasn't great, but I did sort it, so I'm sure that isn't enough to get me binned. That thought is then replaced by the more sinister observation that with Doug gone they may make a few more staff changes—new broom and all that. By the time I'm at the MD's door, I'm thinking about trying to get the best redundancy package and working out whether this will be enough to sort out a few issues with Jack.

A bark from the other side of the door tells me that I can come in and I'm soon face to face with Nigel Stevenson, Managing Director of the WR Newspaper Group, and another couple of Suits, whom I don't recognise but I suppose aren't here to do the cleaning.

"Hello, Paul. Please come in." He stands up and reaches across the desk to shake hands. "I'd like you to meet John Walters, the Group Accountant." He points to a thin pasty-faced man with a prominent chin. "And this is Bob Smart from the legal side." Bob is a corpulent man with a couple of beady eyes, and looks like a Dickensian character who should be called "Bartholomew Whifflepig".

Somehow, I nod and blurt out, "Oh God, what have I done?"

This gets a cheap laugh from the Suits, and I relax a bit as it is clear that I'm not here to be escorted from the building by security.

I sit down, and Money Suit and Legal Suit are still smiling. The grin from Legal Suit is a little forced but as I was expecting to be handed a bin liner and given ten minutes to clear my desk, I'm not complaining. As I'm sitting down, I reflect ruefully on the fact that five minutes ago I was idly contemplating that the job wasn't giving me very much. At least I can now say I've had an interesting day at work!

Focusing on the three of them, I try to look suitably impressed with the assembled company before the MD launches in: "Paul, as you may know, we have moved Doug to another title. We value your work here and Doug has recommended you, so we would like to offer you the post of acting editor."

Words want to come out of my mouth, but my lips are not moving at all. I try to say something, but It sort of dribbles out in a mumbled "canyourepeatha?"

Legal Suit ignores that and says, "We feel that you have the qualities that we need at the moment to get us over this difficult period, now that Doug has moved."

I'm frantically trying not to laugh, but it's really hard; whatever I was expecting when I knocked on the door, it wasn't this. At this point it seems that I'm required to speak, and I try to gather my thoughts and not sound like a simpleton with a speech impediment.

All I can muster to give me some time is, "This is a bit of a shock, Nigel!"

"Yes," he replies, and it's clear that he isn't that impressed by my less-than-enthusiastic response to the issues in hand. Feeling I have to explain, I start by talking about my deep bond with Jack. By the time I finish and start to talk about his impending move down south and my desire to see him more, Legal Suit is looking at his watch and Money Suit is staring out of the window. From this, I divine that I'd better wrap this up quickly.

"The truth is, I was looking to work more flexibly and even consider moving south. Much as I am flattered, I really don't think the time is right for me."

"Right. That is very honest of you, Paul." His tone is difficult to gauge, but the mood music in my head suggests an early exit. Nevertheless, it seems rude to interrupt. " It would be fair to say that you are unable to give us the commitment that we require from someone entering the editorship."

There's a pause as a glorious vision of my name on the editor's door pops into my head. This, however, is rapidly followed by the disappointed face of Jack waiting to see me, only to be told that I can't make our weekly visit because Villa's top player has a groin strain from trying to mount a bosomy WAG in a hotel car park. My mind is quickly made up.

"I'm sorry, Nigel; many people will think I'm stupid, but I would be doing you, my son, and myself a disservice by accepting this position." At this point I stand up, as I need to get the fuck out and gather my thoughts. "Thank you for the offer and good luck with your search."

I shake hands and quickly walk downstairs, avoiding the newsroom as I definitely need a cigarette along with a moment's peace to stew over the monumental thing that I have done.

Chapter Forty-Eight
The Road to Hell

The drive down to Jack's new school starts pleasantly, as Gillian decided to stay over and our goodbyes contained all of the anticipation of lovers' meetings. We talked for large parts of the evening and in the end I had to settle for her usual message of, "Sort Jack out and then we'll make some decisions."

I have to admit that when I'm with her, the idea that this will all turn out OK actually sounds fine and achievable. All my daydreams at the moment normally finish happily with a long kiss, problems solved and finally some lovemaking. Indeed, my happy mood is partly because of this morning's passionate promises about bedtime tonight.

Sadly, by the time I'm on the M25, my old friends doubt and self-deprecation have set in, and I'm paralysed with a feeling I'm finding hard to describe. It's one part fear to two parts melancholy and I've christened it "melanear" or "felancholy"—can't quite make my mind up. That in itself is a suitable metaphor for my feelings at the moment.

The journey on the motorway is, as usual, ghastly. It's depressing being passed by a procession of aspirational motors, all full of energetic and thrusting sales people; all judging my car in the same way my Ex does.

It's hard to express this: I really have nothing against modern cars, but to me they are soulless boxes full of wannabe contestants for *The Apprentice*. You know, the sort of people that talk about "blue-sky thinking" and "imagineering" as a substitute for saying something intelligent. They prowl along the M25 and the M4 corridor with the latest gadgets and a tablet PC, on their way to sell a crappy finance package to some poor Joe who's working his socks off so these hustlers can leech off him.

Ex tried to explain supply-side economics to me once, and I gave up trying to argue that you can't base a whole economy on shopping and credit. Her response to the banking meltdown was to blame it on the poor and vote Tory again. Indeed, I scratch my head as John is being promoted and I'm one of several producers of wealth who could be laid off. If that doesn't take the biscuit, then nothing will. Recently I thought that when the bankers' bonuses were announced large parts of London would be on fire, but somehow most people seemed to be engaging in a bit of post-Christmas revelry and they let it ride.

There are times that I smile when I see the way that the Tories operate: they cut public expenditure and to do so, they leak examples of waste and start to paint everyone who is on benefit as a feckless wastrel. It depresses me that the media just suck up this nonsense without question. In my angrier days, I filed a story about this, and it got spiked quicker than a rat going down a drainpipe. Doug was most upset, and that is where the rot set in with him and me. The fact that he offered me a promotion was a sign of how isolated he had become and how desperate he was to find an ally.

All of this makes me realise how displaced I feel, and it all scares me witless and makes me angry when I let it. The state of modern Britain, in one way, is a bit of an indictment of political spinelessness. I remember my dad saying to me that Labour used to stand for full employment and a decent welfare state. According to him these two things make the system work. Take away one or the other and you have problems, and that certainly seems to be the case. My frequent forays into court and its endless stream of hooded, inarticulate teenagers appear to bear that analysis out. It's depressing seeing this procession of aimless and ambitionless youngsters with nothing at all to motivate them. The complete surrender of any political principle under the onslaught of consumer capitalism is the real message of the Blairite revolution of New Labour. I'm glad that my dad, a true Socialist, died before he could see its more grotesque manifestations.

This dreary reflection seems to make my journey longer, and I put on some music on the CD player. This is my one modern concession in the Citroën, as I couldn't stand having any car without decent music and I have long ago given up finding consistently good sounds on any station that isn't digital. I put on some Bruce and start singing out loud to "Jungleland"—obvious, I know, but it hits the spot.

The traffic on the M25 is just a complete nightmare, and the whole section between the M4 and the M3 is a car park. Of all the places I hate in the world, I hate this road the most. All I want is to get to this bloody school, make the appropriate noises and get back to the Midlands.

The soul-numbing tedium of this journey somehow reminds me of my father. He was from a small town outside Bristol and loved the West Country all his life. He deeply disapproved of me going to college in London, as, in common with most West Country folk, he felt that London was the root of all evil—full of immorality, dogs and cats living together, and too much traffic. A very charming view, in its own way.

Then I found myself at eighteen with some good A-level results (better than I was expecting!), a job offer at Dad's Council Office and a university place.

The fact that I chose to get a degree was a disappointment to him, as I think he wanted me to be an accountant like him. In one of my only positive memories of Dad, he mapped out a career path for me one evening as we discussed my future: two years as an office junior, then onto the Chartered Institute of Public Finance and Accountancy scheme. After that, a long career in local government finance and a pension after forty years of what I would consider penal servitude. A very unappealing vista, I think you'll agree.

To my dad, who grew up with my grandfather's tales of 1930s unemployment and poverty, nothing was more highly prized than a steady job. The thought of staying in one place throughout his working life was a complete blessing to him. A few years before he died, I went to his retirement party, and he was very proud of my achievements but kept saying to everyone, "He's been in the same job for over ten years!" Sad, really.

The traffic slowly starts to move and the DS begins to return to its normal temperature. The stop/start motion of a traffic jam always has me looking anxiously at the temperature and oil gauges, and after some minor holdups I eventually get to my turn-off.

After that, a few minutes' driving and all of a sudden I'm in the country, looking at the leafy lanes of Surrey. You don't have to be a genius to realise that the recession isn't having much of an impact down in this neck of the woods. Indeed, this part of Britain appears unbelievably untouched by economic vicissitude. Bastards!

Soon I reach the outskirts of Godalming, a town I can't help thinking is faintly ridiculous. It just looks like a chocolate-box top and I cannot for the life of me think that anyone in it has anything like a modern thought. It's full of timbered houses, narrow Georgian lanes and narrow Tory minds. Nearby is Charterhouse School, and that should tell you all you need to know about the place: a bastion of Old England and a pillar of the class system.

The drive to the school that Jack is looking to attend would have been beautiful if I was I the mood to enjoy the view. The school I'm looking for isn't Charterhouse, but I suppose I'm inclined to see all these places in the same light. As I drive in through the gate, the manicured lawn and the school cricket pavilion behind the main building begin to speak volumes to me and reaffirm my cynicism. However, the brochure did nod to academic achievement, and I try to get a grip and think of Jack's needs before my prejudices.

After parking up, I walk into the main foyer and am met at the door by a kind-faced lady who sticks out her hand and says, in a friendly voice, "Is it Mr. Castle?"

Trying to smile, I mumble an affirmative, and she asks me to sit, then tells me that she will inform the Head that I'm here. Settling on an inappropriately comfortable sofa, I glance at the stunningly neat display of school brochures and reports on the coffee table.

In fact, the school seems very efficient and neat, and has the hushed atmosphere of a modern library. I was expecting a large trophy cabinet, a smell of institutional floor polish and the sound of cane swishing on backside. However, before my deep-seated stereotypes really start parading in my head, a smartly dressed man strolls across the foyer, holding out his hand.

In a crisp, clear voice he says, "Mr Castle, I'm Malcolm Jardine. So very nice to see you."

Chapter Forty-Nine
Wacko! Perhaps Not!

Walking into Jardine's office, I'm surprised by the informality, the lightness of touch. It has a sofa, an easy chair and a desk that looks straight out of a Scandinavian design house; the whole place has the air of a functional workspace. Of course, I was expecting a cross between *Tom Brown's School Days* and an oak-panelled gentlemen's club in Pall Mall, so my cultural stereotypes are not leaving me. It's as if he's gone out of his way to put me off my guard: bloody unsporting, I call that.

He follows me in, points me to the sofa, and comes straight to the point.

"Mr. Castle, thank you for agreeing to meet me. You've probably got a lot of questions, and I would like to be as helpful as I can. I understand from your ex-wife that you have some reservations about your son coming to this school."

As an opening gambit, his bluntness, delivered in such a smooth way, is very disconcerting. If I was thinking anything at all, I was expecting that he would try to schmooze me and dodge round my objections, but his directness has disarmed me somewhat.

Trying to marshal my thoughts is difficult after this, and I genuinely feel disorientated. Deciding to get my shit together, I test the waters and see whether I can knock him off his stride.

"May I speak frankly?" I ask.

He smiles and answers smoothly, "Of course. Please feel free." His urbane sophistication is beginning to get on my nerves.

At this point it occurs to me that honesty is most definitely the best policy. "Thank you, because I know that Jack is very keen to come here and I would not like to think that any perceived reservation on my part would put his placement here at risk."

The Head smiles. "My word; that is frank!" Despite myself, we're both smiling. He then looks me in the eye: "You do have some reservations, then?"

"Not specifically with this school or its staff, as judging from the brochure it seems to be an excellent place for Jack." I'm trying to sort out my feelings, as I'm not really sure I have anything to say at this point that will do Jack anything other than harm.

Consequently, I decide to go for the truth: "It's just that I'm uneasy about the concept of private education." Deciding not to give him any time to digest that, I add quickly, "However, given the situation that confronts me, especially as Jack is being asked to deal with a lot of changes all at once, I don't want to be a blockage to him getting into the school that he clearly loves."

There is what can only be described as a pregnant pause.

Jardine half-smiles. "Your attitude does you great credit." I try to mumble my thanks, but he carries on. "However, please let me tell you that we don't see ourselves as a regular fee-paying school here. We specialise in an academically rounded education with some specialist add-ons. We look to prepare our pupils for the modern world and in particular for the diverse nature of modern society. You'll find no fagging or Flashmen here."

Unbelievably, I surprise myself by wanting to hear his next sentence, to such an extent that I make an involuntary jerk of the head, which he construes as an invitation to continue.

"What we want to achieve here is a different model of fee-paying school. Most people expect *Goodbye Mr. Chips* and preparation for the Old Boy Network."

He pauses, and I smile to acknowledge his assessment, which in my case is pretty bang-on. That's returned, because it's clear that he knows he has hit the nail on the head.

"The Governors and I believe that there are a lot of parents who don't like the idea of a private education but would like an alternative to the public system."

Nodding as if this thought has ever once occurred to me, I'm keen he doesn't find out that I don't know what he's on about. He cracks on enthusiastically, though, and I feel I've got away with it.

"As I said, we want to forge a different model of private education here. Although I know that you are uncomfortable with the idea of paying for education, you will, I hope, understand that I am rightly proud of the solid record of academic achievement that our pupils have attained. We do all this in an atmosphere that also instils values that will make our pupils comfortable in modern Britain."

At this point, I feel the need to pipe up and interrupt this avalanche of PR bollocks. "Mr Jardine, as I said, I do not want to stand in Jack's way, and whatever my feelings and reservations, these are not relevant. I will, of course, support Jack in whatever way I can if you accept him at your school."

He answers with a merciless question that for a moment leaves me pretty speechless: "Am I right in understanding that you will be staying in Birmingham?"

The fact that he leaves me flat with that question is

testament to his disarming skills and how much I've already accepted that this will be Jack's new school. Before I can gather my thoughts, I get another example of his people skills.

"The only reason I am asking is that your ex-wife indicated that she was keen to keep up your contact. I'm assuming that will be quite difficult?"

Before I can stop myself, I answer in a surly tone, "I'll manage." As it's coming out of my mouth, I know I sound like a prat. I decide on a speedy fix for Jack's sake. "Don't get me wrong; I'm going to make every effort to make my contact as regular as possible. Jack is special to me—precious. I may even move down south to be nearer him."

He smiles, and I can't work out whether it's smugness or genuine warmth. "Of course, Mr. Castle, and we at the school will do everything in our power to facilitate your contact with Jack. You have my word."

I'm stumbling through my thanks when there's a knock at the door and Jardine lets in two sixth-formers, who've been tasked to show me round. Throughout the whirlwind tour, they rave about the school, the lessons, standards, extra-curricular stuff and the facilities. In short I'm treated to a PR blitz by a couple of teenage zealots. They wear down my prejudices and by the time they return me to Jardine's office, I'm feeling like a full-on class traitor.

The next fifteen minutes fly by, and before I know it, I've signed a parental consent form and Jack is a fully signed-up pupil. Very soon, I'm shaking hands and being waved off the premises.

Chapter Fifty
Beam Me Up, Scotty

By the time I get to the restaurant to meet Ex and John, I'm at sixes and sevens and haven't been able to think clearly about any of this. Part of me is delighted that I won't be held responsible for blocking Jack's placement, but you know the rest.

My first job is to ring the Ex and tell her I've arrived and that Jack's place is sorted. She starts to express her gratitude and I find this uncomfortable, so I make an excuse and hang up. Then I text Gillian and the others and wait patiently for John's car to arrive. My only comforting thought is that at least I can see Jack and rescue something from this miserable day.

There's a sense of guilt as I try consciously not to reflect on what I've done and just focus on the benefits for Jack, rather than the perceived downsides. That, as you can imagine, is bloody hard, and it's a relief when I see the three of them walking across the car park towards my car. Jack starts to run, and it's clear that he's happy, and I rush out of my car to greet him. I lift him up and there's a feeling in my head of relief, fear and sorrow, and I want to cry I'm so messed up. I spin him round a couple of times and try to get my feelings together before making a spectacle of myself.

John and the Ex walk over, and he offers his hand; it's clear by the firmness of the shake that he's very happy and grateful.

They are both profuse in their thanks and it's obvious that, for once, the Ex is pleased to see me.

We eventually head into the restaurant, and get seated at a family table. There's an effort to indulge in some small talk, and Ex seems cool about everything, although it's clear that house-hunting isn't going to plan. I've no desire to open that box, and start to chat animatedly to Jack; I think that they get the message.

He starts to ask about the school, and I tell him about the stuff I like and we chat about what fun he'll have. Naturally, I try to enthuse about it all. That's really hard, but he's still at an age where he takes everything at pretty much face value. He wants my approval, and I'm not going to give him anything less than 100%.

John looks me in the eye and mouths the word "thanks", and I just want to grab Jack and run back to Brum as fast as I can go. Obviously I don't, but all of this "niceness" in place of the usual surly hostility is unnerving, and frankly gives me the creeps. What Gerry would make of it, heaven only knows, but the thought of him brings a small smile to my lips.

Suddenly I begin to feel like an interloper, and I want them to go away so I can have time just with Jack, while I can still enjoy it. They, and this place, make me feel uncomfortable and I want it all to end. Knowing that I can't make that happen, I start to feel wretched. Then my telephone ringing saves me.

It's Gillian, and I decide to take the call outside so make my excuses and walk out to the car park. After the "Hi, I love and miss you!" sloppiness, we get down to the nitty-gritty. She is, of course, the personification of understanding.

"So what do you actually think of it?" The tone in which she asks indicates that she wants to hear the unvarnished truth.

Breathing deeply, I gather up some stray feelings for an emotional outburst. "Oh God, I don't know. If it wasn't Jack, I would say that it was it was brilliant. However, it is Jack, and you know how I feel about this stuff. It's not the school; it's just the whole situation."

There's a slight pause, then she says in a calm caring voice, "Darling, I know. When will you be home?"

All of a sudden, I know I just want to be gone from this place.

"I want to get going quite soon. Listen, can I come over?"

This is said in an obviously plaintive fashion, and she fires back the answer: "Come straight to me when you get back. Geraldine is out, so we will be alone."

My answer of "I can't wait!" is followed by the usual phone-ending of two lovers looking forward to being together after a stressful day.

The rest of my short stay is unsatisfactory and I take Jack outside and give him a DVD I bought for him on the journey down. He explodes with thanks, as it is one he's been talking about for a long time. We chat about the weekend and throw some ideas around about things we'd like to do together.

His mother calls him in for some food and offers to buy me dinner. Feeling very flattered by that but uncomfortable about sitting with her and John, I politely decline, much to Jack's disappointment. We hug as I explain that I've a long journey ahead, and he cheers up at the thought of Saturday.

He goes in with the Ex, waving, and I wave back, and after he's in the restaurant I get in the Citroën. The car fires up and I wonder, as I pull out of the car park, whether I can get to Gillian's without breaking down in tears. The car doesn't even reach the motorway before I have my answer.

Chapter Fifty-One
Reflections, Part Three

Have you ever noticed how hard it is to be quiet and that the more you try, the noisier you become? No matter how hard I try tonight, I cannot get to sleep. In the end, I walk over to the window seat in Gillian's bedroom and enjoy a grandstand view of her garden bathed in moonlight; my heart aches at the beauty of it. Of course, my heart doesn't have that far to travel after this afternoon.

I got back to Birmingham at 9.30, and the warmth of Gillian's welcome was a perfect antidote to my downtrodden mood. Of course she was understanding, and didn't press for anything other than the barest details of my day.

Although I'm not an insomniac by any means, tonight just seems full of reasons not to sleep. My mind is definitely not at rest and filled with annoyance and fear. The annoyance is that my son is moving away, entirely due to the ambition and greed of my Ex. The fear's from the realisation that I'm going to have to discuss with Gillian the impossibility of me living in Birmingham while Jack is at that school.

Driving up from Godawful Godalming, it was clear to me that I'll have to be near him. I just couldn't bear seeing him at that distance, becoming even less than the Burger Bar Dad that I've at present consented to be. Jack deserves so much more than that. I could commute each week but all I can see is more meetings in fast food joints, his mother's absences and the pressure of school pulling him to pieces.

In any case, having decided to turn down the editor's job I've little choice but to leave if I want my career to survive. A new editor is likely to shaft me the second he finds out that I was approached, and a new career down south will be more of a necessity than an option.

This all sounds very well, but obviously the fly in the ointment is that my contentment at being close to Jack and my new career challenges will come at the expense of my personal life.

That, I think, is the nub of my sleeplessness: I just cannot see Gillian being happy about fitting in with all this baggage. My time with Jack; the huge weekly trek; captured stolen moments; life lived constantly out of a holdall. There is no way that I can see that being a life that anyone would want.

On my journey up tonight I tried to think of ways of breaking the news:

"Gillian, I love you, but I'm moving down south. How about seeing me a couple of times a week?"

"Gillian, I love you, but can you wait for me till Jack goes to university?"

"Gillian, I'm really sorry, but if you want a future with me you'll have to sell up and come south and live with me."

It's all bloody hopeless, and all I can see is blackness; it makes me truly miserable. Tonight I really did try to tell her that I need to be near Jack. She just put a finger to lips and stroked my hand and kissed me. After that, she took me to the bedroom and made love to me. It was marvellous: a physical nursing of my hurt. That was so beautiful, yet it has delayed the process of dealing with all this. Time is pressing and I need to get a move on, and the pain is tearing me apart. Despite all her protestations and all the platitudes, all the attempts by her to convince me that everything will be all right, I just can't see it.

The real killer is this: manifestly, I know that I'm doing the right thing. I'm looking after my lovely boy's needs and I'm happy to do so. What also kills me is that I know that she will completely understand and try to make this work. On the motorway, I tried to imagine a scenario in which we could make this happen, but gave up because it was too difficult. However, I did decide that I would offer her a *get out of jail free* card, and allow her to walk away.

If she doesn't want that, then I will try with every breath in my body to make this happen and make it work. Sometimes hardships and difficulties make you stronger, don't they? One thing's for sure: I'm not giving up without a fight.

Just as that thought flits across my mind, Gillian stirs and I tiptoe over to the bed; I stroke her hair, and she opens her eyes and asks me the time.

"3.30 in the morning" is my answer, and she lets out a groaning sound and says something that's supposed to sound like "I love you". That's not surprising, given the time. Her eyes open wider and she holds my hand and repeats, "I love you."

Kissing her, a single tear runs down my cheek, from tiredness as much as from emotion. "I love you too, darling." It's about all I'm capable of saying.

She smiles at my answer and pulls me tightly to her, whispering a question: "You can't sleep?" Answering her in the affirmative, we kiss and I lie next to her. We kiss more passionately at her instigation and as emotional and uptight as I feel, I respond to her and she breaks into a smile as she feels my erection against her leg.

Her kisses become more passionate, if that is possible, and soon she is making love to me. Whilst I could not describe it as the hottest we've ever had, it's certainly the most tender. It feels like she is trying to reassure me, which given the circumstances is a pretty big deal.

We finish, and after calming down she gives me a long piercing look and says, "Whatever happens, I'm here for you." The tears really do come this time, and I try to hide my face. Gillian tenderly pulls me towards her. "You want to go down south to be with Jack, don't you?"

The next few seconds are spent in silence as I marvel at her intuition. The answer, when it comes, is from the bottom of my heart. "I dearly want to lie to you, tell you that nothing will keep me apart from you, but I'm so torn."

There's a silence, broken only by the sound of her stroking my hair. Taking my hand, she kisses it gently. "If you think that I am going to let you get away from me, you've another think coming, Paul Castle."

Instantly, my first thought is to shout "Hooray!" and run naked round her garden. However the people of Harborne probably wouldn't tolerate that. As soon as that thought is over, the doubts come flooding back. "What about Geraldine? Your job? Your flat? All the travelling?"

Smiling at me, she answers with a question: "Do you love me?"

After my enthusiastic "of course!" there's a follow-up.

"Do you trust me, Paul?" I nod in response to this and she continues.

"Jack needs you very much now, and as Jack is part of the perfect package that is you, I need you to deal with that." She is saying this at the same time as stroking my hair, and this creates a very strong reassuring feeling.

Call me a wanker if you like, but lot of issues keep going

round in my head; despite her assurances I just can't see the end. Although I'm heartily sick of my doubt and insecurity, that doesn't stop me from indulging them. They're like old acquaintances: not trusted or good acquaintances, but at least I know they will always be there.

"Darling," I say in a quavering voice. "You make it all sound so easy; have you any idea what all this means?" As soon as that nonsense is out of my mouth, the ridiculousness of saying that to a woman who has lived through bereavement strikes me, and I start to apologise.

Again she puts her finger to my lips, indicating the need for me to shut up.

"You're tired, Paul." A sort of half-laugh follows this. "I was going to say that you're tired and emotional, but in your world that's a euphemism for being completely drunk, isn't it?"

Suddenly I'm laughing, and I nod, grab her and kiss her while holding her tightly. Then I remember that it's nearly four in the morning and we start to fall asleep. Finally I begin to lapse into a dream where everything is OK and Gillian and I live happily ever after with Jack. Who says romance is dead?

The alarm sounds its usual battle cry, and we help each other to wake up and eat breakfast together. Her warmth and understanding are evident, as is her concern for my tiredness.

It doesn't take me long to decide that I love waking up at Gillian's place; I feel really at home there. It's easy to love her sense of style: it isn't chintz and it isn't Scandinavian minimalist, but chic and arty and very cool. Above all, her place is meant to be lived-in and enjoyed, but it also reflects her grace and elegance. Everywhere there are touches of class and signs of taste that I approve of. The art on the walls and the fittings are an eclectic mixture of old and modern that works brilliantly.

We eat our usual toast and coffee, and just as I start to tidy up the breakfast stuff, she announces: "Paul, come round here tonight. We need to talk about the future, and I have some things that I need to tell you about."

As insecurity is my default position, this instantly alarms me, and that sense of blind panic must have shown itself. She waltzes over, gives me a long kiss and tells me, "Don't worry—we need to make plans, that's all."

Making the right noises is difficult, and I try very hard to do that without betraying the emotional confusion this has triggered. "OK" comes out of my mouth without much conviction. Realising that if I don't get control of myself soon, I'll be in a cold sweat, I try to ask nonchalantly, "What time?"

Gillian responds with a calmness that is reassuring and suggests that my attempt at nonchalance was shite. "Darling, please don't worry. We need to have a chat about things and make some plans, plus a few other bits and pieces."

You know the sort of silence that follows now, don't you? It's a clumsy quiet, mainly because I'm unable to ask a question since I'm too scared of finding out what the answer might be. Instead of a lengthy objection to all this, I wanly respond with, "Oh, OK." In answer, I get a kiss for not being a complete arsehole.

The kiss is repeated with some violence on the doorstep, and we arrange to meet at 7.00. There's a twinkle in her eye and I want to say "What?" but it just doesn't seem right somehow. Driving to work, I try to sort out a plan of action that makes some sense, and for the life of me that doesn't seem at all possible.

Chapter Fifty-Two
The Cost of Doing Business

My life at work is the usual grind made glorious summer by the thought that I might be leaving soon. Monday is the deadline for voluntary redundancy, and I fancy that I'll spend this weekend with a calculator and a copy of *The Guardian*'s media section. My loose plan, if it can be called that, is to start ringing a few contacts to see whether I can bag some freelance work. Meanwhile, I'll try to buttonhole the new editor (whoever he or she is) to get some stringer work that I can do from London.

My next job is ringing the local estate agent to value my flat and once we get past the "depressed economic climate, blah, blah, blah" and the "buyers' market, blah, blah, blah" I get a time for her to come and look at the place with a view to putting it on the market.

Once that's done, I decide to slink round to Mike's desk to tell him about Jack's school and to thank him for pulling my head out of my arse. When I arrive, he's still miffed about the Suits upstairs and refers to them as the "Value-added Wankers". He adds more detail: "They talked about 'misunderstandings' and how much they value my contribution. I should've asked for more money as they were so far up my arse."

We get onto Jack's school eventually, and he adds a friendly, "Glad you got with the programme; your kid will feel that, I tell you." We both smile, and I'm glad I asked him about it all. I thank him a little too profusely, and he snaps back with, "I told you I'm happily married!" Then, laughing, he picks up the phone, which has been ringing for what seems like ages.

Walking back to my desk, I know that even though the job's drab, the camaraderie offers a little compensation. Whatever things I'll be keen to see the back of, that won't be one of them.

My mobile rings, and it's Gerry, offering to meet for a drink after work. Reluctantly I accept, making plain that I have to be home by seven and not a minute later. He laughs and sings the chorus of The Rolling Stones' "Under My Thumb", which in turn makes me laugh, and eventually we agree to meet in the Crown opposite the Magistrates' Court.

The Subs are hovering, so I decide to pretend to work, and contemplate the fact that I've already started to mentally disengage. Over in the Sports Section there's a bit of a commotion, and it seems that Mike's in the middle of it.

Ben looks over at me and says, "Oh, Christ! Mental Mike's not been sacked again, has he?"

We both laugh, and he goes over to join the hubbub. A strange premonition prevents me from joining him, and pretty soon the whole newsroom is congratulating him. The Suits from upstairs join the throng, as well as the sales people.

The MD comes down and makes the announcement that Mike has been appointed the acting editor. Pretty soon, I find myself outside with a Gauloises, bawling like a baby. Suddenly it seems that the price of moving down south has to be paid in more ways than just my relationship with Gillian. I'm flooded with "what if"s, self-justification and a bit of self-loathing.

Through the glass atrium, I see Ben coming down the stairs. I hotfoot it to the DS to clean up my face, while feeling a bout of rage passing over me, directed at the Ex: the true author of my misfortune.

Gradually, I get my face sorted and walk back to Ben, making a feeble excuse about fetching a lighter from the car. In his hurry to talk about Mike, he accepts this at face value.

"What d'you think of that, then?" he asks.

I decide to play it straight and answer with the truth.

"Mike's OK; a good writer, really. He'll be good, I think."

He looks at me and laughs, then replies, "That'll be a first, then! I mean, management making a good decision!"

We both smile, and whilst I can't say I'm happy, I decide that really I'm sort of OK. "Seems like it," I say, trying to disguise my mixed feelings. Of course, I'm banned from saying "it could have been me".

Sparking up another cigarette we talk about Villa's chances next season, and it's a relief to be thinking about something else.

The day gets a little better, and I'm touched that Mike's first meeting is with me. He coughs up that the first question he asked after getting the job offer was, "Who was the first choice?"

The Suits, in a rare fit of honesty, decided to tell the truth, and Mike wants me to stay. After that, I explain some of my issues, and he offers to let me work flexibly and understands why I'm going. Gratefully, I tell him the redundancy plan and he gives me time to reconsider, with the promise to talk to some contacts on the nationals for some freelance stuff. We run out of things to say and I thank him, and all I can think about is getting the hell out of his office. Sometimes being wanted is as hard as not being wanted.

Then he gets up and shakes my hand. "Paul, just take your time and think things over. I'll make time for you on Monday and we'll square things then, OK?"

"Thanks, Mike. You have my congratulations. I genuinely mean that."

He smiles and replies, "Coming from a writer as good as you, that's a compliment."

We shake again, and I file a few pieces before clearing my desk and shooting off to the pub to meet Gerry. My phone beeps, and there's a text from the Ex telling me she needs to stay in London house-hunting so I won't be able to see Jack this weekend.

That seems to sum up my day nicely.

Chapter Fifty-Three
Drum and Bass

The Crown is starting to fill with the usual collection of lawyers, office drones and homelessness workers trying to get a jumpstart on the weekend. It's a strange pub and it's full of the trappings of the young drinker: TVs everywhere, loud music, blue drinks in bottles, and everything trying to be really edgy. However, you can also see, if you have the imagination, the Victorian splendour that this place must have had in its heyday. It has a sturdy dignity that transcends the gaudy internal décor and the drum and bass screaming from the PA.

Gerry loves this place. He says it makes him feel young. Conversely, I hate this place as it makes me feel old. In many ways that's the difference between us. His desire to be in touch, to be connected, even with this *faux* version of youth culture is something I can't understand. The music on its own wouldn't be long in driving me out of the place, even if I wasn't under orders to be back on time to Gillian's.

Above the din, Gerry is trying to hold a conversation. "So you've seen the school, then?" he asks at a bellow.

I nod in reply. We quickly realise that this isn't the type of place to hold this kind of conversation, and after a few more attempts at shouting questions we give up and discuss unimportant nonsense. He has one last try, though: "Do you want to talk about it?"

Shaking my head, I bellow back, "Nah, you're all right. I need to talk to Gillian first."

He begins dabbing his eyes in a theatrically affected way and comically blubs, "We never talk anymore!"

Although nervous about my upcoming chat with Gillian and the other trials ahead, I richly enjoy giving him the finger as we fall about laughing.

After a short while, he shouts, "Don't worry! I'm sure everything will be OK!" and I nod in hope rather than in expectation. Indeed, I think that I could use some of Gerry's enthusiasm at the moment, as he never loses the ability to make you believe things will be all right. Gillian does it in a much subtler way, and that's like a giant security blanket.

By the time I'm consuming my second soft drink, however, I'm starting to get the yips again and I'm definitely getting fed up with the end of the weak jolliness at the Crown.

Before I can tell Gerry I want to go, he gets a phone call and answers it with clipped, monosyllabic answers, which is very unlike him. He looks at me when he's answering, and when the call's finished he simply says, "OK, let's go." He downs his drink in one and it's clear he wants me to follow suit.

When we get outside I ask him, "What's up?"

He says "Nothing!" with the conviction of a teenager trying to hide something, and I let that ride in my relief to be out of the din that is the modern urban drinking experience. We start to walk to our respective cars and I get a text from Gillian asking me to get some red wine on the way home. As I stop to answer that, Gerry is shuffling from one foot to the other. When I press the send button I ask him, "You OK? You look like you're about to wet yourself."

He laughs and mumbles back, "I have to go. See you later."

He hops in his car after giving me a quick hug, and leaves me on the pavement wondering whether it was something I said. His absence coincides with a re-emergence of the sense of panic that I've tried hard to keep at bay all day. I'm the sort of person who hates surprises, and I want to know everything straightaway so I can process it. This evening is important, and if I'm in for bad news I want to sort it as soon as possible, not wait around for it.

By this time I'm in the car and contemplating the following thoughts:

1.)   Can I even begin to manage all the competing factors in my life and succeed in keeping everything together?

2.)   Can I move forward with Gillian, given that she and I know the distance between us will be a massive handicap?

3.)   I have no idea how I will feed myself, given that there's a recession on and I am about to sign up for redundancy.

4.)   How will Jack be feeling, and how is all this going to affect our relationship?

5.)   Lastly, there will be a mountain of practical stuff: selling the flat, moving, house-hunting and all of that is going to be time-consuming and stressful at a moment when I want to devote more time to both Jack and Gillian.

By the time I reach the flat, I'm a bag of nerves and a bit neurotic, to tell you the truth. Looking up at the window, I see the lights are on and suddenly get a positive rush as I realise she's waiting for me inside. It's a pretty new feeling for me, and it gives me an emotional charge just to look at the window. It's a feeling of security that someone is there for me, and I can't wait to sink into a long embrace that will temporarily take away my troubles.

Just as I arrive at the threshold, the door is flung open for me and Gillian is gathering me up in her arms. The next thing I know is that she's taking me inside, and to my surprise everyone is there: Gerry, Jenny, Archie, Shona, Bonnie and Jim. The food is just about to be served and I'm guided to the table, where in no time *coq au vin* is dished out and some fresh French bread is placed beside it. The fear of the future is left in its proper place, banished by the support of good friends.

The food is wonderful and the conversation is better, especially as no one mentions the Ex, Jack, private school or projected moves down south. It's really hard, but I try to enjoy the evening even though in the back of my mind is the thought that the "big" conversation with Gillian will inevitably follow the scoff.

By the time that the dessert is served, I'm trying to keep a lot of competing emotions together, and all I want to do is talk to Gillian. Whilst I would die before I upset my friends, I feel that if they don't go soon I'll fall victim to spontaneous human combustion. If you're reaching an emotional, dare I say even spiritual, crisis, the last thing most people would want to yak about is the colour of Bonnie's new kitchen units.

Eventually the meal is over, and the atmosphere changes perceptibly. Even with my dull wits, confused with all emotional weirdness in my head, I know that something important is on the way. Slowly I begin to feel my heart beating in my chest, and my hands start shaking.

Gillian reaches over and holds my hand, and then the room goes very quiet as she starts to speak in a gentle tone.

"Paul, I want to say a couple of things and I'm going to ask you to believe that you are so special. In front of our friends, I need to tell you I love you."

Whatever I was expecting, it wasn't this. To say it's a surprise opening is a bit of an understatement.

"I love you too!" is my rather unoriginal response, and I look at her and want to add a lot more than that, but I'm ashamed to admit that, for someone who gets paid for communicating, I'm speechless.

Then another voice pipes up and surprisingly it's Archie's. It's surprising because although Archie is a friendly, warm person, he usually isn't this forthcoming.

"The truth is, Paul, all of us in one way or another have been responsible for getting you two together. There's lots of reasons for that, but the principal reason is that we love you guys very much and we want you to be happy."

I'm a bit stunned with this, but it's clear there's a story coming here. Archie pauses, and I think it's his way of letting me digest that little nugget before he says anything else. Questions are beginning to form in my brain, but before I can make any sense of them he continues.

"We need to tell you that Gillian is actually my sister-in-law; Ray, her late husband, was my brother. Honestly, I can say that we are like brother and sister, and I really wanted her to meet someone who would be perfect for her."

Gerry cuts in: "At the same time, we wanted you to meet someone who would be perfect for you, in circumstances that wouldn't turn you into a gibbering idiot."

Everybody laughs, and I want to be upset but can't manage it; firstly because I'm in such a funk and secondly because I know he's pretty much bang-on.

He doesn't stop there: "Honestly, you're hopeless—all that self-deprecation and lack of self-confidence."

As you can imagine, I'm at a loss to speak, and before I can get myself together, Bonnie wades in.

"Archie and I had a chat and we decided you two should meet. We hoped that you would hit it off, and you did."

Everybody starts to nod and I need to breathe and get

some air; I feel touched, amused, bloody angry and just weird, all at the same time.

Gillian squeezes my hand. "Oh Paul, please don't be upset. I promise I wasn't trying to trap you. I didn't know anything at first. Archie invited me to the dinner party and he told me you were shy; that's all I knew. He told me not to mention anything about being his sister-in-law as he didn't want you to feel obligated and under even more pressure."

At this point, I'm reeling and just can't get my head around any of it. I don't have one clue what to say or what to do. All I can think about is fresh air and my need to get some. It's an overwhelming urge, and I look at them all and say, "I need a cigarette. Give me a minute!"

Getting up, I head for the door. Gerry gets up to follow, but I say to him, "No—I need some time to think this through. I'll be back in a minute."

With that, I head for the door and the comfort and solitude of a smoke.

Chapter Fifty-Four
Confessions

I'd like to say that the doorstep cigarette proves a blessing, but it doesn't, as the smoke passes my lips unnoticed in the light of these revelations and the fact that it's drizzling outside. Questions explode in my brain, and I have no idea of the answer to any of them.

Dully, I try to piece together how I feel and figure out why Gillian is telling me all of this, and why she has kept it from me. Also, why my friends have conspired to make me feel like an idiot! It has been an awful couple of days and now the foundations of my relationship are…well, they're just not what I thought they were.

As I get to the middle of the cigarette, some things begin to pierce the emotional murk my mind has become. It starts to dawn on me that I'm being a bit of a drama queen here and I need to get my shit together. Slowly something else begins to get my attention. Archie and all of them have been very kind to do all of this for us, and considering how much I feel for Gillian, their instincts about how good we could be together are very astute. In addition, now that I know that Ray was Archie's brother, does that really make any difference at all?

Stubbing out my cigarette, I hear myself saying "no". Gillian is the same beautiful, lovely person she was, and I'm the same as well. The fact that she is related by marriage to a mate is a matter of no importance. It dawns on me, too, that they might all be stressing about where I am and what I'm doing, so I decide to hotfoot it into the flat only to find that Gerry's by the door.

"You OK, mate?" he asks in a rather abashed tone, and I look at him and smile.

"Yeah, a bit weird!"

His smile tells me a lot about how he's feeling. We walk through the open door and back into the flat, and Gillian is sitting down looking ashen.

Deciding to make this all right, I walk straight over and kiss her, then sit down and help myself to a coffee.

There's a silence, and everyone is looking at me. At this point, I look her in the eye, and I'm conscious that everyone's hanging on my every word.

"Darling, you said that you didn't want me to feel like I was trapped." She nods and I smile again. "It's just that word 'trapped'. I'm not trapped; I'm happier now than I've ever been."

She breaks into a huge relieved grin, and it's like a vast weight has been lifted off her shoulders. Meanwhile all my friends are cheering, and as I kiss Gillian full on the mouth, they start to clap.

She squeezes my hand and I respond in kind, safe in the knowledge that although the foundation of my relationship may have changed, it's stronger not weaker if I choose it to be. I've now made Gillian happy by allowing her to unburden stuff that made her feel awkward, and that makes me happy too. The fact that she felt that she could trust me with that is actually an endorsement of her faith in me.

Gerry gets up and says, "These two need some space, guys. Let's get out of here."

That's the cue for hugs all round, and in next to no time we are on our own and Gillian is in my arms, crying like a baby. For a long time, that is us: in each other's arms, with her gently weeping. Despite the fact that I'm cool with the whole thing, there are questions that need answering. There is a sort of equilibrium in relationships and when they are out of kilter, I want that to be sorted; otherwise I'm out of my comfort zone.

Biting the bullet, I ask her, "Why didn't you tell me before?"

She smiles, with panda eyes from her running mascara.

"It was Archie. He was so afraid that if you thought that you were being set up, you would feel obligated. He just wanted me to meet you naturally. He didn't even tell me that you were coming to Bonnie's that night. They told me just before you arrived. He and Shona and the others just hoped that we would get on. When we did, Archie asked me not to mention him being Ray's brother when you'd gone out to the toilet. He didn't want you to feel awkward."

"Weren't there times in between when you could have told me?" Even as I'm saying this, I can guess her answer, and it doesn't take long for her to prove me right.

"Of course, but what with Jack and all the other stuff you're dealing with, I didn't want to tell you till we were ready to make some decisions."

That was exactly what I expected, and I'm really happy with the answers, but my questions don't end there. However I don't want to give her the third degree, so I tell her, "I'm sorry. It's just that I need to get my head around this stuff."

As I'm saying this, she is holding me tighter. Her eyes find mine, and she just blurts out: "Archie told me all about you and made me promise not to say anything, and I just went along, and…well, it got out of control, really. After that first night, I told him that I thought that you were lovely, and he told me that you would be nervous and would be all over the place because of the way things ended with your marriage."

Listening carefully, I make a noise that I hope makes me seem thoughtful. Then, before I can stop myself, I ask the next question that pops into my head. "What did you think of me after that first evening?"

Again, she smiles—that lovely, lovely smile. "From the first moment I saw you, Paul, I thought you looked really handsome. Then you started talking, and you were articulate, sensitive, talented, funny, and a loving father."

There's a pause, and I sit there trying to take it all in, trying to make sense of all of this. As I'm doing that, I'm also trying to remember anyone, ever, saying anything as nice as that to me. It's the sort of stuff that you hear at the movies but dismiss as too corny. Amazingly, from her mouth it doesn't sound anything other than beautiful.

There are no words to answer that and all I can do is put it all in a kiss. It contains all my thoughts and feelings and just seems to last forever. After we eventually let each other go, she looks at me in an almost frightened way.

"I was so afraid that you would be upset about this; the others said wait and see, but I knew that you really loved me and I didn't want to hide that stuff about Ray from you."

After this what can I do, but hold her and tell it's OK?

So after another long kiss, I look into her eyes and tell her, "There's nothing to worry about. This makes no difference to the way I feel about you."

The thing is, and this is a real no-brainer, it really doesn't. Looking at her, I can see that she has been labouring under this for ages, and I feel really sorry that she has held all that in for me. Kissing her gently on the forehead, I say, "Let's get cleaned up and go to bed."

Holding me tightly, she whispers, "Tell me that you aren't cross with me!" and for the first time since I walked in the door, I laugh. It's an enormous release of tension and, to be frank, a bit inappropriate.

Eventually getting myself together, I splutter out, "I'm so not angry with you!" Then letting out another chuckle, I add, "I'm really annoyed that my friends conspired behind my back to make me so happy!"

It's a pretty weak joke in the circumstances, but the effect is what I wanted, and we're both smiling as we sort out the dishwasher before going to bed.

Chapter Fifty-Five
The Morning After…

The sunlight starts to make its presence felt, and I wake and she's stroking my hair—a gesture I don't think I'll ever get tired of. Right now, I'm not sure that I want to talk; I only want to drink in the gentle sensation of the tingling travelling through my body. There's a contentment following the storm that was the dinner last night.

We talked before we went to bed, and I came to the conclusion that I was an arse for even temporarily worrying about the past. After all, what does it matter? What matters now is the future and the plans that we will make for dealing with the Jack situation.

My face must show my mood, and she says, "Penny for your thoughts?"

I smile and just look at her, then clasp the hand stroking my hair and kiss it. "I could stay here forever but at some point we have to talk about Jack." She looks at me tenderly as I'm saying this.

"Why don't we stay here for the weekend? Geraldine is at her friend's house in London, and we can look at the options and sit down and make decisions." I groan gently and she reddens a bit. "Paul, we have to get this done. That way we can get all the anxiety behind us and start living with the reality and not with this thing hanging over our heads."

Knowing she's right doesn't diminish the enormity of the task ahead. What has changed is the tone of her voice. Before this morning, she had a reassuring "everything will be OK" tone, and now the message is more like "let's get on with it".

Deciding to make the most of it, I smile and say, "Yes, ma'am!" and we both laugh. She kisses me and I look at the clock, which says 10 a.m.

Then I ask her whether she wants a kiss or breakfast, and she ponders a bit and says, "Kisses are for later. If we get our sorting-out done, we'll have the rest of the weekend to kiss."

"Kiss", you understand, is a pretty poor euphemism for lovemaking, and I cannot help but wonder if that is an attempt to defer proceedings.

However, her determination to get things done is really what is needed here, and I endorse that with a peck on the cheek and a breezy question: "OK! Who's getting coffee and who's in the shower?"

She hops out of bed and walks over to the door. "I'll do coffee, darling; you get in the shower." With that, she blows me a kiss and scoots out leaving me lying in bed.

Suddenly I start thinking negatively again, and it occurs to me that I need to nip this in the bud. There are so many positives here, and I need to think about those rather than obsessing about things I can't change.

Ripping off the bedclothes, I start to get a little angry with myself as I begin the process of getting up. By the time I'm climbing into the shower, I'm practically flagellating myself. I mean, I have a fantastic partner and a fantastic kid, and what is distance compared to that?

At last I resolve to try to get something sorted and try to

make the best out of that. It's going to be hard and it will involve sacrifice, but when did anything good come easily to the likes of me? Besides, looking at all that Gillian went through with her bereavement, I really have nothing to complain about.

The shower is fabulously refreshing and, apart from the fact that I have no clean socks, I emerge from the bathroom much more sorted than I went in. My final thought, as I look for my boxers, is this: Jack knows I love him, as I tell him every day on the phone. That isn't going to change. He knows that I will call him every day and he can rely on me when he needs me. It will be different from my relationship with my dad after he left; better than the occasional trip to the Little Chef, the birthday card with a pound inside and the present on Boxing Day. I may only be a Burger Bar Dad, but he will always know that I divorced his mother, not him.

With that in mind and a determined look on my face, I walk into Gillian's kitchen/diner and sit down to breakfast. The usual toast accompanies the usual coffee, and being here is a great way of starting the day. Gillian runs her fingers through my hair, before going off to her shower while I settle down to eat.

Halfway through the toast, it strikes me hard that I really want to be near her forever and want to share the little things lovers do: the little bits and pieces that make being in a couple so much more preferable to being single.

As I'm pondering this, I can hear the comforting sound of Gillian getting ready, and the positive feelings I had getting dressed are reinforced by the thought that this woman has moved from being a girlfriend to being my partner.

By the time I've finished my coffee, Gillian has emerged from the bedroom in a T-shirt and jeans; as usual, she looks very sexy. Mind you, if she was wearing a bin liner she'd still look alluring. She takes my plate and cup and we set about sorting out the kitchen, and when that's finished we sit down at the table.

Somehow, from somewhere she's produced a notepad and pen, and it's clear that plans are going to be made. With my newfound sense of positive motion, this seems an ideal time.

Gillian smiles and says, "I think we should make a start."

Nodding approvingly, I clear my throat and make a speech.

"Gillian, I want to say sorry for burdening you with all my issues with Jack and all that." She smiles lovingly at me, and I drone on. "My shyness and all of this heartbreak about moving down south. The thing is, I've been thinking, and I want to say that I'm going to listen to you and I'm determined to make this work. I'm with you for the long haul and I'm with you forever."

"That's great!" she says, "I think you need to stop worrying about me running away just because this is going to be difficult." There's a nod from me, accepting that she has hit the nail on the head. Continuing, she says, "You have to trust me. I'm not your Ex and I'm not going to treat you like she did."

The fact she gets that is like a huge relief, and I toy with the idea of telling her about my dad and the impact that his leaving had on my early life. I open my mouth to start, and she interrupts me by saying, "I love you. I think you know what a big deal that is for me, especially after Ray."

I'm hanging on her every word, just nodding. I'm putty in her hands at the moment—and then comes the killer. Her eyes look into mine, and she says, "I also know that you lived through your parents' divorce, and that you don't want Jack to experience his childhood in the same way that you did."

All I can do is stare, and even while I'm wondering where

on earth she got that nugget of information, I reach out and hold her hand. This pause isn't going to end with me breaking the silence, and indeed she has much more to say.

"Gerry told me about your parents and how you grew up not having the relationship with your dad that you have with Jack. So we have to work out ways for you to get sorted and for us to work round that."

The fact that she knows about some of my painful baggage is not at all uncomfortable for me as I've always been open, especially with my friends. In fact, I feel that I can trust her with that, especially as she understands how it impacts on my life. I reach out and touch her hand, and just manage to say "thank you!" before a tear reaches the bottom of my cheek.

"Darling," she says with tenderness, "I didn't mean to upset you." With that, she kisses my hand and says, with a gentle steeliness in her voice: "Now we have to get on and see what we can achieve together."

Wiping away my tearstain, I just manage to say "Thank you!" before she picks up her pen and says with some authority, "Let's get down to business!"

Chapter Fifty-Six
No Ring for Me

Business, it transpires, is a list-writing exercise focusing on the pros and cons of moving down south against staying in Birmingham. Then there are the pros and cons of working up here with the paper and Trevor. That is set against the pros and cons of setting up a new career down south with my redundancy money in my pocket. From there we move on to property issues at my request, and Gillian says she feels we need to focus elsewhere as we're only scratching the surface.

It's soon midday, and we decide to stop for lunch to take stock. None of this has touched on the emotional side of things, which I suspect will to be harder.

Gillian asks me if I want to cook, and I leap at the chance to do something practical. As I'm preparing vegetables, I gently hint at my disquiet regarding the emotional dangers ahead. "I think we've done well; we've gone over lots of practical issues."

She smiles, and is ahead of me already. "Don't be thinking that I've missed out the important considerations."

She knows what I'm thinking, and I shake my head in disbelief, knowing deep down that this woman is so together that trusting her emotional intelligence isn't going to be a problem.

"Well, you know!" is my rather cack-handed response. In my heart, though, I'm just allowing her to take my worries and deal with them, because I feel that right now she can manage all of my concerns. It's like a gigantic surrender, but in a good way.

We have a light lunch of ham and potato with some salad, and we talk nonsense before washing up, interspersed with gentle kisses.

Eventually, we work through all sorts of stuff that helps me to focus on all the issues around us being together and the possibility of me moving down South. The crux of this for her is whether Jack will be at boarding school all week and whether I will be able to see him at weekends.

We decide to phone the school and speak to one of the residential staff. His answer is an emphatic "yes", and he illustrates this by telling us how many of the boarders are away with relatives at the weekend.

We talk over a few more things, and at the end of all that she puts her pen down and looks at me. "So your ideal would be to live down south at weekends and up here during part of the week? That way you can work flexibly with the paper and develop your work as a playwright with Trevor."

I reply hotly, "No, not at all. If I want to stay up here during the week, it'll be so that I can be with you." There's a smile playing on her lips, which is a little charming and a little annoying. However, I feel the need to say a few other things too. "That analysis is good, and if I could swing all that together, it would make life a little better. At least I would see Jack at the weekend, but what about property? I can't afford to work flexibly up here and rent or buy something down there, just to use it at the weekend."

Again, I get the enigmatic smile that's a little bit charming and a little bit annoying.

That leads me to make another point: "If I can't get a property down there, we're left with me commuting every Saturday, and then we'll have little or no time together at weekends. Then there's the fact that I don't want to be arriving tired and grouchy, spending my time with Jack in more fast-food places before a long drive back. I'll do it, obviously, but it just means that that it won't be the quality time that's precious at his age."

Incredibly, I get the now-familiar enigmatic smile. It stops me in my tracks, and all I can think about is what on earth it means.

Gillian doesn't leave me waiting long as she says, "I have a solution to that, if you want to hear it?"

"I'd love to!" I look at her and I can't help myself feeling happy as the enigmatic smile is really catching. She gets up and runs her fingers through my hair, which sends a shiver down my spine. That's soon followed by a kiss on the forehead, which achieves the same result.

"Wait here," she whispers, and I watch her slink to the bedroom. Then there is the noise of drawers being opened and her ruffling about, and she reappears a little later, clearly hiding something behind her back.

Sitting down, she takes a deep breath and says, "I've been thinking about this for ages, and I want you to be with me—to be my partner." There's a moment's pause, and she continues in a more forceful tone. "The last thing I want, though, is for you to be with me and constantly be unhappy about not being with Jack." Nodding because I don't have anything sensible to say, I wait for her next sentence. "I can also imagine that when you're down south missing me, that might have a impact on your relationship with Jack."

At last I feel that I have something to contribute: "That's right!" Not a penetrating analysis, I grant you, but it has the merit of brevity. Gillian then gives me a look that I find really difficult to describe: a kind of smugness; the sort of look a magician would have just as he is about to pull a rabbit out of a hat. There is a strong suspicion that this is what lies behind the smile that I can't quite get to the bottom of.

"Paul, I have a plan. It isn't the answer to all our problems, but it's an answer to some of them." She pauses, and it seems like she's trying to gather her thoughts. "I needed to think it through and talk to Geraldine, and I wanted to get last night out of the way."

I kiss her hand and she responds by gently stroking the side of her face.

Feeling the need to speak, I just say what is patently obvious: "You've given this a lot of thought, haven't you?"

There isn't even a second's pause before she says, "Only from the first time I met you!"

There's a laugh from me, and I exclaim in mock outrage: "For goodness' sake! You'll give me a swollen head!"

I'm grinning from ear to ear. Needless to say conversations like this are a bit of a mystery for me.

"That will never do!" snaps back from her laughing lips.

I walk over to her side of the table and we kiss very passionately. That is abruptly ended as I begin to get an erection, and she pushes me away jokingly and shouts, "Stop that! We need to talk!"

But she's laughing as loudly as me.

When she is fit to talk, she looks at me. "I want to be with you; move in with you or have you move in with me." Stroking my hand, she continues, "You're everything I want: sexy, kind, sensitive, warm and loving."

"OK," I add, "but all of that doesn't answer our problems."

"Let me finish!" she says in a schoolmarmish way that I find disturbingly attractive. "Mr. Paul Castle! You will have to learn to listen." Laughing, I hold up my hands in mock-surrender, at which point she ploughs on. "I've found love and I never thought that would happen. Despite everything that is going on around you—Jack, redundancy, offers from Trevor—you've made me feel like I'm always at the centre of your world."

Leaning over, she pecks me on the cheek in a little romantic gesture, and I reply, "You're so good for me! I want you at the heart of everything I do." Somehow this all comes out without seeming trite or soppy.

There's a silence, and she starts to kiss my hand and I don't quite know what to say. Instead of waiting for me to continue, she looks at me and says, "I have a present for you." I reply with an "ooooh", which she instantly shushes. "Before I give it to you, I want you to promise me that you won't get all male chauvinist on me."

Nodding, I cheekily add, "What can I say? I'm a new man!"

At this point, she reaches behind her and holds out a little bag. "This is for you."

I take it, and she has a serious face as I remove a small jeweller's ring box. Holding out her hand, she places it on the box before I can open it.

"I want us to live together. I hope you do too."

The answer "Of course I do!" instantly comes out of my mouth. My hands are shaking, and to be honest I'm struggling to hold on to the box and to my emotions.

"Open the box, then," she commands gently, and I obey with a heart pounding through my chest.

Presupposing there is a ring in there, it isn't easy to keep my look of surprise from her when I find a key inside. My face clearly isn't the mask of inscrutability that I think it is, and an awkward silence follows.

Eventually I ask, "Is this the key for here?"

Another smile spreads across her face. "No, it isn't. It's a key to solving our problems." As you can imagine, this isn't very illuminating, and I just sit quietly, waiting for an answer to this riddle. Eventually she gives it to me. "We're going to live in two places: you can work part-time for the paper and develop your plays with Trevor." I want to say "but..." at this point; however, she's on a roll and I don't want to stop her. "I was left well-off when Ray died, and he was careful to see about making arrangements like that. I have a place in South London and you are holding the key. It's yours, if you want it. We can go down on Fridays and leave on Monday mornings. That will allow us to spend more time with Jack. Then if it works out OK, we can make a decision to move there permanently. I'm going to cut back on my supply work and we can eventually sell some of the property here when the time is right. I need to be with you, and you made it clear that you want to be with me."

I'm gob-smacked, and that is saying something. I kiss her, and it's a kiss of affirmation; a long, romantic surrender to this most thoughtful of women. I want her to understand that her plan is brilliant, lovely and wise—it means that we're together and can still see Jack.

It's just like a brilliant dream.

Epilogue
(Four Months Later)

Telling Jack that we were going to live in London at the weekend and see him every weekend was so cool. His happiness constantly reminds me that it was Gillian that made it possible. Gillian and Jack get on like a house on fire, and we're having a great day today, happily making plans for the autumn.

Jack loves Gillian's house in London (I still can't get used to calling it "our house"!), and today we're going to look at some holiday brochures. All in all, everything is very cool despite the relentless abuse from Gerry. I'm hopelessly in love with Gillian and my new life. We live together at her place, and that's going fabulously well, and Geraldine has moved into my flat and that's going well too. I've even given up smoking, and as a reward, I've resprayed the DS and it looks better than ever.

Trevor is really happy with the play, which is in production now, and he wants another to work on another as soon as that's finished. The director's very sympathetic to the work but it's a tough business and he's fairly strict about rewrites and stuff like that. However, I love the challenge, and part of my brief is work alongside the actors on the subtext of the play in order to enable them to "immerse themselves" in my writing. It sounds a bit up its own arse, but the company is very committed to the writing and the actors are all edgy kids looking to get the most out of the work.

My journalism is great; I'm employed as a freelancer, and Mike and I get on fine. He's coping brilliantly in the newsroom and the copy is better in all areas of the paper. What's more, the staff seem comfortable about having an old-fashioned newspaperman at the helm. I work flexibly in order to do the play and get the most from seeing Jack, and as you can imagine, that's fantastic.

So all in all: a result, courtesy of the great woman Gillian! We've all been to a movie today, and Jack really loved it. As usual, I ask him where he wants to eat.

"Can we eat at Gillian's house?" He hasn't got used to calling it "our house" either. "I read in a book somewhere that you shouldn't have too much fast food, and I want to eat healthily. We can still have one every now and again, if you want."

Smiling, I look at Gillian and I think how cool my kid is. I love the idea of being more involved in Jack's life: helping him make decisions; doing all the stuff that parents do—being more than a Burger Bar Dad.

After my reflections, he pipes up again. "Dad, can we have the radio on? I want to hear the football."

Score!

Acknowledgements

I would like to thank the following for making *Burger Bar Dad* a reality: Nick Foot for his honesty and encouragement, Trevor Johnston and Lorraine for the spur to finish. Also I need to mention Carlo Gebbler and my friends at the Fermanagh Creative Writers Group who first gave me the idea I could write well. Then there is Séamas Mac Annaidh, who read my first jottings and told me to write more. Also Jay, Connor and the other young people from FUEL. Thank you also to Philip Goulding.

In addition to these I must include Jon Priest as his skills are essential to this success, and obviously Mark, Maria, Richard and everyone at M P Publishing, who have been brilliant right from the start of this adventure. There is also a need to thank Tony Viney, Ken Ramsey, Wayne Hardman and Peter Byrne for their help and for laughing at my jokes, as well as Hugh Mannix, who never stopped telling me I could do this.

Last but not least, all thanks to my partner, Heather, who made it all happen in the first place.

Printed in Great Britain
by Amazon.co.uk, Ltd.,
Marston Gate.